ESCAPE TO THE COUNTRY GARDEN

HANNAH LANGDON

Storm

This is a work of fiction. Names, characters, businesses, places, events and incidents are either the products of the author's imagination or used in a fictitious manner. Any resemblance to actual persons, living or dead, or actual events is purely coincidental.

Copyright © Hannah Langdon, 2025

The moral right of the author has been asserted.

All rights reserved. No part of this book may be reproduced or used in any manner without the prior written permission of the copyright owner. This prohibition includes, but is not limited to, any reproduction or use for the purpose of training artificial intelligence technologies or systems.

To request permissions, contact the publisher at rights@stormpublishing.co

Ebook ISBN: 978-1-80508-713-7
Paperback ISBN: 978-1-80508-715-1

Cover design: Rose Cooper
Cover images: Shutterstock

Published by Storm Publishing.
For further information, visit:
www.stormpublishing.co

ALSO BY HANNAH LANGDON

The Feywood Sisters

Escape to the Country Kitchen

Christmas with the Lords
Christmas with the Knights

For John

*At last,
My love has come along.*

ONE

'At the bottom of the drive is fine, thanks.'

Frankie didn't want to risk the taxi driver's welfare on Feywood's treacherous and neglected drive. It was full of potholes and lumps only partially hidden by the thin, patchy layer of gravel no one had raked or replenished for years. She supposed the roof must come first for repairs, but in the months since her last visit, it still showed no signs of attention.

Frankie hoisted her bag onto her shoulder and started trudging towards the house she had grown up in, hoping that her family would pay her as little heed. Her two sisters and father loved her, she knew that. But she also knew that they would, understandably, want to know what had suddenly made her turn tail and return home, after living in London for months with her boyfriend, Dylan Madison. She had shrugged off everyone's warnings that Dylan, the latest bad boy darling of the art world, was bad news; but that was exactly what he had turned out to be. If – *when* – she was asked about it, she would pull out the old Frankie bravado, but really all she wanted to do was to creep back home unnoticed and hide under her duvet for a month.

There's no way anyone would allow that, though, so you'd better get your act together.

She pushed open the heavy oak front door, which immediately shrieked out its customary greeting from the five-hundred-year-old hinges, which were never oiled, despite everyone complaining about them regularly. Practicalities such as a squirt of WD40 never occurred to the Carlisles, who seemed to think that boring day-to-day tasks would resolve themselves as magically as the art that came to each one of them in a different way.

Well, not anymore. Frankie shoved the door shut. *I'll have to get a proper job now.* Tears rose suddenly to her eyes and she scrubbed them away furiously. *Not sure there's much call for self-pity, Frank. Most people don't have a massive family home to come back to when things go tits up.* Now, she had made herself laugh. *Good. But I've never been good at anything but art, and bloody Dylan even took that away.*

'Frankie!'

The voice made her jump. She hadn't had time to recover herself when her oldest sister, Martha, wearing her usual shapeless smock, her face and hands covered in smears of oil paint, came rushing towards her and flung her arms about her. Reluctantly, Frankie let herself be hugged for a few moments before wriggling away.

'What are you *doing* here?' her sister said breathlessly. 'Why didn't you say you were coming to visit? Everyone will be so pleased to see you, it's been months.' She paused and looked at Frankie's pale face, and concern shadowed her pretty amber eyes. 'Are you okay?'

'Absolutely fine and dandy,' said Frankie breezily, starting to move towards the magnificent staircase. 'Hungover, of course, but what's new?'

That wasn't true. What *was* new was that she hadn't had a drink for nearly a week, but she wasn't about to tell Martha that. It would set off too many unnecessary alarm bells and another raft of questions, and she couldn't be bothered talking about it. The last time she'd got drunk had resulted in such horrendous hangxiety. Had she made a complete fool of herself, yet again, or was it just good old Frankie being hilarious? She no longer knew, but she had decided to knock off alcohol for a while to see how she managed without her usual social crutch.

'Well, let me take your bag, at least. How long are you staying for? I must tell Juliet; she'll be so pleased to see you.'

She dashed towards a closed door at the side of the hall and disappeared. Surmising that Martha had gone to the small library, where her second oldest sister, Juliet, could often be found if she wasn't in her light-filled studio above the cookery school in the old stable block, Frankie started to climb the stairs. She wondered if she should hide in one of the unused bedrooms and buy herself some time before facing the inevitable onslaught of her sisters' well-meaning inquisition. No such luck. She had barely reached the galleried landing when Juliet shouted 'Frankie!' and started up the stairs two at a time. She gave her sister another hug, briefer but no less warm and welcoming than Martha's had been.

'It's so good to see you, although you look bloody awful,' said Juliet, less tactful than Martha. 'Shall I go and get Dad? Or Sylvia? They'll be glad you're here.'

Frankie shook her head furiously. Her messy hair, with its dyed blonde streaks growing out, whipped around her face.

'I want to get to my room. This hangover won't sleep itself off.'

Juliet frowned. 'All right, but Martha and I are coming with you.'

She glanced at her older sister, who had caught up with them and now nodded.

'Yes. Do you want a cup of tea?'

'Or something stronger?' suggested Juliet with a grin. 'I

know it's only eleven in the morning, but that's never stopped you before. You've always sworn by the hair of the dog.'

Good old Frankie.

She rolled her eyes.

'I don't want anything,' she said, and set off again towards her room. Pushing open the door, she felt an overwhelming sense of relief at being back in familiar surroundings, and she threw down her bag then sat heavily on the side of the huge old four-poster bed. Her sisters immediately climbed up onto the bed as well, and she felt her initial resistance to them ebb away as the familiar scene of the three girls – so different in so many ways yet united in their loyalty and love for one another – took shape. She pushed off her shoes and pulled herself over to the pillows, propping herself up on one and hugging another to her. Juliet was sitting with her back against one bedpost, and Martha was lying on her stomach, her chin in her hands. Frankie opened her mouth to speak, when there was a gentle scratching sound at the door.

'Ava!' said Juliet, jumping down and opening the door to admit a sweet little dog with long silky ears and a gentle face. 'You see,' she said, picking her up and plonking her on the bed next to Frankie. 'She's pleased to see you too.'

Frankie pushed aside the pillow she had been holding and drew Ava to her, letting the dog lick her face as she cuddled the ecstatically wriggling body. She felt the last of her stiffness dissolve and looked up at her sisters.

'Look, girls, I know it's too late for you to roll out the red carpet, but I'm back at Feywood for good,' she said. They both beamed and opened their mouths to speak, but she pushed on, feeling that if she didn't say it all right now, she might never tell them what had happened. 'I know you were worried about Dylan, and I said it was all right, but it wasn't. So don't say "I told you so", because I *know*,' she finished fiercely, pressing the heels of her hands into her eyes to try and stem the tears.

Martha and Juliet exchanged concerned glances. Dylan Madison, Frankie's boyfriend of nearly a year, had always been a worry to them. An artist with a huge following, whose paintings sold for thousands of pounds, he was also a notorious hell-raiser who had been in trouble with the police countless times for brawls and suspected drug offences. When Frankie had taken up with him, she had insisted that this side of him was diminishing and they were muses to each other; indeed, when Juliet had tracked them down to a sordid housing project in London, she had seen some of Frankie's best work, and little evidence of anything concerning other than a few bottles of wine. Knowing that trying to persuade or lecture their youngest sister would only backfire, she and Martha had agreed to watch from a distance, always ready to welcome her home and help her, if needs be. It looked like that time had come.

'We won't say a thing,' she said now, reaching out to squeeze Frankie's thin foot. 'We're glad to see you home. What happened?'

'Well, you know I like a party, and don't worry, that hasn't changed. I'll still give you two a run for your money, even Dad.'

Juliet and Martha grinned. Their father, the famous sculptor Rousseau Carlisle, was well-known for his stamina.

'But it was the drugs,' Frankie continued. 'I mean, there's fun and there's fun, but that's not my scene, never has been. He was taking more, saying it helped his work, and he kept saying I should too. But screw that. I'm already too much fun when I've had a drink; I don't think the world is ready for Frankie on a real high.'

Martha swallowed.

'So you didn't?'

'Of course not,' said Frankie vehemently. 'I know everyone thinks I'm wild, but it was only ever the booze, never anything else. And none of that, now. Not anymore. Well, not for now, anyway. I'd started to rely on alcohol too much to get me through social stuff, so I'm trying to find out what I actually enjoy doing, and who I get on with. Take the piss if you want to, but I've had enough.'

'We wouldn't,' said Martha, distressed. 'Of course we wouldn't. We're here to support you.'

Frankie glanced up, a spark of the old fire showing in her tired eyes.

'Oh, go on, just a bit, if you must. I'm glad of the support but don't get all saintly on me. Especially not you, Juliet – the halo wouldn't suit you.'

Juliet grinned. 'Phew. I thought for a moment I'd have to improve my bedside manner which, as you know, is non-existent. Martha's good at that stuff; I'll stick with being more bracing.'

They laughed and Frankie began to relax.

'Thanks. I know I've been stupid, but I know now I was kidding myself. Work was going so well, but even that's crap these days.'

'Aren't you hoping that being back at Feywood will help?' asked Martha. 'You're such a talented artist; it will come back, it has to.'

'I'm not that bothered,' replied Frankie stubbornly, and untruthfully. 'I've lost my touch and it's embarrassing trying anything. I have to accept that I had my time and it's over. Pretty embarrassing, given that I've grown up here and been given everything, even the right genes, but there it is. I'm going to find something else to do. Maybe Léo and Aunt Sylvia can teach me how to cook.'

Juliet let out a snort of laughter.

'Really? Frankie, after me, you're the worst cook Feywood has ever seen. Léo and Sylvia are the kindest, most patient teachers in the world, but I think you'd be the one to break them.'

Léo Brodeur, Juliet's boyfriend, and the girls' Aunt Sylvia, their father Rousseau's sister, ran a cookery school in the old stable block where Juliet had her studio. They had also released a successful cookery book together, inspired by Feywood and illustrated with Juliet's photos and drawings. Discussions of a second book had already begun.

'Ha ha,' said Frankie, sticking her tongue out at her sister. 'But maybe you're right, I don't want to poison anyone. Well, no one in this house. Or, should I say, no one in this house right at this moment. Give me time. Come on, enough of my boring life, what's been going on here recently? Still no work started on the roof?'

'Not yet,' replied Martha, 'but soon, Dad says. The bank is pleased with what we're doing. It was amazing of you to carry on paying rent even when you weren't living here.'

Frankie shrugged. 'I wasn't paying anything in London, and we had promised to help. I didn't mean to move out, it just happened. Anyway, talking of things that take a million years to get done, what about you and Will? Have you made a move on him yet?'

Martha blushed to the tips of her ears.

'No, I haven't, and you know I'm not going to. I couldn't. We're good friends, that's all. But Dad and Sindhu are going strong – she's here almost all the time now. Will you be all right with that?'

Frankie nodded. 'Yeah. I know I was a bit funny when they first got together, but I hardly think I'm the one to be judging other people on their relationships. Do you like her?'

Both girls nodded.

'She's nice,' said Juliet. 'No aspirations to be our mother, which is what I was worried about. One mother was more than enough for me. I think she's good for Dad too. Lets him get on with his work because she's got her own life going on.'

'Her jewellery's exquisite,' added Martha. 'Look, this is one of hers.'

She showed her sister an intricate silver pendant she was wearing, studded with a rainbow of tiny, semiprecious stones.

'And what about Aunt Sylvia?' asked Frankie. 'I can't wait to see her.' Her sisters' faces darkened, and she looked from one to the other. 'What is it? What's wrong?'

'Well,' said Juliet slowly, biting her lip. 'She hasn't said much, but she's still having lots of appointments and she's weak, although she tries to hide it. She doesn't talk to any of us about it. Léo says we have to wait for her to tell us in her own time, but we're so worried.'

Martha nodded.

'She doesn't look at all well, but she's trying to carry on as normal. Come on, let's go and find her and Dad; they'll be so happy you're back.'

The days turned into weeks as Frankie settled back into life at Feywood. She shut up her studio – the room next to her bedroom – and stuffed the key into the pocket of an old coat hanging in her wardrobe. She got in touch with a couple of friends, but couldn't muster up the energy to meet up with them. One after another, her family and the others living at Feywood tried to persuade her to start work again, but she always had an excuse not to, laughing it off to Juliet, saying she was trying to decide between accountancy or insurance brokering for her next move. She became impatient with Martha, pushing away her timid enquiries and demanding to be left alone. She told her father and Sindhu that she was taking a break and would work again soon.

It was only Sylvia who came anywhere near the truth, finding her niece one day in the old orangery, where she had taken to hiding. She had appropriated a few cushions from around the house and made a sort of nest with these on an old cast-iron bench in the corner of the once-magnificent nineteenth-century glasshouse, its white paint flaking away as rust took over. She spent long periods here, reading, when she wasn't wandering around the gardens or trying to make herself useful in the cookery school by offering to wash dishes, which usually needed quietly doing again after she had drifted away.

'Hello, darling,' said Sylvia, picking her way across the floor, its paving stones cracked and invaded by moss and ivy. 'Mind if I join you for a bit?'

'Of course not,' said Frankie, slipping an old receipt into her book to mark the page and rearranging some of the cushions so that her aunt could sit down.

'Thank you. I brought some tea,' said Sylvia, producing from her bag a flask of hot water, swiftly followed by two china mugs, a small box of teabags and a little bottle of milk.

Frankie grinned. 'You're so civilised. Please tell me there are biscuits as well?'

'Naturally,' said her aunt with a wink, producing a tin. 'Léo made these this morning – those lemon ones he's so good at.'

Once they each had a cup in their hands, and Frankie was nibbling a biscuit, Sylvia spoke again.

'Darling, I wanted to talk to you about – well, about *you*.'

Frankie tensed up and she shrank back into her nest. Talking about herself was the last thing she wanted to do, but how could she rebuff kind Sylvia, one of her favourite people in the world?

'What about me?' she muttered, trying not to sound too ungracious.

'I know you had a terrible time with Dylan,' her aunt continued, 'and I am so proud of you for leaving. It can't have been easy, when you loved him.'

Frankie looked up sharply. 'Loved him?'

'Yes, loved him,' Sylvia repeated calmly. 'Which I think you did?'

Frankie dropped her eyes and nodded miserably.

'I did. The others don't know. They think I was rebelling or messing about.'

'I wouldn't be so sure. They're wiser than perhaps you realise – and we are all immensely proud of you for having the strength to leave. But maybe it is time to summon that strength again and to ask yourself: what's next?'

Frankie forced her eyes to meet her aunt's.

'I don't know. I'm pretty bloody useless. I thought I was being helpful here, at Feywood. I have tried to tidy up the gardens a bit. Will's given me some jobs. I thought I could, sort of, get good at that. Maybe.'

Sylvia sighed.

'Dearest Frankie, meekly going about the place washing dishes and poking around aimlessly in the flowerbeds is not what you were put on this earth to do. You know that. Have you tried going back to your studio?'

Frankie shook her head.

'I don't want to,' she insisted. 'I'm a wreck after everything that's happened. If I start working again – being *me* again – I'll find myself rocketing off. I don't know how to put the brakes on when that happens – I always go too far.'

'So you're going to shut yourself up here, are you? Safe and sound for the rest of your life?' Frankie shrugged and her aunt continued. 'I know you need to recover, in many ways, but this listlessness is worrying us all.'

'What do you mean? That I should go away from Feywood? I know it's pathetic to run home like this and believe me, I know I'm lucky that I can, but I can't go, not right now, Aunt Sylvia, I just can't.'

'I don't mean that. But you do need to start taking some risks again. You have had a painful lesson, one I wouldn't have wished on you or on anyone, but the point of lessons is to learn from them, to let them propel you forward.'

'All I have learnt is that I can't be trusted,' said Frankie with a dry laugh. 'You all already knew that, but now I understand too. Wayward, wild Frankie, always up to something stupid, always ready to be reckless. Well, I'm not doing that anymore.'

'No one's asking you to,' said Sylvia calmly. 'But it's time to get busy with *some*thing. Why don't you try working again? It might help.'

'I don't feel ready,' said Frankie stubbornly. 'I'll find something, Aunt Sylvia, but not that.'

'All right. I'm not going to try and force you. I think your father had an idea for something. I don't know if he's done anything about it yet, but at least give it some thought if he does.'

She stood up to go and Frankie opened her book again, but she took in nothing of what she read. The truth was that she desperately missed Dylan and her colourful life in London. Trying to fill her days with menial household tasks and trashy novels left her feeling apathetic yet agitated. She also felt a darkness around the edge of her spirit, a darkness she knew could close in dangerously, as it had threatened to do when she was a teenager. She dreamt sometimes of working, of creating powerful sculptures that came from her very soul, but when she woke, always around three in the morning, the inspiration and motivation had drained away, and she lay until dawn wondering what the hell she was going to do with the rest of her life.

TWO

Nathan Brooks gazed out over the Tuscan countryside as he sipped his coffee. The sun shone on the tall, slender cypress trees and warmed the stone buildings that peppered the landscape. Several of them belonged to his brother's wife's family, whose home this was, and where he had been living for the past couple of years. The peace all around him was palpable, the only sounds being the distinctive gentle hooting of the hoopoe birds and the clattering of pans in the kitchen beneath the stone balcony he stood on as Giorgia, the housekeeper, started preparing lunch. He sighed as he drained his cup. He knew that he ought to return to the preliminary designs he had agreed to do for the council, but was reluctant to pull himself away from the glorious view only to continue some dusty, boring work he had no interest in beyond the fat wage it would bring in. A footstep behind made him turn: his brother, Henry, who smiled as he came to stand next to him.

'Never gets old, does it? You've only been here for two years; I've been drinking it in for nearly seven and I could still stare at it all day.'

'It's outstanding, but I should be getting back to work.'

'What is it this time? Another council commission?'

'Yeah, well, a bid for one anyway, but I'd be surprised if they didn't choose me again. They like the fact that I live locally, and they can keep an eye on me to stop things getting too interesting. It's yet another tired town square in need of replanting.'

'And how long will this one take?'

'About six months. And then there's a nearby park that has a patch of scrub they want redesigning into a picnic area. So I'll be busy till the end of the year.'

'Doing commissions for other people.'

Nathan stared at the view for a moment before replying.

'I can't bring myself to turn them down. The money's good and I've nearly got enough saved now for a deposit on my own home. I've found some places near here that I'll be able to afford soon. Allegra's parents have been indescribably generous letting me live here for virtually nothing, but I can't stay forever.'

'You can,' said Henry mildly. 'They're generous, but they're also ridiculously rich and they like having you here, you know that. Partly for you and partly because, as my brother, they consider you family.'

'I know, and I feel the same about them, but it's important to me to support myself again. When we lost everything – and I *know* it wasn't my fault – but when we lost everything, all I ever wanted to do was to get it back again. I can't let Mum and Dad's fecklessness impact my life forever. They did enough damage in the first thirty-five years.'

'It was your own designs that supported you then; I don't understand why you stopped. You're still in demand.'

'Only for bids... there are no guarantees.'

'I hate seeing you unhappy. Just turn down the commission and start working for yourself again. Allegra's parents would be delighted, they're dying to be patrons of the arts in their very own home.'

'I will when I can, safely,' said Nathan, his mouth setting into a line.

Henry shrugged.

'You know best, but at least consider it. Anyway, lunch in about forty minutes. Giorgia said not to be late on pain of a severe scolding: she's made prawns and, apparently, they need to be eaten at precisely the right moment or the world grinds to a halt.'

Nathan laughed. 'Now, there's an artist. Of course I'll be on time. Thanks, H, I will think about it, but maybe one last commission.'

With a final glance at the hazy hills, Nathan turned and walked through the high-ceilinged drawing room into the hallway and up the marble staircase to his suite of rooms which comprised a bedroom, a study with a small balcony and a bathroom. It was the most wonderful place to live. His rooms were light and airy with views across the extensive gardens to the Tuscan hills beyond. Henry's in-laws were not only generous and welcoming but hugely sociable, and the house was often filled with guests for weekend stays and evening parties, when the laughter and chatter went on into the early hours. Nathan usually chose to sit on the outskirts of these events, happy to people-watch and continue picking up Italian, but there was never any pressure to participate – he could just be himself.

He opened his laptop to read again the email from the council, outlining their requirements for the garden, but another message caught his eye. It was the reply from a man he had emailed recently, when his frustration at the endless dry commissions, which seemed to have become all he ever did, had overwhelmed him. Nathan had met Rousseau Carlisle a few years ago, at his mother's funeral. Rousseau had lived for some time with his parents in an artistic colony in the south of England, before returning to Oxfordshire when he inherited the family pile, Feywood. A recent Google search had shown this to be a ravishing stone Tudor house, built in an 'L' shape with a magnificent porch and long gravel drive. Nathan had asked Rousseau if he might come to England for a mentorship in sculpting, something that had always interested him alongside his garden design. He had commissioned sculptures for gardens he was working on, and it intrigued him how the artists managed to create them for the spaces. In return, knowing that he could not possibly pay the great Rousseau Carlisle anything like what his mentorship was worth, he had offered a quid pro quo: to create a design for part of Feywood's gardens, then produce it. But he was already regretting the email. After all, why should he want to jettison the secure, comfortable and, let's face it, luxurious life he had in Italy, for a stranger's house in England? His idea that it would give him the opportunity to stretch himself and his creativity beyond the council commissions already felt foolish. But he couldn't possibly ignore Rousseau's email, and he clicked on it.

Re: A proposition

Dear Nathan,

Many thanks for your message, which I read with the greatest interest. It has, I know, been a long time since we saw one another on the sad occasion of your mother's funeral, but I have thought of you often since then, and followed your career. I would be delighted for you to come to Feywood, on the terms you describe. It is many years since I have taught, but it was always something I enjoyed, and I have a feeling you would be a most rewarding student. I confess that I also find it hard to turn down your offer of working on the gardens, although I have to warn you that, for the most part, they are more of a jungle. The lawns and roses are kept in good shape, as well as the kitchen garden, but other than that they are woefully neglected. Feywood herself, whilst beautiful, is, I'm afraid, a crumbling relic of a bygone era, but we are all far too romantic to let her go. However, if you would still like to come to this shack, we would be glad to welcome you. Feywood might be a bit rickety, like the best of us, but it is a splendid place to live.

I wonder if I might make one final request? My youngest daughter, Frankie, has had a difficult time and recently returned home. She is, I'm afraid to say, rather aimless, although she seems to enjoy spending time in our ramshackle orangery, which could certainly do with some attention. I thought she might find some purpose in being a sort of assistant to you in the garden, and maybe learn some garden design skills from you too, if you were to agree.

Warmest wishes,
Rousseau Carlisle

Nathan looked up from the screen and stared unseeingly at the plastered wall in front of him. He had heard of Rousseau's house, Feywood, and knew of his and Lilith Carlisle's three daughters. Martha, the eldest, an accomplished portrait painter. Juliet, in the middle, had produced witty, acerbic cartoons for newspapers until she changed her path and now worked with watercolours and photography, choosing mostly subjects from nature. Frankie, the youngest, was a wild child known as much for her partying as for her brilliant, difficult sculptures, which he admired and found impossible to understand in equal measure. He wasn't sure what kind of assistant she would make, but he could hardly refuse.

He had not entirely expected Rousseau to agree to his suggestions, and now he felt torn. If he agreed to go to England, to Feywood, it would mean no council commission. The thought at once thrilled and horrified him. It meant no guaranteed fat pay cheque but also no time and energy spent creating a dull green space that may be exquisitely executed, as all his work was, but would be mostly ignored by the people who hurried by or through it in the town square, going about their daily business. As he contemplated this potential new chapter in his life, Nathan felt a swell of excitement. He was being offered the opportunity to be part of an artistic household, with the great Rousseau Carlisle, and to live in the space where Lilith Carlisle had produced her masterpieces.

Nathan was grateful when he glanced at his watch and realised that he was nearly a minute late for lunch. Dreams of his future were one thing, but if he wasn't on time for Giorgia's prawns, he might not live to see them realised.

The rest of the family was already sitting at the table on the shady terrace when he slipped into his chair with muttered apologies.

'Don't worry, Nathan,' said his sister-in-law, Allegra, in a stage whisper. 'Giorgia's not come out yet, so you're safe.'

He grinned his thanks, then looked across to the kitchen door, where the housekeeper was emerging, bearing a large, steaming platter of prawn linguine bursting with ripe cherry tomatoes grown in the grounds and flecked with parsley. A delicious smell of garlic wafted over, and Nathan was glad he had made it on time. The food was set on the table, and Giorgia vanished again to continue preparing the second course, as the family dug in, chattering loudly about their mornings. It was only Nathan who didn't join in the conversation, but ate slowly, savouring the flavours and deep in thought. The family were used to him being quieter than they were and made no comment on his silence as they laughed and talked together. From the snippets that he understood, he worked out that they were talking about a recent visit they had all made to a nearby vineyard where the same family had been producing their exquisite wines for over a hundred and fifty years. Immaculate lines of vines stretched in the sunshine over acres of steep hillside and the grapes they grew made red and white wines as well as grappa and one of the most delicious sparkling wines he had ever tasted. The owners of the vineyards liked to declare that their wines were so fresh and carefully made that they would never give you a hangover, and Nathan grinned as the family loudly and robustly refuted this claim and described with increasingly dramatic words and even actions their suffering the following day. Nathan remembered his own sore head with some affection, as it had been a wonderful outing.

There were seven of them at the table that day: Nathan himself, his brother Henry, Henry's wife Allegra, her younger sister Lucia, their parents and their grandmother Donata. Nathan had no idea how old she was – surely at least ninety? – but she had the energy to match that of her granddaughters and was now roaring with laughter over some anecdote that Lucia had shared. A momentary lull in talk followed this hilarity, and Nathan knew from experience that, if he did want to speak, he had to do it quickly or lose his chance.

'Could I ask everyone's advice?' he said in his hesitant Italian, only the slight tightening of his fingers around his water glass giving away his discomfort at drawing attention to himself.

For a moment, there was silence as six faces turned towards him, then Antonio, Henry's father-in-law, smiled broadly.

'But of course! You've certainly come to the right place: everyone here will be delighted to offer you their opinion.'

Everyone laughed again and Nathan relaxed slightly.

'I am in line for another commission from the council, but I have been offered a different opportunity today: to go to England and work with Rousseau Carlisle, learning sculpture from him and, in turn, working on the gardens there, with one of his daughters helping me. I'm not sure how long it would be for, but I would live with them at Feywood, their house.'

'So, what's the question?' asked Carla, Antonio's wife, gently. 'That sounds like an amazing opportunity.'

Everyone agreed loudly, and it was a moment before Nathan spoke again.

'It is. I suppose I'm worried about turning down the council commission, and the money that would come from it. I'm so close to being able to afford my own place again. And what if England is a disaster? What if I'm useless at sculpture and I waste my time?'

'And what if you don't?' said Allegra. 'What if it is incredible, if you take well to sculpture, if you start working on your own designs again rather than those endless boring commissions? What if you continue on the path you started several years ago to design gardens that bring pleasure to people in need? What then?'

'The commissions may be boring,' said Nathan, stung. 'But they have filled up my bank account. Our parents, as you know, put their art before everything else – even their own children – and that didn't end well.'

It was Henry who spoke next, his eyes full of compassion for his brother.

'That's true, but you're not our parents – neither of us is. You've already proved that, over and over again, through the years. I agree with Allegra. What if this is the break you need? And you can always return to the commissions if things don't work out, you're in such demand. You asked for advice. Mine is: grab this opportunity with both hands. You and I have spent years undoing our parents' reckless choices; I think you deserve something different.'

Nathan looked around at the concerned, loving faces and gave a small smile.

'You know it's not that I don't love living here with you all, and that I'm so grateful for everything you've done for me...'

Across the hubbub of agreement cut Donata's voice, still strong enough to silence everyone:

'*Chi non fa, non falla.*'

Nathan frowned. His Italian was good, but some expressions were still new to him.

'It means "if you don't make mistakes, you make nothing",' explained Allegra in English. 'I don't know if you have a similar expression, but for Italians this is important.'

'Who dares, wins?' suggested Henry, then returned to speaking in Italian. 'It's time for you to take a risk. We all love you, but we'd like to see you go.'

Laughter and vigorous nodding met this statement, and Lucia mimed shooing him away, chanting until they all joined in:

'Va, va, va!'

Go, go, go!

It was only Giorgia appearing with the second course of baked sea bass that distracted them and left Nathan to mull over the decision that could change the course of his life for the better or could set him back and spoil everything he had worked for.

After lunch, Nathan went for a long walk through the countryside, passing through small towns where he saw the occasional person sweeping their doorstep or sitting in the shade with a cold drink. Many of the streets weren't wide enough for cars, so he passed uninterrupted down narrow roads flanked by pink stuccoed and plain stone buildings, troughs of cheerful red geraniums balanced precariously on the windowsills. It wasn't the time of day that most Italians would choose to walk several miles, but it was still only spring and

Nathan found the temperature pleasant and the peace therapeutic. He considered dropping in on friends who lived nearby, but decided that would only mean putting off doing the serious thinking he needed to. As he walked, he turned Rousseau's email, Henry's family's opinions and his own feelings over in his mind, and when he returned to the villa, he knew that, while he had managed to answer few of his questions, he did know what he wanted to do. With a wave at Giorgia, who was snapping jackets into order on the hall stand, he ascended the stairs and went to his rooms, where he headed straight for his laptop.

He read the email through one more time, then composed his answer, thanking Rousseau and politely agreeing to have Frankie as his assistant. He outlined some initial arrangements for his visit and pressed 'send' before he could change his mind. Part of him wanted to. He was flinging open a door he had, for years now, been too timid even to tap on, and perhaps shutting one that had meant security, even if that had been at the expense of creativity. Well, the deed was done. The best thing for him to do now was to push aside the dry emails from Francesco Lombardi, the twenty-third mayor of the town, who had a special interest in drainage, and start working out what he needed to take with him.

He hoped that work would help squash the insistent inner voice that was currently panicking and demanding that he backtrack immediately.

'Nothing like making it easy for yourself,' he muttered.

THREE

Frankie was spending more and more time in the orangery, but rather than reading – or staring unseeingly at the pages of a book – she had started trying to tidy it up. She had little hope of returning it to its original magnificent state, but she found the almost Sisyphean tasks of pulling up ivy, which seemed to return again almost immediately, and cleaning windows, which were determined to smear even more when she wiped them, comforting and purposeful rather than frustrating. The progress was slow, but undeniably happening. One morning she was working on clearing a stone bench, which ran around the domed end of the structure and was filthy as well as overgrown with weeds, when Sylvia came in.

'Good morning, darling. You're doing so well in here! Can I give you a hand?'

Frankie looked doubtfully at her aunt's thin frame and pale face and hesitated. But, knowing that the offer was genuine, and understanding from her own experience that work could slowly become something healing, she nodded.

'Yes, please. Could you take the secateurs and attack some

of the thicker stems? Then I can clear the plants much more quickly.'

It was a job that Sylvia could do sitting down, and which would be truly helpful.

Look at me, thought Frankie sardonically. *Actually thinking about someone else. Wonders will never cease.*

They worked in silence for a while, then Sylvia spoke.

'How are you feeling about this garden designer coming to stay?'

Frankie paused for a second, then resumed ripping out the plants with renewed vigour.

'Bloody Dad,' she said, panting slightly with the effort. 'I'm furious, but I couldn't exactly say no, could I? I can't believe he volunteered me as his assistant without even asking me. I've read a bit about this Nathan and he's very *serious*. He'll probably hate me messing around with his begonias. What do I know about plants?'

'Not a lot,' replied Sylvia. 'But that doesn't mean you can't learn. You might find you're good at the design part if nothing else. Rousseau was just trying to help.'

Frankie stopped again and pushed her hair back off her face with her forearm.

'I know that, but I'm honestly not worth it. I've had a knock, but I'll probably bounce back eventually and then everyone can stand down from the Florence Nightingale routine.'

'It wasn't that long ago,' said her aunt mildly, chopping at a particularly thick stem, which yielded to her secateurs with a satisfying crunch, 'that you were telling me how much you *didn't* want to be the old you.'

Frankie grinned.

'Oh, I know. I don't want all that again. I suppose I'll have to make the best of it. I will try, you know.'

'I know you will. And Frankie, I gave Juliet some advice not so long ago, and I think I can say the same to you now: you're very young. You can do this, give it a good go, spend time on it – and then forget it if you want to. Yes, you're looking at me in much the same way as she did, but I mean it. You've got time to try a dozen different things, to try them then reject them, to find you're good at something you hate and terrible at something you love. You might learn something about gardening with Nathan for six months, then go and be a... a... a trapeze artist.'

Frankie laughed.

'I'm not sure anyone wants to see me in a spangly leotard. Although if I was also risking my life forty feet above the ground, there might be a few takers,' she added ruminatively.

Sylvia smiled. 'Well, maybe not that. But you see my point. You have the luxury of youth and you can see what works.'

'Not Juliet's expensive face cream,' quipped Frankie. 'But don't tell her I've been nicking it.'

'Oh, be serious for a moment,' said Sylvia with uncharacteristic impatience. 'I'm trying to help. I'm glad you're regaining your sense of humour, but I know you, Frankie, and I know you're scared. And I'm trying to make it easier for you, although truthfully, I think that if you don't find a way to move forward from what's happened, it would be a great shame.'

Frankie stood upright and stopped yanking at the ivy. 'You do?'

'I do, and so do you and so does everybody else. Darling, at the moment, your self-esteem is at rock bottom, but Rousseau wouldn't have done this if he didn't believe in you. Keep putting one foot in front of the other, but grab the opportunity you've been given, please.'

'And if it doesn't work out, there's always the circus?'

'Well, quite.' Sylvia glanced out of one of the smeary panes of glass. 'Ah, good, here are your sisters. Open that flask that's in my bag, will you, and we can all have tea.'

Juliet and Martha pushed open the heavy door and came into the orangery, picking their way over the rubble-strewn floor.

'It's years since I've been in here,' said Juliet. 'Do you remember we used to have fairy parties when we were little?'

'Oh yes!' said Martha. 'They were lovely. We thought the fairies of Fey Wood would enjoy a special day out now and again, and we made little chairs and tables out of sticks and left iced gems for them.'

Frankie nudged her eldest sister.

'And I bet you'd do that again, given half the chance.'

Martha smiled dreamily.

'I probably would. I've never quite given up on believing there are fairies at the bottom of the garden, especially when that's such a special place.'

Frankie and Juliet exchanged glances, but neither said anything more. Frankie had been accustomed to teasing the gentle, whimsical Martha quite relentlessly, but felt less like it after her experience with Dylan. Maybe there was more to be said for believing in fairies at the bottom of the garden than in looking for your answers at the bottom of a bottle.

'Well, I'm glad you're all here,' said their aunt, handing round mugs of tea and pulling the lid off a biscuit tin. 'Léo made this shortbread yesterday, do try some. He used borage from the kitchen garden and wants some opinions on whether it works or not.'

Everyone took a piece, and they sat down on the stone bench, the rusty bench and Sylvia in a folding chair she had brought with her.

'Now, girls, I didn't only bring you here to eat shortbread – I'm afraid there's a rather more serious reason for our meeting.'

The sisters glanced at one another. *What could it be?*

'As you know, I have been unwell for a while now with my

heart and the doctors have decided that an operation is in order, after a few more weeks of treatment.' She paused, before continuing. 'They've also found a bit of cancer in my lung...'

There was a collective gasp at this, but Sylvia kept speaking, her voice steady. '...so they're going to take that out at the same time. Now, I know this is a shock, but we can't get too upset about it. My doctor is very pleased they've spotted it early, and I should be as right as rain once it's done.'

A shocked silence fell as this news was digested, eventually broken by Juliet, tears rolling down her face.

'But why have you got lung cancer? You've never smoked.'

The other two girls nodded vigorously, as if this statement could somehow prove that the diagnosis was wrong and they could all carry on as before.

'No, I haven't,' replied Sylvia. 'But I worked in so many restaurants before any smoking ban had even been thought of, let alone come into action, and they think that's the probable cause. Second-hand smoke.'

'But that's so unfair,' burst out Frankie.

'Unfair it may be, darling, but it is what it is. I'm lucky it's not much worse and I'm lucky they spotted it on a scan when they were looking at my heart.'

'What can we do to help?' whispered Martha, dabbing at her eyes with a tissue. 'We all want to.'

They all nodded again, and Sylvia smiled.

'That's more like it: let's talk practicalities. I've already told Rousseau, and he went into a bit of a panic, which I expected. But he did manage to suggest moving my bedroom downstairs for a while, which I've agreed to. I've always fancied that back parlour, with its view of the gardens, and it will make it much easier for me if I don't have to climb a lot of stairs all the time. I'm going to speak to Léo when we're done here, and once I've finished mopping up his tears' – she grinned at Juliet, who smiled weakly back, acknowledging her boyfriend's emotional openness – 'we can make a plan for the cookery school. The recipe book has been remarkably successful, which has boosted the coffers, and I'm going to keep working in some capacity, as much as I can. It's the physical stuff that will be difficult for a while, but that doesn't mean I can't think up recipes, or deal with admin, or whatever.'

'Shouldn't you be resting?' asked Martha.

'I think too much rest would probably be the worst thing I could do,' answered Sylvia. 'I might go crazy as well as having to recover from an op. I don't want to be wrapped in cotton wool, and I won't let you do that. I want to be supported to get back to normal as quickly as possible. Understood?'

The sisters nodded and Frankie reached out to take her aunt's hand.

'Yeah, I get that. We'll look after you, but we won't treat you like an invalid. And I promise I'll try with Nathan.'

'Good girl. Right, wish me luck, I'm off to see Léo.'

The three sisters sat in silence as Sylvia left the orangery, each lost in her own thoughts. It was Martha who spoke first.

'Oh, poor, poor Aunt Sylvia. She's being so brave about it.'

'Best thing to do,' replied Frankie. 'There's no point in her dwelling on it and we mustn't either.'

'I wasn't going to,' said Martha, sounding offended.

Frankie went over and sat down next to her, slipping an arm around her shoulders.

'I didn't mean it like that. I meant that the best thing we can do to help right now is to get on with life the best we can, not give her anything to worry about. So, I suppose I'll have to try to make the best of things with this Nathan bloke.'

Martha summoned up a small smile.

'Yes. I'll get to work clearing out that back parlour and make sure it looks welcoming and pretty by the time she needs to use it.'

'And I'll help with the cookery school,' said Juliet, then, clocking her sisters' concerned faces, added, 'Not the cooking, don't worry – I'm sure the thought of that would make Sylvia feel even worse. I mean I'll do the admin until she can take it back again and I'll make sure Léo doesn't freak out too much. Honestly, that man could make a drama out of any crisis.'

Her fond smile for her passionate, emotional boyfriend belied her sharp words and her sisters smiled too.

'He'll make a lovely nurse when she comes out of hospital,' said Frankie. 'I can just see him fluffing pillows and trying to tempt her with tasty morsels.'

'Poor woman,' quipped Juliet. 'She'll make sure she speeds up her recovery if he's fussing around taking her temperature every five minutes.'

'A case of *Don't* Carry on Nurse,' said Frankie, dissolving into giggles, in which she was quickly joined by the other girls.

'Oh, I do feel better!' said Martha. 'I'm not sure it's the right time to laugh, but it's helped. Poor Léo, he's such a dear, and I know he'd laugh, too, if he was here.'

'Of course he would,' said Juliet firmly. 'Now, what about Nathan Brooks? I remember an article in the paper about his work a few years ago, but I haven't heard anything about him in ages.'

'Let's look him up,' said Frankie, taking out her phone. 'I might as well see what I'm in for.'

The three girls crowded around the small screen as Frankie tapped his name into the search engine, then narrowed the results down to images only.

'That must be him,' said Martha, leaning forward to tap on and enlarge a picture of a man with auburn hair, brown eyes and a serious expression. 'Ooh, Frankie, he's very good-looking.'

Frankie wrinkled her nose.

'I suppose so, and I have always had a weakness for redheads. But he looks a bit severe.'

'Perfect for keeping you in line, then,' replied her eldest sister, grinning. 'What about his work?'

'That's the design that was in the article I read,' said Juliet, pointing to a picture of an ethereal space laced with ferns and wispy nigella. 'It's staggeringly good. I don't know how he managed to get so much feeling into it, but I stared at it for ages even though I know nothing about plants.'

'It *is* good,' said Frankie. 'How on earth is he going to teach me anything? This is genius level, not colour by numbers.'

'He won't start with stuff this tricky,' said Martha. 'I bet you'll start with weeding or something. And when it comes to drawing up designs – if he lets you get past yanking out dandelions – don't forget that you're pretty much a genius yourself, so don't start thinking he's better than you.' She turned her attention back to the phone, ignoring the flabbergasted stares of the other two at the usually gentle Martha speaking up so fiercely. 'He did that a few years ago. What's he doing now?'

Frankie tapped away some more and several pictures appeared.

'Ooh, they're a bit different,' she said, studying one photo of a city square lined with box hedges but with colourful plants interspersed and people enjoying the shade of well-placed trees. 'It's good – really good – but hardly the same as that other one. Look, it says it's a commission from a town in Italy.' She went back and chose another, similar, picture. 'This one's a commission too, and this one.'

'That's weird,' said Juliet. 'Why would such a talented designer take on such boring commissions? He can't have much time left over for his own work. Google him again, Frankie, and see what else you can find out.'

But Frankie turned the screen off.

'Sorry, I don't feel like it. I keep thinking about Sylvia. Oh God, what if she dies?'

The sisters looked at one another, their faces grave. Eventually, Martha spoke, her voice steady.

'We have to take one day at a time, and we can't let ourselves get bogged down with thinking about that. Sylvia needs us to be strong. We've got each other; we'll do this together.'

FOUR

As the taxi bumped over the cattle grid and moved slowly up the gravel drive, Nathan peered around the driver to see the house he was going to be living in. It stood in an 'L' shape, stone built with stone-mullioned windows and a huge wooden front door behind a large porch. The roof's red tiles were encrusted with moss – or was it lichen? – and there were bare patches where the tiles had fallen off. The drive was flanked by large lawns, which were beautifully mown in neat lines, and made a contrast to the house, which looked rather run-down, if extremely beautiful. His car drew to a stop, and he and the driver both got out. As the driver popped the boot and handed Nathan his bags, he grinned.

'Staying with the Carlisles for long?'

'I'm not sure – certainly a few weeks.'

'Hope you've brought plenty of aspirin – they like a party, especially Frankie.'

Nathan felt his stomach flip as he took the bags and dug in his pocket for the fare.

'Well, I've come to work, so I'm sure I'll be concentrating on that.'

He knew he sounded prim, but he didn't want to hear anything else from this man, who obviously thought that staying at Feywood was a hilarious prospect. He compounded this now, with a loud snort of laughter.

'Good luck, mate. You'll either last five minutes with that lot, or you'll surface in twenty years' time wondering what the hell happened.' He slammed the boot shut. 'Well, you've got my number if – when – you need taking away.'

With a final cackle of laughter, he gave Nathan a mock salute, got back into the car and drove off, spraying more dust than gravel from the threadbare drive.

Ignore him. Nathan strode towards the front door, hearing loud music behind it as he approached. *You're here to work and to learn and God knows you've had enough challenges in your life to be able to focus on what matters.* He rapped hard with the heavy knocker and waited, but there was no response. Apparently, the music was drowning out his knocks. He sighed. There was probably no point in trying again, so he flicked open Rousseau's last email.

If there's no one around when you get here, there's a spare key in the pot on the recess to your left.

The porch was about six feet long, with wooden benches running along each side – both of which looked too riddled with woodworm to put any weight on – and stone recesses in the walls above. In the left-hand recess there was, indeed, an earthenware pot, which Nathan took down now and tipped over. A large, iron key dropped into his hand. *Bingo.* He slipped it into the keyhole, and it turned with a satisfying *click.* He picked up his bags again and pushed the door open, hinges shrieking, the music now blaring around him with an upbeat pop song he vaguely recognised. He took in the enormous wood-panelled hallway, with the stairs rising upwards and a gigantic portrait that he recognised as Lilith Carlisle hanging above them, and a muddle of coats, shoes and dog leads. There was also a rather terrifying 1970s shop mannequin sporting a skew-whiff wig and an orange kaftan which, he supposed, made a change from the suit of armour one might reasonably expect to see in a house like this. He was pushing the door shut when a woman burst through a door to his right, wearing nothing but a towel and clutching a small dog to her. She was singing along loudly to the music and dancing with abandon, not seeming to have noticed Nathan at all.

'Hello?' he said politely, as she shimmied past the bottom of the stairs, facing the portrait. But the music was too loud. 'Er, *hello?*' he said again, almost shouting, and the girl turned, saw him and screamed, half dropping both the towel and the dog as she clutched them to her frantically and yelled:

'Alexa! Stop!'

The music was instantly terminated and the two of them stood in silence for a second. Nathan had recognised the woman straight away. There was no doubt that this towel-clad, screeching, whirling creature with her cropped blonde hair and incredible bone structure — only slightly marred by the accompanying scowl — was Frankie, Rousseau Carlisle's youngest daughter and Nathan's soon-to-be assistant. He began to summon up a smile but was swiftly cut off.

'Who on earth are you?' demanded Frankie, her imperious tone somewhat at odds with the desperate grasping as both towel and dog threatened to fall to the floor.

'I'm Nathan Brooks. Sorry, Rousseau told me where the key was and to let myself in. I, er...' He trailed off, his heart leaden. *What was I thinking, coming here?* His mind drifted back to the peaceful Tuscan villa and even lingered regretfully, for a moment, on Francesco Lombardi and his drainage maps. *This girl is going to be impossible to work with.*

'Well, there's no need to glare at me like that,' said Frankie.

'I'm Frankie – sorry I can't shake hands. Look, take Ava for a moment, will you?'

Nathan blinked at her, bemused.

'The dog?' said Frankie.

'Oh, right.'

He stepped forward and tried to extract the wriggling animal without touching Frankie's bare skin or further dislodging the towel. Both these things proved impossible, so eventually, he grabbed the dog and pulled her to him, turning away as he did so, both for Frankie's sake and his own. Annoying she undoubtedly was, but even given her current dishevelled state, she was undeniably beautiful and had a lively sparkle in her eye that made him want to abandon dog, towel, his bags and all reason, scoop her up and spend the rest of the day in bed. It had been a long time since he had felt that way about anyone and, although there had been girlfriends over the past few years, the relationships had been polite rather than passionate. He had tried to make them work as, rather like the commissions, they offered safety and security. But ultimately his heart hadn't betrayed him and wouldn't let him sustain them for longer than a few months, whispering quietly but insistently that *there was more to life than this, whether you like it or not.* He smiled down ruefully at the little dog in his arms, who responded by licking his chin.

'You can turn round now,' said Frankie. He did so. 'Sorry about that. Shall I take Ava again?'

He handed her back.

'She's a very nice dog.'

Frankie smiled at him and his heart skipped about seventeen beats.

'She's the best. We rescued her from the bottom of the drive when she was a tiny puppy and all nursed her so that she lived. You'll get on all right here if you like dogs.'

'I do.'

'Good. Well,' she said abruptly. 'I'm going to go and get dressed.'

She straightened her shoulders and turned to march towards the stairs, promptly tripping on the first one and landing on her knees, nearly losing dog and towel again. Nathan took a step towards her.

'Are you all right?'

She didn't turn, but stood up. He could see her take a deep breath.

'Couldn't be better. See you later. Alexa! Resume!'

The deafening music started up again as Nathan watched Frankie walk up the stairs, flick a V-sign at her mother's portrait and then disappear along the landing. He stood motionless for a minute or two, as the song ended and quiet fell again. There was no indication that anyone else was there. He looked around the hall, trying to avoid the lugubrious gaze of the mannequin. Although on first impressions it was impressive, with a closer look it was clear that it had seen better days. The stone-flagged floor was dirty and scuffed, although a small patch at one side glowed where someone had scrubbed and polished it; whether the start of a later abandoned attempt at restoration or an experiment to see how easy it would be to spruce up the whole floor, he could only guess. The wooden panelling, which lined the entire room, was scratched and dull and – could he be right? He stepped a little closer and bent down. Yes, it had undeniably been nibbled. He gave a shudder at the thought that rats might be responsible. And with teeth marks that big they would have to be *giant* rats. He stood up abruptly and returned to the relative safety of the middle of the floor. What now?

FIVE

Frankie shoved her bedroom door shut behind her and sat down heavily on the side of the bed, pulling Ava up to her face and breathing in her comforting dogginess.

'Oh, Ava, how cringey was that?'

The dog offered a reassuring lick in response.

'Yes, I know you don't think it was that bad, but you see me prancing around to Taylor Swift in my towel *all the time*. It wasn't the first impression I wanted to make on Nathan Brooks.' Then a giggle escaped. 'Oh dear, but Ava, did you see his *face*? Poor man! He must have thought I was deranged.'

More laughter bubbled up inside her, until she was lying on the bed helpless, with tears pouring down her cheeks. Ava, confused, licked them away. Eventually, the giggles subsided, and Frankie lay back on the bed, pulling the little dog onto her stomach as she gazed up at the ceiling.

'Ugh, look at those cobwebs,' she said. 'I should probably climb up with a feather duster, but I never will.'

Now the laughter had left, she was filled instead with melancholy.

Maybe it's not so funny. What on earth can he have thought of me? I must look a complete state.

She got down from the bed and went over to the mirror.

'Worse than I realised, Ava.' She picked up a strand of hair and let it drop. 'At least it's clean, but it could do with about four hours at the hairdresser.'

She unwrapped the towel, which she flung over a nearby chair, then pulled some underwear out of a drawer. Next, she burrowed under the damp towel for some clothes. Shaking out a black T-shirt she had scrawled across in bleach: 'Sculptors do it with their hands', and a pair of ripped jeans, she sniffed them, deemed them acceptable and pulled them on. She was reaching for her phone when there was a tap on the door and her sister Martha put her head round.

'Come in,' said Frankie. 'I was just thinking about making a hair appointment. My friend Marnie used to do it for me in London. Or would you cut it for me, darling Martha?'

'I can if you like,' said Martha, coming in and sitting on the bed next to Ava. 'Are you going to go back to your natural colour?'

Frankie shrugged.

'I don't know. I know I should do something, but I can't be bothered to think about it.' She threw down the phone and said casually, 'That bloke's arrived, the one Dad invited.'

'Nathan Brooks? Have you met him?'

'Yeah, you could say that. I was having a post-shower boogie and he walked right in and found me. I nearly dropped my towel, and he had to hold Ava while I sorted myself out.'

Martha put her hand to her mouth to stifle a laugh, earning a glare from her youngest sister.

'I'm sorry, Frankie, but it does sound funny. I didn't hear the door over your music, and I was pretty engrossed in my work, anyway. Where's Dad? Poor Nathan should have had a proper welcome – or maybe he enjoyed being greeted by you with your towel falling off.'

Frankie rolled her eyes.

'He looked like he was about to pass out, probably wondering what he's let himself in for. I'm not sure I like being disapproved of as much as I used to.'

Martha stopped laughing and stood up to give her sister a hug.

'I'm sure he won't even remember. And when he gets to know you, he won't care, anyway.'

With a sceptical snort, Frankie shrugged her sister off but reached to give her hand a squeeze.

'Thanks, M.'

'Did you recognise him?'

'No, that's even worse. At first, I thought he was an intruder. I hate to admit it, but he's even better-looking than his photo, and when I suddenly saw him standing there, I couldn't decide if this hottie appearing in the hallway meant my luck was in or out. It's a shame you refuse to get over Will – you might like this one.'

Martha reddened.

'Will and I are friends and I'm not looking for romance, anyway.'

'I don't see why not. You can't still be getting over that awful fancy-dress shop man. What was his name? Roger?'

'Ralph, and it was academic dress for the university, as well you know. Of course I don't care for him anymore, I'm far too busy.'

Martha's voice sounded tight, and she bit her lip. Frankie softened her tone.

'Sorry, M. I know what a wind-up merchant I can be, and I'm trying to pack it in. Believe it or not, I'm a bit more clued up now I've had my own heart broken.'

Martha, ever-forgiving, smiled warmly.

'I'm sorry that you've been hurt, but I can't pretend I'm sorry that Dylan's in your past. You deserve so much better.'

'Thanks, but I'm taking the same stance as you: no romance for me. I'm going to focus on this garden business and helping Sylvia – that's quite enough. Poor Dad, I bet he never thought Juliet would be the only one of us fixed up. Wasn't this place a convent about four hundred years ago? We could start it up again: Sisters of the Broken Hearts. It would be beautifully tragic. And the wimple would mean never having another bad hair day. Come on, don't say you're not tempted.'

As Frankie had intended, Martha laughed.

'Well, it might make life easier, but I'm not going to give up on love yet, and neither are you. Nun indeed. Even if you could manage the chastity bit, you'd be awful at obedience. Mind you,' she added, 'a convent might be cosier than Feywood sometimes. You were lucky you missed the winter here. Dad was so paranoid about the gas bills that we were eating salads, showering every three days and using extra blankets rather than putting on the heating. Of course, that meant things got terribly damp, so we've got even more peeling wallpaper than before. Léo and Sylvia were quite pleased, though, because we all kept wandering casually into the cookery school offering to do the washing up as it was the warmest place.'

Frankie laughed.

'I can imagine that.' Her face became more serious. 'Do you think Feywood will ever be sorted out? I hate to say it, but Dad and Sylvia could sell.'

Martha sighed.

'Never going to happen. Dad has been talking to the bank loads, and we've all been doing our bit, so hopefully things will improve before too long. I want to suggest opening to the public in some way, but it's too decrepit at the moment. I don't think anyone would pay to see where that enormous rabbit of yours chewed all the panelling.'

'Gulliver was a one-off,' said Frankie. 'But I admit that his legacy isn't exactly Anne Boleyn's prayer book. I'm not sure it would bring in paying visitors.'

They both giggled.

'Oh well,' said Martha, giving Ava a kiss on her head and sliding off the bed. 'At least we're all together again. I missed you so much when you were in London. Right, I'm going to go and introduce myself to Nathan – are you coming?'

'No,' said Frankie. 'I think he's seen enough of me for a while. Repair my reputation with him if you can; I'll see you at supper.'

When Martha had gone, Frankie stood up, too, and paced around the room. She was used to quelling this sort of agitation with wine or even vodka, then going out and partying with anyone who would join her, whether she liked them or not. She could feel the temptation rising within her.

Go on, nip down the back stairs to the dining room, no one will see you. There's plenty to choose from in there. There's always some vodka in the cabinet, and gin, and if you had some of that expensive whisky, Dad would never notice. You could get a taxi and be in Oxford within the hour.

'No,' she said out loud, banging her hand on the wall and making Ava jump. 'Are you serious?'

Okay then, whispered the voice. *What about some wine? Wine is fun and not so strong. Dad has plenty in the cellar, so you could grab a bottle and have a single glass. It must be wine o'clock somewhere and it's not like you're an alcoholic. You haven't had a drink for ages, and a small glass would make it easier to talk to Nathan. It would probably be a good thing.*

Pushing her hands through her hair, Frankie hauled in a huge breath.

'I do *not* want a drink,' she said, then turned to the puzzled little dog. 'Ava, I do *not* want a drink. Well, I do, but I'm not going to.'

She sighed as she gazed at Ava's sweet, uncomprehending face.

'Do you want to go out? We could go to the orangery and get on with some stuff there.'

She pulled on some trainers, scooped up Ava and slipped out of the door.

'Now, where is everybody?' she whispered. 'It would be just my luck to run into them all.'

She stood for a moment and listened.

'I can't hear a thing. We'll have to take our chances.'

She turned left and walked silently down the landing away from the main staircase and past several closed doors until she entered what was called the 'new wing' – new in that it had been built in the seventeenth century, rather than a hundred years earlier, as had been the oldest part of the house. Léo and Juliet had their room here, but she expected them to be in the old stable building where Léo had the cookery school and Juliet her studio in the space above. Indeed, it was all quiet and she slipped unseen into a bedroom sometimes used for guests and across to what looked like a perfectly ordinary wall. She knew the exact spot where the wallpaper was slightly worn, and it was here that she ran her fingers until she found a little catch. She twisted it and pulled, and a door opened, admitting her to a dingy staircase, its only illumination struggling its way through small windows that desperately needed a wash. But Frankie had never minded the gloom of these hidden servants' stairs and had used them often as a teenager to slip in and out of the house unnoticed, not that her parents had ever been particularly censorious about curfews. She ran lightly down them until she found herself behind another door, which she pressed her ear to. Silence. Again, she located the catch and pushed at the old door, peering through the gap. When she was as sure as she could be that the room beyond was empty, she opened it fully and slid through into the dining room. Turning her head away from the drinks cabinet, Frankie darted to the French windows and was outside.

'We did it, Ava,' she said triumphantly, but quietly, putting the little dog down. 'I know I'll have to meet Nathan properly later, but I need some sort of help first, and if I'm not going to have a drink, then the orangery will have to do its bit.'

Knowing she may now be seen, she ran swiftly around the side of the house and pushed open the heavy cast-iron and glass door. She entered her sanctuary thankfully. Glancing around at the rubble and wildly overgrown plants, she felt a sense of relief. Here, in the milky green light, she knew exactly what needed doing next. Here, she would not be met with questions, opinions or concerned looks. Grabbing a pair of shears, she got to work.

SIX

Nathan shook off thoughts of giant, wainscot-nibbling rats, but picked up his bags and put them on a nearby table, just in case.

'You can keep an eye on these,' he said to the kaftan-clad mannequin, then rolled his eyes at his own whimsy. Maybe the taxi driver had been right and Feywood would suck him in inexorably. No, he was going to keep his reason and take charge of the situation. Next job was to find somebody. It would do more harm than good to go chasing up the stairs after Frankie, so he'd have to try the ground floor. A kitchen would be ideal; there was likely to be someone passing through at some point and he could make himself a coffee. The entrance hall offered four closed doors. The first revealed a cavernous lavatory which smelled incongruously, but not unpleasantly, of Christmas spices and on whose walls were pinned dozens of children's drawings and paintings, interspersed with several clearly drawn by talented adults and coloured in by childish hands.

'The family archives?' murmured Nathan, pulling the door shut again. 'Probably worth a fortune.'

Behind the next door was a large living room in which stood huge, faded sofas strewn with books and magazines. A couple of used glasses and mugs were abandoned on side tables and there was a saucepan on the windowsill. The third revealed a vast hall, empty save for a few ghostly stacks of what he assumed was furniture, shrouded in white sheets. It was cold in here, despite the warmth of the day, and it had a forlorn, unloved air about it, unlike the living room, which had felt homely and well-used. He left the room gladly, and headed for the fourth and final door, which revealed a long passageway. Shrugging, Nathan stepped in and started heading towards the back of the house. A door to his left opened into a dining room, so he headed the opposite way. Would he ever find what was supposedly the heart of the home: the kitchen? Idly, he wondered what it might be like – nothing would surprise him. Maybe the Carlisles cooked their food over an open fire, or in a five-hundred-year-old bread oven, or maybe they had all the mod cons in the form of a black leaded, red-hot Victorian range. Or perhaps a Carlisle down the years had reimagined the kitchen as cottagecore with oiled wood worktops and cheerfully striped fabrics. The thing that would surprise him the most, he ruminated, as he reached the end of the passageway and a final door, was if all the money that had clearly not been spent on the rest of the house had instead been ploughed into a state-of-the-art modern kitchen, all shiny marble and grey cabinets without handles.

When he opened the door which finally did lead him to Feywood's kitchen, he nearly burst out laughing. It had managed to surprise him, after all. The one thing he had not anticipated was the rather tired, nineteen seventies affair that stood before him, with its dark green units and textured laminate worktops. He stepped inside and touched the moulded tiles, in orange and olive with a starburst design, then glanced rather doubtfully at the oven, which looked as if it came from the same era. Surely it must be dangerous? Gratefully, he spotted a yellow plastic kettle and, hoping the plug adhered to modern safety standards, he filled it and gingerly switched it on, whereupon it started heating up with a cheerful enthusiasm that gave him a modicum of confidence. There were some bits and pieces of washing up in the metal sink and, rather than rummaging through the cupboards, which felt intrusive in a house he hadn't even been invited into, he extracted a used mug to wash. It had the words 'What would Mick Jagger do?' emblazoned across it, along with a caricature of the star, all lips and hips. Instant coffee was in a tin on the side, and within a few minutes, Nathan was feeling more in control as he sat down at the faded Formica table and pulled out his phone. He texted Rousseau and sent a photo of the mannequin to his brother, Henry. He had drunk about half his coffee when the phone rang. It was Rousseau.

'Nathan! I'm so sorry that no one was there to greet you.'

'No problem, I'm having a coffee in the kitchen.'

'Splendid. I hope you found everything you needed. I've called Léo and Juliet. They were in the cookery school, so they'll join you in a minute or two. Can't get hold of anyone else although all the girls are at home as far as I know. But then *what* do I know?' Nathan did not mention the fact he had already met Frankie. 'I won't be long myself.'

'See you later.'

He put down the phone and continued drinking his coffee. Would anyone mind if he looked through the cupboards for a biscuit? It was a long time since breakfast. He had decided that no one in this family would care less if he cooked himself a three-course lunch, and was seriously missing Giorgia, when the outside door to the kitchen opened, admitting a smiling man and woman. The man was tall, with shaggy hair and friendly brown eyes, while the woman had dark hair caught up in a ponytail and porcelain-perfect skin. He recognised them from his brief research into the family as the middle daughter, Juliet, and her French chef boyfriend

Léo, who ran the cookery school at Feywood with Rousseau's sister, Sylvia.

'Hello,' said Juliet, holding out her hand. Nathan rose to shake it, followed by Léo's. 'Dad rang to say you had to let yourself in. I'm so sorry, I thought Martha and Frankie were here – we hadn't forgotten you were coming.'

Nathan sat down again, feeling awkward.

'Er, well, I did meet Frankie, briefly.'

'Oh dear, was she *very* rude? She doesn't mean to be, but she's gone through a tough time.'

'I think I took her by surprise, suddenly appearing in the hall.'

Juliet looked sceptical, but let it go.

'I'm glad you made yourself a coffee, anyway. We've brought some biscuits over from the cookery school, if you'd like one?'

She went to fill the kettle again, while Léo sat down at the table and opened a couple of glass boxes.

'There are biscuits, but also I thought you might like some quiche. Travel always makes me hungry. This is brie, mushroom and thyme, which always seems to be popular. Let me get you a plate. I have brought some olive oil and rosemary *tortas* as well – a sort of Spanish cracker, I suppose – for you to have with it.'

Soon Nathan was gratefully tucking in to one of the most delicious lunches he had ever eaten and telling Léo and Juliet all about his sister-in-law's family's house in Italy, and the stellar cooking they were lucky enough to enjoy from Giorgia.

'How long are you going to be staying here?' asked Léo, finishing off his biscuit.

'I'm not sure,' said Nathan, treading carefully. In one way he was ready to belt back to Italy when he had finished his coffee rather than stay and try to work with Frankie. 'I have an enormous amount to learn from Rousseau, and with working on the garden as well, I think it will be at least a month. Oh, look, there's Frankie now.'

He pointed out of the window, and they turned to watch as she ran past a little distance away, Ava gambolling around her. Juliet turned back to speak to him.

'Please don't be too hard on her. I don't know what happened when you met her earlier, but I wouldn't be surprised to hear that Frankie didn't show herself in her best light. Don't let that put you off, though. She's wonderful, really, so funny and quick and insanely talented. She's had a bad time with her ex. I wouldn't wish it on anyone, let alone my little sister, but at the same time it does seem to have – oh, I don't know, helped her grow up a bit, or something. We were so glad, Martha and me, when Dad said that he'd volunteered her to help you.' She let out a little bark of laughter. 'As far as we're concerned, you're her knight in shining armour, but whatever you do, don't tell Frankie that.'

Nathan smiled drily.

'I take it she was rather less pleased to be volunteered? Don't worry, I won't say anything.'

'Thank you. Would you like me to show you your room now?'

They returned to the entrance hall, where Nathan reclaimed his bags and followed Juliet up the stairs then around to the right.

'This is the new wing,' she explained, pushing open a door. 'Not the best name, given it was built about four hundred years ago, but it was new to the house then.'

He followed her in apprehensively. Given the state of the parts of the house he had seen so far, his expectations were low, and he wouldn't have been surprised to find a camp bed and gas fire, or an itchy straw mattress contemporary to the age of the room, but he was pleasantly surprised. The room was large and filled with light from the tall windows overlooking the front of the house. The frame of the double bed looked old, but the linen was bright and modern and the pillows plump, which gave him hope for the mattress. The room was papered in cream with a fresh pale pink and green Chinoiserie pattern of birds, leaves and flowers and there were several faded but pretty rugs on the wooden floor.

'I hope it will be okay,' said Juliet. 'It's one of the rooms we spruced up for the cookery school clients – they sometimes stay for weekends – so the bed should be comfortable and there's a bathroom through that door over there.'

'It's a lovely room, thank you.'

'Good. If you leave your bags, I'll show you the room we've put aside for a studio. We would have used Frankie's, but she won't go in and anyway, this is better for the garden.'

They went back downstairs to the entrance hall, then over to the door that Nathan, from his earlier explorations, knew led into the comfortable living room. Juliet crossed this, opening a door at the other side of the room that he hadn't noticed before, and ushered him through into yet another unexpected space.

'Oh, what a wonderful room!' he exclaimed. 'Feywood is full of surprises.'

Juliet grinned.

'Isn't she? This is the garden room. It was added on to the house about a hundred years ago, and I'm afraid that nobody uses it much because it's so tucked away and very cold in the winter. We tend to collapse on the sofas in the sitting room before getting here, or use the garden in the summer. But it should be warm enough at this time of year, and the light's amazing. It's a miracle none of us ever claimed it for a studio, but that's your good luck.'

It certainly was. The room was hexagonal with huge windows overlooking the lawns and flowerbeds to the side of the house. The floor was of red quarry tiles, mostly intact, and at some point, someone had painted trailing ivy leaves on the stonework that formed the main part of the room. Two massive Victorian green glazed jardinieres, empty, stood to one side, but otherwise the room had everything he had asked for or had sent: a sturdy table, some coiled-up extension leads, his tool box, garden tools, a couple of bags of soil, a pile of terracotta plant pots and his precious – and very expensive – tech, which looked like it had arrived unscathed.

'I hope we found everything you need?' asked Juliet. 'There was great excitement when your toolbox arrived – we couldn't imagine what was inside.'

'A lot of little saws and trowels, mostly,' said Nathan, smiling. 'It all looks great, thank you. You've even set up a sink, that's amazing.'

'Yes, you said it would be useful, but there wasn't anything in here, of course, or very nearby, so Will – Dad's estate manager, you'll meet him later – rigged this up. It took him two days and it works perfectly.' She went over to the large ceramic butler's sink and turned on a tap to demonstrate. 'He even made the stand and draining rack for it, out of a couple of horrid nineteen sixties chairs he found in one of the outbuildings.'

'Thank you,' said Nathan again.

'Well, I'll leave you to sort things out how you like them,' said Juliet. 'Supper's at 7.30, but we usually get together for a drink first in the living room – so next door to here.'

She went out, leaving Nathan alone to take in his surroundings.

Looking around the eclectic, beautiful space, Nathan felt the tension in his chest begin to ease. The familiar tools of his trade were laid out before him, grounding him in the work that awaited. For the first time since arriving at Feywood, his heart lightened. Maybe he had made the right decision, after all.

SEVEN

The orangery had its usual calming effect on Frankie. When she next looked at her watch, an hour and a half had passed and she had a huge pile of creepers beside her, which she had pulled away from the window frames and the stone bench.

'Look at that,' she said to Ava, who was curled up on Sylvia's camping chair. 'Next time maybe I'll bring a cushion for you, and you can snooze in style.'

The little dog wagged her tail agreeably in response.

Frankie started gathering up the foliage and carrying it to a compost heap she had started nearby, and in another twenty minutes, she could stand back and admire the results of her work.

Maybe I should become a gardener. It's certainly less tricksy than creating art.

It was pleasing to see the ironwork, windows, bench and floor revealed and feel an ache in her arms and hunger pangs in her stomach from the exertion. But what would working alongside Nathan be like? His stiff disapproval earlier had shaken Frankie, and after she had rinsed her hands under the garden tap, she went to see her father, tapping gently on the door of the long room at the back of the house that he used as his office and studio.

'Hi, Dad,' she said, entering the room. 'Have you got a moment?'

'Of course,' said Rousseau, looking up from some papers on his desk with a strained smile. 'I'll be glad not to be reading through yet another missive from the bank.'

He stood up and they went to sit together on his old sofa beside one of the windows, which smelled comfortingly of years of ingrained marble dust, white spirit and wax.

'Are we still in trouble with the bank?' asked Frankie.

'No, no, quite the opposite. They've finally agreed that we've been doing well enough to let us borrow a bit more to mend that blasted roof. I might not look delighted, but I am. There's a lot of paperwork, and you know that's not my strong point.'

Frankie grinned. 'I'm my father's daughter in that respect.'

'Well, I'm sorry to have passed it on,' said Rousseau with a matching smile. 'Now, what did you want to talk about? Nathan's arrived, by the way, have you met him?'

'Er, yes, very briefly.' She didn't elaborate. 'And Dad, it's that I wanted to talk to you about. Look, I don't think I can go through with this assistant thing, I'm sorry. I'll find something else to do and stop just hanging around.'

Rousseau looked down at his scarred hands and sighed.

'I was afraid you would feel this way. And maybe I shouldn't have volunteered you without asking first. But Frankie, I still think that this is the best possible next step for you. I know you're terrified...' He broke off and clasped her shoulder in his hand. 'Yes, you are, even if you won't admit it, but you need *something*, and I want to help. Also...'

He paused and Frankie looked at his face, which suddenly

seemed so old and tired. He didn't look like her usual youthful and charming father. She swallowed her objection and asked:

'Also what?'

'Well, I don't want to emotionally blackmail you, but I was so *relieved* when you agreed to working with Nathan. Getting the money sorted for Feywood has been a strain, even with the help of you wonderful daughters and Sindhu, and now I'm desperately worried about Sylvia.'

Frankie went cold. How could she have been so selfish?

'Dad, I'm so sorry. We're all terribly worried about Sylvia, but we're going to rally round – and she'll be all right, she has to be. Forget I said anything about Nathan. You're right, I'm scared silly, but if Aunt Sylvia can face all that horrible treatment and the operation with a smile on her face, then I haven't got a leg to stand on. I'll do it and it will be fine – better than fine. And I am grateful to you for sorting it out.'

'Thank you, darling. You said you'd met each other? Didn't you get on or something?'

Frankie tried to suppress a smile, but the ridiculousness of their meeting earlier had caught up with her. An image flew into her mind of trying to preserve the vestiges of her modesty with a small towel and an even smaller dog while poor Nathan stood there flanked by rabbit-gnawed Tudor panelling and a crazed vintage mannequin and a giggle bubbled up through her chest and erupted into a blast of laughter before she could stop it.

'Sorry, Dad, sorry, it was just so *awful*,' she screeched, grabbing his arm as another wave overtook her. 'He must have thought I was appalling, oh, poor man!'

Eventually, she calmed down enough to explain to her father what had happened, and soon he was laughing too.

'Oh dear, Nathan has always been quite serious. I can't imagine what he thought of some semi-clad nymph pirouetting through our disreputable hallway, then scolding him before flouncing off. I'm not sure it was the sort of artistic environment he had in mind. Ah well, we'll all probably do each other good.'

'Thanks, Dad,' said Frankie, standing up and rubbing her side where it ached from all the laughter. 'It'll work out, all of it.'

EIGHT

It was with some apprehension that Nathan got ready for dinner that evening. While he had enjoyed meeting Juliet and Léo, and felt particularly well-disposed towards her for showing him that wonderful room he was to use as his studio, he wasn't looking forward to seeing Frankie again. She was every bit the *enfant terrible* he had expected, and as far from being the person he wanted to spend time with every day as could be possible. Even though she was undeniably gorgeous, it didn't make up for her attitude. He inspected his appearance in the full-length, mahogany-framed mirror, hoping it would pass muster. *This could be a long few weeks.* Shrugging at his reflection and slipping his phone into his pocket, he headed for the door and towards the stairs, when he saw a woman coming towards him. She had long, wavy chestnut hair and huge amber eyes and was beaming at him in delight.

'Oh, hello, how super to meet you!' The woman threw her arms around him and pulled him into a warm embrace, which he received stiffly, in his surprise. 'Oh gosh, I'm so sorry, I haven't introduced myself,' she said, laughing. 'I'm Martha – you're Nathan, aren't you?'

'Yes, that's right. So you're Frankie's eldest sister?'

'That's me. Shall we go downstairs together? You're probably much braver than me, but I'd hate going on my own into a room full of people I don't know.'

He smiled. 'Thank you.'

'Although I suppose you know Dad, don't you?' she said, as they started walking down the stairs. 'And Frankie told me you met her earlier.'

'Mmm,' Nathan answered noncommittally. *What had Frankie's side of the story been?*

'Don't worry,' said Martha comfortingly as they reached the hallway. 'She's mortified about it and honestly she's calmed down loads since...'

But Nathan wasn't to find out since what, as Martha pushed open the door of the sitting room he had seen earlier, and they walked into a room which seemed to be heaving with chattering strangers. *You should have stayed in Italy,* said a cross little voice in his head. *One of the best things about gardens is the peace and quiet and general lack of other people.* But he forced a smile to his face as Martha kindly steered him straight over to Rousseau, who greeted him enthusiastically.

'Nathan! How wonderful to see you! I'm so sorry we haven't caught up before now, but Juliet told me that she showed you where everything is?' Nathan nodded. 'Splendid. Martha, do get him a drink, and one for yourself, of course. Everyone!'

His call was barely necessary as everyone had already stopped talking and were looking over at Nathan curiously. He tried to look back at them all but felt his eyes sliding away from their faces, hating being the centre of attention. At least he could now take in the fact that, rather than hordes of unfamiliar people, there was actually only a handful of people in the room, with two or three he hadn't already met, although he hadn't spotted Frankie at all. Rousseau continued.

'Everyone, this is Nathan Brooks, the marvellous garden designer who has come to study sculpture with me and work on a new design for part of the garden with Frankie. I know you will all make him very welcome and be as excited as I am to see the magic he will weave at Feywood.' He raised his glass in the air as Martha pushed one into Nathan's hand. 'Welcome!' announced Rousseau, and everyone echoed the word. Nathan took a sip of his drink and recoiled slightly at the strength of the gin and tonic Martha had poured. Rousseau saw his expression.

'Too much gin and not enough tonic? Martha's drinks are never what you expect – she gets distracted halfway through pouring one thing or the other and you always end up either with something eye-wateringly strong or disappointingly watery. Here, let me get you another and then I'll introduce you to everyone.'

Furnished with something more drinkable, which Nathan was grateful for in the circumstances, even though he never usually chose spirits, he submitted to being taken around the room.

'You've met Juliet and Léo, of course,' said Rousseau. 'Léo runs the cookery school with my sister, Sylvia.'

Nathan exchanged handshakes and murmured greetings with a slight woman, her hair in a neat grey bob, who was sitting at the end of one of the sofas next to Juliet with Ava, the little dog who had been with Frankie earlier, on her lap. Moriarty, the family's other dog, was lying next to her.

'Forgive me for not getting up,' she said. 'I'm not a hundred per cent at the moment, but I am so looking forward to seeing what you do in the garden. I potter around out there a little myself, but it's the kitchen garden that mostly keeps Léo and me busy.'

'Well, I promise I won't go anywhere near that,' said Nathan, liking the look of Sylvia, who reminded him a little of Carla, his brother Henry's mother-in-law, with her soft smile and kind eyes. 'Although if we make any headway on the orangery, you may have some citrus fruits to use at the cookery school.'

'How wonderful!' said Léo. 'Not many places near here can boast locally grown oranges.'

'Feywood always keeps giving,' said Rousseau sentimentally. 'And draws to her people who will bring out her best. Now, come and meet the others.'

With a nod goodbye, Nathan followed Rousseau over to the next group.

'You have, of course, already met Martha and nearly been poisoned by her.'

Her sweet face looked up in concern.

'Oh no, what have I done? Was it the gin and tonic? I'm so sorry, I did wonder if it might be a bit strong, but a fox was running past outside and it had such a beautiful, fluid movement.'

Everyone laughed, including Martha.

'No harm done,' said Rousseau. 'Nathan, this is Sindhu, my partner...'

Nathan shook hands with her.

'Welcome to Feywood,' she said with a twinkle in her eye. 'It will be nice for me not to be the new girl anymore.'

Rousseau slipped his arm around her shoulder.

'Sindhu made me very happy by moving in a couple of months ago. The rest of us have been here forever, I'm afraid.'

'Not me,' said the third person in the small group, a man about the same height as Nathan, with dark gold hair and a shy smile. He held out his hand, which Nathan shook.

'So sorry,' apologised Rousseau. 'I'm as bad as Martha, always getting distracted. The girls will tell you about their strategy for getting people through the hallway when we have parties: I'd keep them out there talking all evening. This is Will, my wonderful estate manager. He hasn't been here forever, that's true, but long enough to be part of the family and for it to be impossible to imagine Feywood without him.'

As Rousseau realised that Sindhu's glass was empty and took her to get another drink, the two men fell into conversation.

'It's great that you've come,' said Will. 'I do what I can with the gardens but only in my spare time, and then it's mostly the roses and the lawn. The kitchen garden is Sylvia and Léo's territory, and it's come to life under their care, but the rest of the grounds are in a mess, beyond basic maintenance. There are some formal areas and another lawned part, which is more or less a meadow now, not to mention the pond, although that looks after itself remarkably well.'

'I'm looking forward to it,' replied Nathan. 'Although there will be a limit to what Frankie and I can achieve. But I'm going to show her how to draw up design plans, what to consider and so on, so you'll be able to take it all forward in the future, even if you don't have the resources now. But we should be able to sort out the orangery. I've seen photos – it's magnificent.'

'Yes, it certainly is,' agreed Will. 'And surprisingly the structure seems sound, so it's more cosmetic work that needs doing. Frankie's made decent progress clearing it, but...' He tailed off and reddened slightly. Nathan looked at him questioningly and he continued. 'I'm not comfortable talking about her when she's not here. It's none of my business, but you know she's had a difficult time?' Nathan nodded. 'Well, she's been taking it out on the weeds, although I don't think she's thought about it beyond that.'

Nathan started to reply, when the door opened, and in came Frankie herself. She was wearing a black band T-shirt and a short denim skirt over black leggings, with heavy boots. Had it not been for her earlier behaviour, which had left on Nathan the impression that she was super confident, he would have sworn she looked nervous.

'Ah, Frankie,' boomed Rousseau. 'Good to see you. Léo has

vanished, so I think that means we're going in to eat quite soon. Let me get you a drink.'

As Nathan started to tell Will about his plans for the orangery, and one of the formal yew hedge gardens, which was almost obliterated by overgrowth, he watched Frankie out of the corner of his eye. She accepted a glass from her father, stopped to exchange a few words with Sylvia, and then headed in his direction.

'Hi, Will, sorry to interrupt, but I need a word with Nathan.'

'Of course,' Will replied. 'I'll look forward to talking more another time,' he said to Nathan, and went over to join Martha and Sindhu.

Nathan took another sip of his drink. *What was Frankie going to say?* He wouldn't be surprised if she called the whole thing off, but then how would he repay Rousseau for his mentorship? Her next words were the ones he was least expecting.

'Look, I'm sorry about before. I usually greet visitors fully dressed.' She paused. 'Yeah, not always, but usually. You've probably already heard all sorts of horror stories about me, if you've looked me up.' Nathan opened his mouth to speak, but she continued. 'It's all right, we've Googled the heck out of you, so I expect you did the same. I've not been the most sensible, but the stuff with Dylan was a wake-up call. I'm even sticking to the ginless tonics.' She raised her glass, took a sip and screwed up her face. 'Disappointing at first, but you get used to it. Can't say I miss the hangovers. Anyway, not sure I'll be much good as an assistant, or very teachable, but welcome to Feywood, anyway. Hope I didn't put you off too much, cavorting around in my towel. I do own clothes.'

'I can see that,' said Nathan stiffly. After this rather ungracious speech he felt like telling her not to bother helping him.

He was glad to be spared from further conversation by the reappearance of Léo.

'Please come through now, supper is ready.'

Nathan had seen the dining room before, briefly, when he had searched for the kitchen, but the room looked much livelier now than it had that morning. A cloth had been placed over the large table, and there were candles flickering merrily. There were plenty of glasses and plates laid out, none of which appeared to match, and three large dishes of food. One held a fragrant, steaming pile of basmati rice, one was brimming with curry wafting its rich, spicy scent across the room and on the third was a towering pile of naan bread. He found himself sitting between Frankie and Rousseau and opposite Léo who grinned over at him and said:

'I hope you like curry? This is paneer with peas and spinach, rice, as you see, and coriander naan bread. Help yourself, please.'

'I love curry,' replied Nathan. 'We don't often have it in Italy, so this is a real treat, thank you.'

He reached for the spoon as Frankie said, a teasing note in her voice:

'Léo, this doesn't seem too local. Don't tell me you're venturing outside your usual five-mile radius of Feywood. Or are you thinking about a new book – *Feywood and Friends*, maybe, or *Feywood on Tour?*'

Noticing Nathan's confused face, Léo raised an eyebrow at Frankie and spoke directly to him.

'Frankie mocks me because I try to be sustainable at the cookery school and use local produce as much as possible. You may know that we recently published a cookery book with recipes from the house and family and guidance on how best to find food that is produced nearby. What she does not know—' He broke off to pull a face at her, and Frankie stuck out her tongue in reply. 'What she does not know – yet – is that I made the paneer myself with milk from a farm less than one mile away. The lemon I needed was given to me by a friend who owns a home near here with a restaurant and a few citrus trees which she grows in a conservatory. I confess that the spices were, indeed, imported.'

Unabashed, Frankie laughed.

'I'm impressed. And maybe if Nathan and I get the orangery in shape, we'll be able to grow our own for you. Is that right?'

She turned her twinkling eyes to him.

'Well, yes, we could certainly try. They need a lot of nannying in the winter, though, to keep them alive. And there are plenty of other things you can grow here to add to your curries – if you don't already?'

He turned to Léo, who shook his head.

'We focus for now on the kitchen garden, with a few herbs on the windowsill. What did you have in mind?'

'Bay, of course, and ginger and turmeric are quite easy, although you'll need to be patient and they'd need a greenhouse. We could also plant some fenugreek and coriander, for the seeds, and chillies are no problem. Things like cumin and cloves would be harder, but there are some clever people out there who know exactly which English-grown plants taste similar.'

'How fascinating,' said Sylvia, who was sitting next to Léo and had been listening to the conversation, whilst picking at what looked to Nathan like a tiny amount of food. 'Maybe it's something I could research while I'm recuperating.' A sudden hush fell at the table, as everyone's attention turned towards her. She looked around at each worried face and when she spoke, her voice had an edge to it. 'Please stop looking at me like that. I said recuperating, not lying-in-state and it's not going to help me get better any faster if you all behave as if I'm knocking on the pearly gates already. You should save your sympathies for Léo, who is going to be all alone in the cookery school.'

A beat of silence followed this speech, broken by Frankie.

'I agree. I will, of course, be up to my arms in weeds, but I can graciously offer my services in my spare time. I'm sure you would be glad of them, Léo, as would your students. For my first class, I will teach them how to microwave a packet of rice and grate some cheese over the top.'

There was a ripple of laughter, and Juliet snatched up the baton.

'And I know that having me there will be a great comfort to you, *mon amour*, given my culinary prowess. I will offer classes in making toast in the toaster, with a special module on using the 'bagel' setting, which I think you'll agree I have mastered.'

'Ah, *bon*,' said Léo, kissing his fingertips in an exaggerated gesture. 'You see, Sylvia, with these wonderful helpers you have nothing to worry about.'

She smiled.

'So I see. I look forward to my convalescence even more, in anticipation of this nourishment. But seriously, there is something I am worried about, and that is how I am going to get to the damn appointments. There are several where they fuss over this and that before they let me go under the knife.'

Martha gave an involuntary squeak, then apologised.

'Sorry, Aunt Sylvia, I'm trying to be as brave as you are, but it's hard. In terms of helping, I wish now that I'd learnt to drive, but I'll gladly pay for taxis and come with you any time.'

A chorus of voices arose with similar offers, but it was Will's words that cut across them.

'I'll take you, Sylvia – if that's all right with you, Rousseau?' Rousseau nodded vigorously. 'My work here is generally flexible, I have a car – *and* a driving licence – and besides, I'd like to.' He paused and looked around, taking a deep breath before continuing. 'My mother went through something similar, years ago, and I wasn't living near enough to be of any help. I'd be grateful if you would allow me to accompany you. Then everybody else can make sure that everything is perfect for you here.'

Nathan noticed Martha discreetly dabbing at the corner of her eye with her napkin, watching the adoration on her face as she looked at Will, and how she quickly concealed it when he glanced at her, therefore missing the fact that her feelings were, quite clearly it seemed to Nathan, returned.

'Thank you, Will,' said Sylvia with dignity. 'I would be glad for your help.'

'Well done, everyone,' said Rousseau, standing up and lifting his glass. 'I never cease to be grateful for the wonderful people who end up under Feywood's roof, leaking though it still is, and pull together to be part of this family – and yes, Moriarty and Ava' – he tipped his glass towards the two dogs, who were snuggled up together on an antique tapestried chair – 'I include you in this. I invite you all to join me in a toast. To Feywood!'

Chairs scraped as everyone rose to their feet and joined him: 'To Feywood!'

Sitting down again, Nathan looked around the table. Although he knew he wasn't nearly bonkers enough to be one of them, for the first time since he had arrived, he felt glad that he was there, and a creeping confidence that his stay could be a success.

NINE

Frankie awoke early the next morning, groaning when she glanced at the clock and saw the time. She didn't need to be up for a couple of hours, but try as she might to get back to sleep, it stubbornly evaded her. If she snuggled under the duvet, she was soon too hot. If she tossed it off, she felt chilly. She flung herself about from side to side, tried lying on her back and then on her stomach, but nothing worked. No matter what she tried, one thing was abundantly clear: Frankie was nervous about the day ahead.

'Fine,' she said out loud, after another ten minutes' writhing. 'Fine, I'll get up.'

She went into the bathroom and stood in the shower as the thoughts roiled around in her head. Last night, supper had gone well, even if the talk of Sylvia's operation had added another layer of worry, no matter how much they had joked about the cookery school. Nathan had been polite but evidently enjoyed talking to Léo and Will more than he did to her, conversing freely to them about planting stuff but giving her tight little answers. Mind you, she mused, turning off the water and rubbing herself vigorously with her towel, you could hardly blame him. She couldn't stop herself making stupid jokes instead of having a proper conversation and she hadn't shown much enthusiasm about working with him. He was probably dreading spending time with her. She dressed quickly and went down to the kitchen, where she found Rousseau dolloping mixture into muffin tins.

'Hi, Dad.'

'Good morning, my darling. It's very early for you. Have you slept well?'

Frankie sat down at the table and started picking at a chipped piece of Formica.

'Ish. I woke up early and couldn't get back to sleep.'

'Here,' he said, putting a chopping board, a bowl and a pile of fruit in front of her. 'Start cutting this lot up, please. It'll give you something to do with your hands other than wrecking that poor table.'

She picked up a banana and started peeling it disconsolately.

'Look, Dad, much as I'm sure I'd be the most fabulous asset to Nathan, and he'll be devastated if I don't turn up to help, I think we should forget this assistant business. I mean, I was just mucking about in the orangery, really, and Nathan – well, he's a proper person, he knows what he's doing. I can already tell he's wondering what he signed up to, getting stuck with me, and this morning is going to prove all that.'

Rousseau slapped his hand down on the table, making her jump.

'Prove all *what*, exactly?'

'That I'm totally clueless.'

'Rubbish. You always had a beautiful, fanciful imagination, and you loved the garden when you were a little girl. I know it's hardly your image these days, but you would create enchanting watercolours of the pond and the flowers and the woods, flickering with little fairies.'

Frankie sliced into the banana sulkily.

'Well, that was years ago. I'm hardly likely to impress Nathan with fairy drawings now.'

'I disagree. And that, my darling, is why Martha and I had a rummage through the family archives...'

'By which you mean those mouldering old boxes in the attic...'

'By which I mean those mouldering old boxes in the attic, and we found some of your old drawings. These are for you.'

Rousseau disappeared briefly into the larder, then brought out a parcel wrapped in brown paper and placed it on the table beside the chopping board, which Frankie pushed out of the way with a frown.

'Thanks, Dad, that's sweet of you, but I don't think these can be any help. I barely remember doing them.'

'Open it.'

She unwrapped the paper to find four framed pictures, which she looked at in turn, excitement mounting as she examined each one.

'Oh yes, I *do* remember this! It seemed such a shame that the fountain never worked, so I imagined what it would look like all spruced up, with lilies and things – and the fairies, of course. It's rather pretty... maybe we should get it going again.' Her face fell. 'Although I don't think that's what garden designers do – you should have got in a plumber.'

'Look at the next one,' said Rousseau gently but firmly.

'It's the orangery! I don't remember painting that. Gosh, it was in a bad state then, but nothing like it is now. Look at that, I've painted the fairies sorting it all out – these ones are pulling out the weeds and these ones are bringing in new plants. They look like palms – and is that an orange tree?'

'It is. You went through a whole phase of reimagining the garden. I'm amazed you don't remember, but then perhaps that's what children do. Look, the third one is that yew garden, which you can barely see any more, and the fourth is what is now the kitchen garden.'

'Oh yes! Better not tell Sylvia and Léo I had plans for it to be a rockery, complete with waterfalls.'

Rousseau laughed.

'Might not be as useful for their quiches. But you see, this is in you. It came out at your lowest point, even if you think it was nothing but a distraction. Give it – and Nathan – a chance, won't you?'

Frankie nodded slowly.

'Thanks, Dad, I will. I do feel better.'

'Good. Will has put some hooks up in the garden room so you can hang these there to remind you. But now hurry up and get that fruit chopped, or there will only be half a breakfast for everyone.'

'Do you mind if I have mine in here? I could do without Martha wittering on about how good I'll be with a pair of secateurs and Nathan glaring at me over his cornflakes like he's made the biggest mistake of his life.'

Rousseau put his arm around her shoulders and gave her a squeeze.

'If it will help you to take a moment to yourself, then you must do so. Do you want some chamomile tea to help things along?'

Frankie grinned.

'I'll stick to coffee, thanks, Dad. I may be a reformed character, but I still need my caffeine fix.'

When it was nearly time to meet Nathan in the garden room, Frankie's nerves, which she had managed to get a grip of over breakfast, returned with a vengeance. It was Martha who found her in the bathroom, throwing up everything she had managed to eat.

'Oh, Frankie!' she said, kneeling down beside her sister and rubbing her back gently. 'Are you ill?'

Frankie shook her head, then sat back on her heels and broke off some loo paper to wipe her mouth and streaming eyes. After a few deep breaths, she managed to speak.

'Not ill, no. I'm stupidly scared about this whole bloody venture. I've never been scared of anything like this in my life, so I don't know what's wrong with me.'

'There's nothing wrong with you at all,' said Martha in her gentle voice. 'You've been through a horrible time and you've pushed it all down, but these things have to come up somehow.'

'Quite literally in my case,' groaned Frankie, flushing the loo and staggering to her feet.

'Well, you never were one for half measures of any kind,' said Martha, dampening a flannel under the tap and handing it to her.

'Ugh, don't mention measures, I'll be sick again.'

'At least it's not a hangover. I feel awful after last night; I must get the hang of pouring gin.'

'You couldn't get me one now, I suppose?'

She summoned up a weak smile and Martha threw her arms around her.

'I would if I thought it would help. Do you feel well enough to start work?'

'No, but I'm going to go down anyway and get on with it. I don't want to be late and give Nathan any more reason to disapprove of me.'

'I'm sure he doesn't. Come on, I'll carry these,' said Martha, picking up the framed paintings. 'Do you remember them?'

The sisters started down the stairs.

'Not really, but Dad did a good job of trying to persuade me that working on the garden is my inner calling.' She stopped and faced Martha. 'I'm going to make a proper go of it, I promise. Now, give me those – I don't need an escort, even one as nice as you.'

With a final hug, Martha handed over the paintings and Frankie strode off in the direction of the garden room, trying to exude more confidence than she was feeling. She hoped that her churning stomach would settle down now that it was comprehensively empty. She pushed open the door to the garden room and was relieved to see that she had arrived before Nathan. She spotted the hooks that her father had mentioned and started hanging the pictures, taking a moment as she did so to look at each one more closely. She hadn't been entirely honest with Rousseau or Martha. The truth was that she *did* remember painting them, remember how absorbing and satisfying she had found them and how she had longed to bring them to life in the neglected gardens. She wasn't sure why she hadn't said all this to her family; maybe because it felt too exposing, too intimate somehow, to admit to this sense of oneness with the natural world. Easier to fill the role of the tearaway that had been assigned to her somewhere in adolescence, the role that everyone seemed to think fitted her and that was so easy to personify. Fun as well, of course, she couldn't deny that – but its time was up, and now she was going to have to expose her soft underbelly to this complete stranger, who already looked at her as if she was an unexploded bomb.

'Good morning.'

Nathan's voice behind Frankie made her jump, and she nearly dropped the final picture. At least it gave her something to do with her hands as she replied:

'Oh, hi. Dad gave me these to hang, hope that's okay.'

He came over and stood next to her, his fresh, just showered smell reminding her that she was probably none too fragrant herself, given the nerves and the vomiting.

'These are great... who did them?'

She moved away slightly, running a hand through her still-uncut hair and hoping that she was far away enough that any foul odours she might be emitting wouldn't reach him.

'Erm, I did, when I was a kid. Dad looked them out; he thought it would be nice for me to remember how much I used to love the garden here.'

Nathan walked slowly around the room, looking closely at each picture, as Frankie dug into her pocket and gratefully found a squashed packet of chewing gum. She popped one in.

'They're great. I like this one – I think I saw that yew garden yesterday. If you still like this design, we could use it. But I think we should start with the orangery.'

Frankie shrugged.

'Okay. It's where I've been working up till now. Haven't you seen it yet?'

'Only a few photos that your father sent. I think he wanted you to be the one to show it to me.'

'All right, let's go there first then.'

Nathan had been perfectly pleasant, even praising her child's efforts at garden design, but Frankie still didn't much feel like spending the morning with him. She reluctantly went to open the door into the garden, but it resolutely refused to budge. She jiggled the handle fruitlessly, then jumped as Nathan came up beside her.

'It's locked,' he said, producing a key and opening the door quickly.

'Locked?' said Frankie, stepping outside. 'I didn't even know that door had a lock, it's always been open. It was our way in and out of the house when we were teenagers and belting home from the pub and the woods at all times of the night.'

Nathan raised his eyebrows.

'I'd love to hear more about the three of you when you were younger – I bet there are some stories. Sorry about the door. I found the key balanced on a window frame and now I understand why it was covered in dust. There are a couple of pretty expensive computers in there, so it seemed like a good idea to lock the door, for the insurance if nothing else.'

Frankie grinned.

'Now, there are some words that have never been strung together before at Feywood, at least not by anyone but Will: *good idea, lock, insurance...* You'll be telling us next that we have to pay tax.'

'You don't pay...' started Nathan, then stopped and pulled a face. 'You're joking.'

Frankie laughed.

'We're bad, but not that bad. Look, here we are.'

Nathan looked up at the glass, stone and iron structure in front of him and let out a low whistle.

'This is impressive. So many of these old orangeries didn't survive – they got pulled down or fell down. A lot of them are being rebuilt now, but to have an original like this is pretty special.'

Frankie pushed open the heavy door and they went inside. For a few moments, she watched Nathan as he examined the space. First, he stood quietly and looked all around him, then he walked around slowly, moving plants to peer more closely at a wall or window, then suddenly crouching down to run his hands over the stone tiled floor or inspect a planter. Eventually, he came back over to her.

'Stunning,' he said, and she glowed with pride. Maybe this whole project wasn't going to be as bad as she had anticipated. 'So, what's your overall plan for it?'

Her smile faltered.

'I'm not sure I have one. I just thought, you know, that I'd pull out all the overgrown plants and see what was there and, er, take it from, well, there...'

He raised his eyebrows, and she felt twelve years old again, standing in front of the headmistress who wanted an explanation of the comic strip Frankie had created when asked to write a history essay plan.

'I see. Have you not considered what you're going to plant, if the building is structurally secure, what you're planning to use it for when it's finished – even what the plants are that you've yanked out with such vigour and whether pulling them off that stonework will do it any damage?'

She rolled her eyes.

'I reckoned it would look better cleared back – and it does. I thought I'd made pretty good progress.'

So don't you come in here criticising it all.

'Hmm. Well, before we do anything else, we have to inventory everything that's growing here, find a floor plan or draw one if there isn't one, assess the structural integrity of the building and decide on a direction.'

Frankie shrugged, annoyed at his peremptory manner, even though she knew that was exactly what he was there for. She had come to think of the orangery as *her* space and had been proud of the work she had done. She was about to reply when she spotted something moving on the floor by one of the huge terracotta pots.

'Oh!'

'What is it?'

'I think it's a bee.' She darted over and pulled back the fronds of the large fern growing in the pot. 'Yes, look. Oh dear, they *will* come in and then they can't find anything to eat or drink and they die, it's so sad.'

She gently picked the bee up on a stray leaf. Grabbing a small bottle and a spoon from the table, she headed back out to the garden, Nathan following. She went to an overgrown but colourful flowerbed and carefully placed the bee on the grass by it, then squeezed a few drops of liquid out of the bottle onto the spoon.

'It's sugar water,' she explained, leaning over to see if the little creature was drinking it. 'Oh, look! She's having a sip! Oh, well done, darling,' she said to the insect. 'Now, lie there in the sun for a while and hopefully you'll soon feel better enough to have some nectar and go back to the hive.'

'Do you rescue many bees?' asked Nathan, looking amused.

'When I find them,' replied Frankie. 'They're so important, we should all be trying to help them.'

'I quite agree,' he said. 'Right, shall we get on? Even though it's not the first thing we need to do, I have a feeling that sketching out some ideas first might be a good way for you to work. It would help to have the original floor plans of the orangery – do you have any idea where they might be?'

Frankie shook her head.

'Not a clue, but Dad or Sylvia might know. Let's try the cookery school.'

She led the way across the lawn to what had, at one point in Feywood's history, been the stable block. Now, it had been sympathetically converted into a modern, but still cosy, kitchen and it was here that they found Sylvia, peering into a bubbling pan while Léo made notes at the large table.

'Hello,' said Sylvia as they entered. 'What can we do for you? It is about time for a midmorning snack – we've got some honey and orange blossom tuiles coming out of the oven in a minute.'

'Ooh, good timing,' said Frankie. She hadn't eaten since being sick earlier and was hungry. 'Shall I put the kettle on?'

Soon they were sitting down with steaming cups of coffee, watching Léo as he deftly peeled the hot tuiles from the parchment paper and wrapped them around the handle of a wooden spoon to make neat cylinders.

'You can tell us what you think of the flavour,' he said, sliding a fifth onto a plate. 'They should cool and harden a little more, but I have a feeling they will not last that long. The ones we will eventually make in the school will be shaped around a little glass, *voilà!*' He pressed the next warm biscuit around the bottom of a shot glass, quickly moulding it, then tipped it off gently to show a flower-shaped cup. 'These will be filled with flavoured cream and hopefully be *délicieuses.*'

'They look it,' said Frankie. 'Always glad to be called on for testing whenever you need it, but that was a happy side effect of today's visit. Aunt Sylvia, we wanted to ask you if you know where the original floor plans are for the orangery.'

'Oh gosh,' she said, taking a sip of coffee. 'You're talking about documents that are about two hundred years old. Let me think.' There was silence for a few moments, then Sylvia put her mug down with a triumphant flourish. 'Ah! I was thinking about all those cabinets in Rousseau's office and what hell it would be trying to find anything at all in them, although he never seems to have much trouble. But then I remembered our mother had a fairly brief period of interest in Feywood's history and got a local historian to help her gather stuff together and store it all safely. I think you'll find it in one of the attic rooms. There are various cabinets and boxes up there, but I don't know which one specifically the plans would be in – if they've even survived this long.'

'Wonderful!' said Frankie.

'Yes, thank you so much,' added Nathan. 'We'll go and look straight away.'

'Good luck,' said Sylvia, as they stood up. 'There's a lot of stuff up there.'

They headed back towards the house, Frankie now fizzing with excitement.

'This is like a treasure hunt, isn't it? It feels like we might find Feywood's missing millions up there, or at least a map to find them. That would cheer Dad up no end.'

'*Are* there missing millions?' asked Nathan, as they went back inside the house.

'Not that I know of,' said Frankie cheerfully. 'But it's a nice idea.'

'It is,' replied Nathan. 'Although we need to focus on finding those plans.'

Feeling slightly squashed, Frankie led the way upstairs and along the landing and opened a door tucked away at the end which led, not to yet another bedroom, bathroom or cavernous linen cupboard but to a narrow wooden staircase.

'Nobody ever goes up here; it's the old servants' quarters. We debated using the rooms for the cookery school clients, but they would have taken far more renovation than we could afford even if we could have done the roof in time, and they're all stuffed with old furniture and bits and bobs.'

'It's a magnificent house,' said Nathan as they emerged at the end of a long, bare boarded passageway with sloping ceilings.

'It is,' agreed Frankie. 'We all love it so much. Now, which room are those cabinets in?'

She opened the first door, revealing a small room full of wooden chairs stacked on top of each other.

'Not this one, keep going.'

They opened three more doors, finding similar piles of furniture, many shrouded in white sheets. It was the contents of the fourth room that looked more promising.

'This looks like it could be Feywood's archives,' said Nathan, standing in the doorway behind Frankie. His sudden proximity startled her, and when she turned to look at him, she noticed behind his tortoiseshell glasses that his eyes were a complex mix of green, amber and brown: quite mesmerising. Martha should paint his portrait. 'Are you okay?' he asked, a slight frown creasing his forehead.

'Me? Oh yes, perfectly fine,' she replied as breezily as possible. 'Yes, this room looks excellent.' She hurried inside and looked around at the several large filing cabinets and boxes. 'But where on earth are we going to start? Sylvia was right, there's masses of stuff here.'

'We're looking for floor plans. They're usually large, and if your grandmother's friend knew what he was doing, they'll be stored flat, not rolled or folded. So we need a big enough cabinet... Look! What about that one?'

He pointed to a large wooden cabinet of waist height, long drawers across its width, with brass handles. Frankie went over and pulled open the top drawer, to reveal a large pale ivory folder. She opened it carefully, then said excitedly:

'Yes, look, these look like plans.'

'They definitely are,' said Nathan, coming over to see. 'They're so faded, but you can see that this is part of the ground floor. I think these are much older than the ones we're looking for, but they're amazing.'

Frankie tried the next drawer, to reveal similar documents, but it was the third that revealed what they were looking for.

'This is it!' exclaimed Nathan, taking out the folder and placing it on top of the cabinet. Frankie glanced at his face as he examined the pieces of paper, noticing how those beautiful eyes had lit up and how he was even more handsome in his delight. *You would have dismissed him as a nerd a few months ago*, whispered a little voice in her head. *I would,* she answered it candidly, *but that might have been a mistake.*

'Look,' he said. 'You can see how carefully it was designed so that it let in as much light as possible. Lots of orangeries weren't built with big enough windows, so they never got enough sunshine to cultivate the exotic fruits people were so keen to grow.'

'Not just oranges, then?' asked Frankie.

'No. Citrus fruit trees were all popular, but people also grew palms, of course, and pomegranates and they attempted bananas. There was a huge craze for growing pineapples at one point, but I don't think that we should run before we can walk. Come on, let's get these downstairs and onto the computer so that they can be put away again as soon as possible.'

Once back in the garden room, Nathan placed a machine on the table, comprising a large, sturdy black mat with a sleek adjustable metal arm that rose over it. He plugged it in.

'This is an overhead scanner,' he explained, switching it on. 'It won't damage the paper. It's not quite big enough for this work, but I couldn't bring anything bigger with me, so we'll have to piece the images together.'

'I haven't got a clue what you're talking about,' said Frankie. 'Maybe I should let you get on with that while I do something I'm actually half good at.'

TEN

As Nathan carefully lifted the first piece of the plan onto the scanner, he was aware of Frankie on the other side of the table. She was spreading out a large piece of paper, on which she was rapidly sketching. They both worked in silence, but every so often she would come around and stand next to him, inspecting one of the plans, before returning to her task. Nathan was fascinated by his work, combining as it did two of his loves: garden design and technology. Even so, he had to force his mind back to the job on several occasions, and away from Frankie. She exuded an effervescent energy, even as she worked quietly, and he longed to stop what he was doing and go around the table to see her drawing. Maybe she would glance at him with her dancing eyes and quick smile. But he made himself refocus and continue the scanning, admonishing himself as he did so.

You're here to work and to mentor her, so get on with it. Remember yesterday's first impression? Maybe it was unfair, but maybe not, and God knows you don't need any chaos in your life, just as things are settling down.

Thus, he managed to complete the scanning and soon he was carefully closing the folder over the precious drawings, tucking them away from the damaging light until someone else might need them in the future.

'Have you finished?' asked Frankie, looking up.

'Yes. Do you want to see the plans on the screen?'

'Sure.'

She put down her pencil and came round the table, pulling up a chair next to him. Her casual proximity unsettled him, and he fussed with his laptop to try and conceal his reaction.

'Here they are, look, you can see so much more detail now.'

'That's amazing,' Frankie said, leaning closer still. Nathan felt his body stiffen with confusion and she edged away slightly with a murmured 'sorry', then continued. 'I can see the shape of it, obviously, and the stone bench, but what's that? It doesn't look familiar.'

She pointed at a square drawn on the plan, its corner cut out with a second, smaller square.

'I don't know,' said Nathan, relaxing again as his interest was caught. 'Let's zoom in.' He pressed a few buttons and squinted at the screen. 'Look, I can make out the words – it says 'fish pool'. How fantastic!'

'Well, I don't know how you can read it,' said Frankie, screwing up her face. 'But I believe you. What's the corner bit?'

Nathan grinned.

'I'm pretty used to looking at these old plans; you get used to the writing. They're even worse in Italian, believe me. I don't know why the corner has been cut out, though; it hasn't been labelled. I think we'll have to do a bit of detective work on the site.'

'Can we go now?' asked Frankie. 'I'm dying to know, and maybe we can get the pool working again, with fish in it!'

Nathan looked at her shining eyes. He fought back the urge to throw his arms around her, then rush off to the orangery and start ripping out plants with wild abandon purely to please her.

Really, get a grip. You're here to do a job, which you seem to have forgotten yet again.

'First things first, I'm afraid.' He hated the pompous tone in his voice and the way it made her face fall, but he pressed on. 'We don't want to go in carelessly and cause any damage. We still need to start by making an inventory of what's already there – that will take a few days – and then, if we still want to start with this area' – he pointed to the fish pool on the plan – 'we can approach it with more information.' She looked disappointed, and he longed to make things better. 'Can I see what you've been drawing?'

'Sure.'

His heart squeezed at the dullness in her voice after the excitement, but he followed her around the table to look at her work, emitting a little gasp when he saw it.

'You've done so much already – this is incredible. How did you draw out the outline so quickly? You can only have glanced at it.'

He leant down to pore over the paper, taking in the swift pencil strokes and the flashes of colour which instantly brought the orangery to life both on paper and in his imagination.

'It's just a quick sketch – silly, really. I wanted to try to remember what it was like to be a kid, imagining whatever took my fancy. I'm going to add some fish in now, even if you won't let me in real life.'

She reached across the drawing and her pencil flew around for a minute or two, before she stepped back and let Nathan see. When he looked, he burst out laughing. The fish pool had been populated with a fantastical variety of sea creatures – tropical fish, electric eels and an octopus slinking its tentacles around the border of the pool. There was even a small shark's fin making circles in the water at one end.

'Well, I don't see how we can't attempt at least some of that. It's ambitious, but hey!'

He laughed again, then saw Frankie looking at him with curiosity.

'I was being silly – I thought you'd tell me off.'

His face fell. He had only wanted to be professional, and get the job done well, and now she obviously had him down as some sort of humourless martinet.

'Well, come on!' She nudged him with her elbow and shot him a humorous look under her lashes, which tightened his squeezed heart even more. 'I wasn't sure you'd be into a full sea world display, but now I know differently I'll get on to a local walrus provider I know.'

The iron grip on his heart released and he raised an eyebrow at her.

'Good idea. Only one or two though, we don't want to overdo things. Seriously, though...'

'Of course,' put in Frankie.

'...I do like the flowering creepers you have growing on the west side.'

'Well, they're already there,' said Frankie. 'You'll be glad to hear I haven't pulled them out. I didn't know if they were weeds or not, but they flower like mad and smell divine.'

Nathan peered more closely at the picture.

'I wonder if they're a sort of clematis – they were popular in the eighteenth century. I *must* get started with the inventory. We can't make any decisions until I've done that.'

'What shall I do? I barely know a daisy from a daffodil at the moment, so I wouldn't be any help.'

'It would be a good way to start learning, but given the tangle that's there at the moment, I think I'd better make a start so that I can show you the things that are worth keeping. So, for this morning, why don't you do some research on typical plants that would have been grown there originally? I've got a list of websites I can email you, but you've probably got some contemporary books in the house that would give you a truly authentic idea. Then when you come back into the orangery, you can see if you can spot any matches.'

'You mean things might still be growing there from two or three hundred years ago?'

'Well, perhaps not exactly the same plants – though it's possible with some trees and palm-like plants in the right conditions. With things like ferns, there's no reason why some of their ancestral lineages couldn't still be growing. The neglect could even have encouraged some of them.'

'Well, that's something,' replied Frankie wryly. 'I'm glad to know that the Carlisle family style is good for some things, if not necessarily wood panelling and roofs.'

'Well, quite. I did want to ask...'

'What?'

'I *had* wondered exactly what had, er, nibbled the wood panelling in the hallway.'

Frankie clapped her hand to her mouth to suppress a giggle.

'Sorry, you look so horrified! I suppose it *is* horrifying, but it wasn't rats, I promise. I used to have this giant rabbit called Gulliver. He was a house pet and lolloped about everywhere. He was very sweet, but he did gnaw. I do miss him.'

Nathan wasn't sure how to respond to this, so settled for nodding in what he hoped was an understanding way.

'The dogs are nice, though,' he said. 'And they seem like best of friends.'

'Oh, they are!' said Frankie. 'We rescued Ava from under a bush where some horrible person had left her and her mother and brothers and sisters when they were tiny. She was the only one who survived, and Moriarty has taken it upon himself ever since to look after her. She's Juliet and Léo's dog really, they're the ones who found her and did most of the nursing. I'd love a dog of my own, but I think I'd better be satisfied with the orangery for now.'

'Quite, and talking of which...' Nathan looked at his watch

in horror – how had so much time slipped away? He was usually much more workmanlike than this. 'I'm going to go and get to work. See you later.'

He left the room abruptly, snatching up his phone and a bag with his sketch pad and notebooks, appalled at his own lackadaisical attitude. He was here to work, not chat away about dogs and rabbits all morning. He strode quickly back to the orangery, pushed open the heavy door and felt a certain peace steal over him as he stepped inside.

The stone, ironwork and glass structure was beautifully designed to let light pour in throughout the day, with the glass dome at one end. Although currently stained inside and out with moss, lichen and grime and invaded by overgrown plants, it was nothing short of magnificent. He couldn't tell if it was original or a nineteenth-century modification. The orangery stood separately from the house and maybe it was this that gave it its peace; no one would wander through or even think to look for you there. Maybe this was part of the reason why Frankie had chosen to spend so much time in it. He set his bag and phone down on the table, noting the nest of blankets and pile of books, the top one of which he picked up: *Pride and Prejudice*. This supposed wild child apparently liked to snuggle up in this secluded place with a dog and a classic romance novel. These were pastimes he could relate to far more easily than all night partying and freeform art. As he flipped open his notebook and prepared to start his inventory, Nathan acknowledged to himself that Frankie was far more complex and intriguing than he had imagined. And he couldn't pretend that he did not want to find out more.

ELEVEN

Over the following two weeks, Nathan and Frankie fell into a pattern of working on both the orangery and the abandoned formal yew garden. Much to her surprise, Frankie found this both stimulating and calming. He had shown her how to use the garden designing software and, although doing creative work on a computer was very new to her, she was fascinated by how she could incorporate her hand-drawn designs and then bring them to life, including in 3D.

She found Nathan, who had initially appeared so critical and as if he were pouring cold water on her ideas, to be patient and humorous, while teaching her with such skill that she felt empowered and capable. What a difference from Dylan who had, on the one hand, accepted her talent, but then was more likely to berate her for not using it than to help her by talking through any sticky patches. Instead, he would flounce off, either to throw paint at what the artistic community would surely laud as his latest masterpiece, or to disappear for hours, sometimes days, only to return dirty, foul-tempered and uncommunicative.

'Do you think we could do this?' she would say to Nathan,

turning the laptop to show him a design of the orangery as a stunning palm-filled space, laced through with flowering creepers and dotted with exotic fruit trees. He would study it seriously for several minutes while she grew impatient, wishing he would enthuse immediately, but then ultimately grateful for his respectful and considered feedback.

'I love the way that you've used the shape of the building to decide on the plants,' he would say. 'And the combination of foliage, flowers and fruit is what we want to aim for. But have a look at those palms. I'll send you a link so that you see how much space each one needs to be healthy, and you can also check if there are different species that might fit the bill. We should keep the vines – I hadn't considered those. Will they fruit, given the average temperature?'

'I'm not sure,' Frankie would say, clicking through the software with interest. 'I just thought "vines", but I'll look and see which ones will do best. It would be such fun to produce Feywood wine, even if we only got enough grapes for one bottle.'

She was also enjoying the more hands-on aspects of the work, especially once Nathan had finished the inventory of what was growing in the orangery. Only then was she allowed to resume ripping out weeds, even if she had to take more care with the fabric of the building they clung to than she had before. The yew garden was harder work, but as they climbed ladders and hacked at the bushes, she noticed more and more changes in herself as well as the garden.

'You're looking very tanned,' said Juliet one day, as she passed by where they were working. 'And I think that might be a little muscle popping up in your arm.'

'I know, right?' said Frankie, lowering her clippers and looking down at her sister from where she was balanced on a stepladder. She flexed her arm and grinned. 'Just call me

Popeye, although I'm chopping at the greens rather than eating them.'

'Are you making progress on the garden as well as your physique?' asked Juliet, peering in vain over the yews. 'It still looks pretty tangled. Oh! Is that Nathan in there?'

'Yes, he's doing all the careful stuff while I massacre things safely, happy for hours like a toddler with plastic scissors and an old magazine. He likes to pretend he's terribly pragmatic, but actually he's an old romantic, hoping to find some evidence of an Elizabethan knot garden that we can coax back to life.'

'I heard that!' came a disembodied voice from the shrubbery.

Frankie and Juliet looked at each other and giggled.

'I'm going to leave you to it,' said Juliet, then, raising her voice, added, 'Nathan's certainly a brave man, letting you loose with a pair of shears!'

Deciding it might be a good time to take a break, Frankie shouted to Nathan that she was going to get them both coffee. Then she went to the kitchen, spooned some instant coffee into a couple of mugs and started flicking through Facebook on her phone as the kettle boiled. She had taken a break from social media after leaving Dylan, but was slowly being drawn back in. She had extricated herself from many of the groups and friends that she found damaging and started using Facebook more than other platforms as it was too passé for most of them. She had caught up with some old friends, and enjoyed doing so. At Nathan's suggestion, she joined a couple of groups for aspiring garden designers where she was, tentatively, starting to share some of her own ideas and was finding a warm and supportive reception. Scrolling through her feed now, her attention was caught by a post by a local area group and she felt a rush of excitement. She sloshed some water and milk into the mugs and carried them back out to the garden as quickly as she could. As she approached, she saw that Nathan had emerged from the tangle and was looking up at her work of the morning. He turned as he heard her.

'You've done well here,' he said. 'You've got a neat line across the top. You'll have to learn some topiary next.'

'Never mind that,' said Frankie, thrusting one of the mugs at him. 'You've got to see this.'

She put her own mug down on one of the ladder's steps and pulled her phone out of her back pocket, swiping the screen impatiently to unlock it, then holding it up for him to see. He looked at it, then at her and said, looking puzzled:

'It's a peacock.'

She tutted and scrolled down to the text beneath the picture.

'Yes, it's a peacock, top marks, but it's actually two peacocks and they are desperately in need of a home, poor things. Look, it says here that they were handed in to a sanctuary in Belminster – that's about five miles from here. They're too small an outfit to be able to keep them and they're looking for somewhere which has at least four acres for them to wander around in and no close neighbours.'

Nathan took the phone and read for a moment, then looked slowly up at Frankie.

'Are you saying that you think Feywood is the perfect home for these peacocks?'

'Yes! There's plenty of room and they'd be in keeping with the house and your knot garden. I'm sure Henry VIII loved them.'

'Maybe roasted on the dinner table.'

'Oh! Don't be awful. I love the noise they make, like throaty seagulls, or malevolent cats.'

'Sounds delightful.'

'It would be. And they're so beautiful and vain and funny.'

'It says here that they need an aviary for the first six weeks and somewhere secure to sleep after that if they're free range the rest of the time.'

Frankie waved a hand.

'Oh, that's all perfectly doable, I'm sure. We had chickens a while ago, we've probably got all the stuff. Will won't mind, oh, I don't know, extending it a bit or something. Come on, admit they'd look fab walking around. Everyone would look after them; the whole family's mad about animals.'

Nathan laughed and held up his hands in defeat.

'Well, I'm not going to stand in your way if you want to talk to your father and Will about it. But you'd better be quick: it also says here that they can only look after them for another few days and then they'll be in a quandary about their future.'

'Then we *must* act quickly! I'm going now.'

Frankie gulped down her coffee and ran up to the house, bursting into Rousseau's studio, where he was staring intently at a large block of marble.

'Frankie! Are you all right?'

'Not really, Dad, look!'

She showed him the article and he read it carefully, then tutted with compassion.

'What a shame, such beautiful creatures. I agree with you that they would fit in beautifully at Feywood, but we must consider their welfare, the upkeep and the expense.' He looked again at the photos and smiled. 'Get some more details, darling, and if it looks possible, then I don't see why we shouldn't help.'

'Great!'

Frankie was about to dash from the room when she paused by a smaller block of marble near the window, which someone had started carving.

'Whose is this – not yours? Is Sindhu working again?'

'No, that's what Nathan has been working on in our sessions. I'm not sure you were supposed to see it actually, so don't tell him.'

ESCAPE TO THE COUNTRY GARDEN

With a promise of silence shouted over her shoulder, Frankie ran back out to Nathan.

'It's a *yes* from Dad if I can work out the logistics. I'm going to ring them right now.'

Two hours later, having made several phone calls and a visit to Will, who had been working on the estate's accounts and was glad for a reason to think about something else, Frankie had everything she needed in place. She had secured a large aviary on loan, a promise to build a night-time shelter from the old chicken coop and delivery the next day of two Indian blue peacocks, not to mention the gushing gratitude of the Belminster sanctuary.

The next afternoon, the whole household was waiting outside the front door for the birds. Will, Frankie and Nathan had worked from early that morning to put together a suitably large and strong structure for the peacocks to sleep in, with a little run outside for them to peck around in if they woke up early. They had also prepared a patch of ground for the aviary that would arrive with the birds, making sure there was nothing that could harm them and that it had sufficient light, shelter and space for them to be comfortable for the next six weeks before they could be allowed to roam free. Even Sylvia, who seemed to her loved ones to grow paler and more breathless every day as she waited for her operation, had made it outside, and was sitting on a canvas camping chair that Rousseau had carried out for her.

'I think this is them!' said Martha, as a four-by-four dragging a huge trailer came bumping across the cattle grid and up the drive. Two people stepped out, a man and a woman, who both shook Frankie's hand with wide smiles.

'I'm Louisa – we spoke on the phone. We can't tell you how grateful we are to you for taking this pair. We aren't set up for peacocks, and Arthur and I thought they would be almost impossible to rehome.'

'They're quite easy to look after,' added the man. 'Especially once the first six weeks' confinement is over. Shall we set up the aviary, and then you can meet your new additions to the family?'

With everyone helping, it wasn't long before the aviary had been unfolded and clipped together and two peacocks were strutting around inside, pecking at the food and water they had been given.

'They'll start to lose their tail feathers quite soon,' explained Louisa, 'but they'll grow them again in the autumn and they're still stunning without them.'

'I think they're wonderful,' said Frankie, gazing through the mesh. 'I don't care what they look like, I'm glad we could give them a home.'

'Let us know how you get on,' said Louisa. 'And if you think you've got room for anything else, give us a call. We're always looking to rehome all sorts of creatures: cats, dogs, chickens, ferrets...'

'That'll do for now,' said Will firmly, glancing at Frankie and Rousseau's enraptured faces. 'But we'll certainly let you know.'

Once they had left, everyone gathered around the pen to watch the magnificent birds.

'What are you going to call them?' asked Sindhu. 'They'll need good names so they can be part of the family.'

'It's hard,' said Frankie with a sigh. 'On the one hand, I'm tempted to call them something funny, like Laurel and Hardy, but then I think they deserve something much more dignified.'

'Morecambe and Wise?' proposed Martha. 'Or Abbott and Costello?'

'Or what about Jeeves and Wooster?' said Sylvia. 'Although neither looks bright enough to be Jeeves, I'm afraid.'

'No, true, but I like the literary reference, it seems suitably dignified.'

'How about Aramis and Porthos?' said Léo. 'Rather elegant and French, of course.'

'Although then you'd need another two to have all the musketeers and we are *not* going there,' put in Rousseau firmly.

'You could go down the Harry Potter route and call them Harry and Ron,' said Juliet.

'Not striking enough for this pair, I don't think,' said Frankie. 'It's tough.'

'I have an idea,' said Nathan, and everyone turned to him. 'You already have this handsome chap, called Moriarty.' He bent down to pat the scruffy black dog who was entering into the whole episode with his characteristic enthusiasm and good will. 'So, why don't you call them Holmes and Watson?'

A second's silence met this suggestion and then Frankie let out an ear-piercing shriek and threw her arms around him, before quickly backing off.

'Sorry, but that is such a good idea! It's the perfect names. I love them, don't you?'

She looked around and everyone agreed and congratulated Frankie on her exciting new addition to Feywood, before drifting off back towards wherever they would be busy that afternoon.

'Thank you for helping,' said Frankie to Nathan, when it was the two of them left. 'I didn't expect you to do so much, but their bedroom looks amazing and they've got so much room while they settle in.'

He smiled, and Frankie felt an involuntary quiver in her stomach. *Probably a bit of leftover excitement from getting Holmes and Watson*, she told herself.

'No problem. I must agree that they're what every Elizabethan manor needs, and I admire the way you flew into action to get them instated. Now, do you think you could apply some of that energy to the north wall of the orangery? I'm going to test out the fish pool to see if there's any chance at all it might be watertight.'

The pool had been one of the first things they had uncovered, once they had identified it on the plan. It was about two metres long by one wide and appeared to be in good condition. The cut-out square at one corner had turned out to be a small plinth, and further investigation uncovered some broken pieces of marble.

'It looks like it might have had a little statue on it at some point,' Frankie had said, examining the pieces and the discoloured patch on the plinth carefully. 'Look, I think this is an elbow. Maybe it was a little cherub holding a fish, or Neptune, or a water nymph with a shell. Dad might be able to take a better guess.'

'I'll take him the pieces when we have our next lesson,' said Nathan, gathering them together carefully.

'How's it going?' Frankie asked.

'Okay, I think. I mean, I'm not ever going to make a living out of it, but I'm enjoying learning the technique.'

Frankie hadn't pushed him any further, although now she had seen a glimpse of what he was working on, she was much more curious, and at his mention of the fish pool, she wondered again what he could be making. But she didn't have a chance to ask as he started off purposefully towards the orangery, leaving her to bid adieu to Holmes and Watson and follow him.

The peacocks settled in quickly and seemed remarkably content in their new home. Although, as Juliet pointed out, how one was supposed to spot a gloomy peacock was up for debate. Frankie often took a cup of tea down in the morning when she fed them, then sat and sipped it while they pecked about, squabbled occasionally and made their curious miaowing call. About two weeks after they arrived, she was in her usual spot when she decided to check her email. Scrolling through the screeds of junk and adverts, she stopped with a sharp intake of breath. There was a message titled 'Invitation to private viewing of "Dylan Madison: Retrospective".' With some reluctance, she tapped on it, and the email, sent by the gallery where the exhibition was to be held, opened.

You are invited to a private view of
DYLAN MADISON: RETROSPECTIVE
a fascinating timeline of the work of this fresh and eclectic genius

It went on to give the time and date of the exhibition, but further detail was scant. Returning to her inbox, she continued looking down the messages, finding what she had hoped for: a personal one from the gallery owner, Fabian Shuttleworth, who she knew reasonably well.

Dearest Frankie,

How are you? Very well, I hope. I was so devastated to hear that you and Dylan were no more, but I suppose it is only natural that two such bright stars could not burn together for long.

Frankie raised a sardonic eyebrow and kept reading:

I have sent you an invitation to Dylan's latest exhibition – a retrospective is, I confess, unusual for someone with such a relatively short career behind them, but we felt it would be fitting, given his stratospheric rise. I invite you, darling, partly I admit for selfish reasons. I know that Dylan gifted you many works during your time together, and I wondered if I might be able to persuade you to part with any of them. Early works, in particular, would be very welcome even to loan to the exhibition if you are not willing to sell. There are also some pieces for which you were the muse, and I thought you would like to see them before they disappear into the hands of eager private collectors, as they inevitably will.

Do be in touch,
Fabian.

She turned off the phone's screen and sighed, then dropped her head down onto her hunched-up knees. The sudden reappearance of Dylan into her life was not, she supposed, wholly unexpected, but it had stirred up her thoughts and emotions in a way she never would have believed possible. Images of her and Dylan together spun through her head, bringing with them all the feelings she had pushed away, both good and bad. She had loved him, that much was true. He was exciting, daring and careless and got away with everything and she had been up for that ride, over and over again. But he was also spiteful and critical, and that carelessness extended to everything, including her feelings and well-being. She had so nearly followed him down a dangerous and destructive path that she might never have turned back from, and she was glad every day that she hadn't, even if she did, at times, miss him. She missed his sharp sense of humour that zinged with hers so well, she missed his blazing talent that caught her up and allowed a little of the stardust to rub off. But she had been happier away from him, that she knew, even without all she had lost along the way, not least any ability or inclination to work on her own sculptures again. And Fabian was right: she did own several of Dylan's works, as well as sketches and notes he had made in her books that any archive would leap on. They were all locked away – not to keep them safe, even though she had some idea of their value, but because she couldn't bear to see them. They would surely bring his ghost to bother her and tempt her to dark places where she never wished to return.

She dug her hands into her hair and raised her face to the early morning sky, shouting out a single, loud swear word.

'Frankie?' She spun round and saw Nathan, holding a mug and frowning. 'Everything all right?'

They had built something of a friendship over the past few weeks, and Frankie was enjoying each day working with Nathan more and more. She looked at him now, his kind and steady face concerned for her, and decided to confide in him.

'It's this,' she said, bringing the phone's screen back to life and handing him the email from Fabian. He read it slowly, then turned his troubled face to meet hers.

'You haven't spoken much about Dylan,' he said, handing her the phone.

'No.' Frankie shook her head. 'I can't – I can't bear to rake it all over. I know that I've been an absolute fool and to be honest...' She looked up to see nothing but care etched on Nathan's features, and a lump formed in her throat. 'To be honest, I'm so *ashamed* of myself and the way I've behaved, who I am...'

'And who's that?' asked Nathan in a quiet voice.

'A bloody idiot who skips about through life having fun and not taking stuff seriously, letting everyone else pick up the pieces. I can't pretend I haven't enjoyed it, though – it's not like anyone was forcing me.'

'And then the fun stopped?'

'Yes. It all got so dark and scary, and that wasn't what I'd signed up for, but everybody thought I'd be up for it.' She brushed away an escaped tear. 'That's who they thought I was. I– I don't know how I let it get that far. I didn't think that Dylan was... so *serious,* I suppose, about the drugs and stuff. And coming away from it, and back to Feywood, has felt like I've been rescued from drowning in a tempestuous sea, and although I'm glad to be here and out of all of that, I'm scared that once I feel better, I'm going to start doing it all over again. Be "Fun Frankie", who's up for a laugh and a drink and doesn't mind anything much.'

A long silence followed this speech, eventually broken by Nathan, who cleared his throat several times, then said, 'Frankie, I don't know you well, so I hope you don't mind me saying...?'

She looked up at him and shook her head.

'Please, I'd appreciate your opinion.'

'Just that, having got to know you a little bit, I don't see any of that. I can't say if you've changed, or who is the real you, but I have found you to be authentic. You don't seem as if you're concealing or suppressing anything. You *are* fun, and daring, much more than me, but there's nothing wrong with that – and I think that Holmes and Watson would agree.' He grinned at the two peacocks strutting around in their cage. 'You're amazingly talented as well. Look, when I first came, I had read about you, of course I had, and I was dreading it.'

'Oh, thanks!'

'Sorry. I'm not good with words. I'm trying to be nice. What I was going to say is that I was dreading it because I did think you were all those things you've said – reckless and careless and chaotic – and that stuff makes me uncomfortable. I grew up with it.'

'Really?'

'Really. So I have a very good radar for it. And Frankie, now I know you a bit better, you don't set that radar off. You have terrific energy, verve, but you're not wild. I don't think. Sorry.'

'Don't be. Thank you. You're probably right. I know I sound all 'poor little rich girl', but growing up here, surrounded by amazing people... well, I often felt so inadequate. Even more, now that I'm not sculpting and Dad had the idea of asking you to help me. But oddly enough, I'm getting to prefer pathetic Frankie to wild Frankie. At least she's not making problems for everyone else.'

'So, you're worried that if you go to the exhibition...'

'It'll all be unleashed again? Sort of, but I'm more scared that I'll feel boring or something, that I'll hate myself even more. Oh, I don't know.'

'You don't have to go. Just delete the messages.'

'I could, but the thing is, Fabian's right. I do have some of Dylan's work, and if I sold it, I could give the money to Dad to help with Feywood. I'd like to. I'd also like to see some of the other stuff, I can't deny that.'

'Mmm. You have time to think about it. Why don't you put it on the back burner for now and let it percolate? The answer might be clear after a few days hacking back yews and cleaning windows.'

'Oh good, I'm glad you've saved me all the glamorous jobs,' said Frankie, nudging him with her elbow. 'But you're right. Just in case you hadn't noticed, I do tend to rush into things.'

'Oh really, I never would have noticed,' said Nathan, looking pointedly at the two peacocks. 'Come on, let's get started. Oh, talking of exhibitions, there is something I wanted to ask you. It's more of a display, of garden design in one of the Oxford colleges, and I was hoping you'd let me submit one or two of your drawings?'

'Do you think they're good enough? I've only recently started all of this.'

'But you're a professional artist, which doesn't hurt, and you do seem to have some sort of natural affinity for all this. I'm sure they'd be accepted. Can I?'

Going pink with pleasure, Frankie agreed, and as they walked through the garden, she felt herself standing a little taller. Why was it that she found herself opening up to this quiet, diffident man? Why was his approval so important to her? Why did it touch her more than the years of accolades from art school and the forceful praise Dylan specialised in? She shrugged as she picked up her shears. No doubt it was the novelty of support from such an unexpected source. It would probably wear off.

TWELVE

As Nathan had expected, the organisers of the garden design showcase at St Delphina's College jumped at the chance to display Frankie's work. They chose both a hand-drawn picture and the computer-created design that she had developed from it.

'Everybody else is going to think I'm a terrible fraud,' she grumbled, as they got ready to leave the house to go and see the display. 'They're all properly trained. Mine might be pretty, but they'll spot me as an amateur immediately. Oh, look, maybe I won't go. You can go and see it and tell me about it later. I'll go and clean out Holmes and Watson.'

Nathan had been through various permutations of this conversation several times with Frankie over the last couple of weeks and he was running out of ways to answer her. He took off his glasses and wiped them on his shirt.

'Frankie, the peacocks are fine. Your drawings are great. We need to leave or we'll be late. I have every faith in you.'

'Really?'

'You know it.'

She nodded, and he held the door open for her, then shut it

swiftly behind her again, before she could change her mind. Juliet had offered them the use of her small car and they threw their cases in the back, then climbed in. As Frankie started the engine, Nathan decided to change the subject.

'So, what's the hotel you've chosen like?'

'Didn't you look it up when I sent you the details to pay?'

He shook his head.

'No, I just sent you the money. I was late up that night after working with your father on my sculpture. Talking of things people don't want to go to, I'm dreading tomorrow night's dinner, but it could be good for business – there are a couple of people going who want to ask about Italy.'

'So, why are you dreading it?'

'I'm not great in big groups like that. I prefer being in the garden or in front of my computer to the networking side of things. Some of the people going represent huge outfits with massive turnovers… It's not my sort of thing.'

'Maybe it's time for me to give you a pep talk, then,' said Frankie, driving up the slip road onto the motorway. 'You've already said that people want to talk to you – not only because of Italy, I bet, but because you're a brilliant designer *and* you have the Italian connection. You've got plenty to offer.'

He gave no more response than a noncommittal 'mmm', but had to admit that hearing Frankie's encouragement *did* make him feel better. He was usually such a one-man band, living in his own echo chamber and hoping that the work that emerged was what people wanted, that hearing validation from someone else, particularly Frankie who didn't hesitate from offering an honest opinion, was a breath of fresh air. *She's good to have around,* whispered that little voice. *You're good at bolstering each other up, and you're getting on well all these weeks later, working together. Don't you think…*

'So!' he said suddenly, seeking to silence that inner voice. 'Tell me about the hotel.'

'It's small,' said Frankie. 'And looks terribly old-fashioned, but they've done something clever – made it feel all nostalgic but not missed any of the mod cons. It's comfortable and has great views of the Bodleian.'

'I'm surprised it wasn't more expensive.'

Frankie winked.

'I might know someone who gave us special rates,' she said. 'We're even going to be able to park, which is almost unheard of in Oxford.'

They chatted about the garden for the rest of the journey, until they reached Oxford and Frankie nipped expertly through the narrow streets, finally saying a cheery 'breathe in!' as she squeezed the car through a tiny arch entranceway to a walled, cobbled courtyard.

'It feels as if we should have come here in horse-drawn coach,' said Nathan, taking the bags out of the boot. 'I like it already.'

'Good,' said Frankie. 'Just wait until we get inside.'

They walked to the front of the building, entering through a heavy, paned wooden door into an entrance hall with a black and white tiled floor, elegant palms in huge ceramic pots and deep leather armchairs with extravagantly curved arms and smooth, gleaming walnut backs. Ahead of them stood a shining marble reception desk to the right of which a marble staircase with a geometrically patterned carpet and brass banisters ascended.

'Frankie, it's stunning!' said Nathan, gazing about at the art deco splendour. 'When you said "old-fashioned," I was expecting some tired boarding house with curling lino on the floors and nylon sofas. This is spectacular.'

Grinning, Frankie opened her mouth to answer, when a man with thick, neatly combed white hair and wearing an impeccable grey suit appeared from a door behind the desk then, spotting them, came over swiftly, his face wreathed with smiles.

'Frankie, my dear, how wonderful to see you. Welcome back to Lamotte's!' He seized her hand and shook it warmly, then turned to Nathan, who Frankie introduced, and who was greeted equally warmly.

'Delighted to meet you. I am Walter, the general manager. Let me show you to your rooms.'

He turned swiftly to the front desk and hit a small bell, upon which appeared a young, uniformed porter who wordlessly took two keys from hooks, picked up their bags and followed them as Walter swept them up the staircase and along a carpeted corridor.

'You are here, Frankie,' he said, beckoning to the porter, who scurried over and unlocked the door, then deposited Frankie's bag inside.

'Oh, it's as perfect as ever,' she said, gazing around. 'Thank you, Walter.'

'My pleasure. Sir, would you follow me to your room?'

'I'll knock for you in a bit,' said Frankie, and they went to the room next door. When Walter and the porter had gone, Nathan had the chance to look around his home for the next couple of days. As Frankie had said, the room had an old-fashioned feel, firmly rooted in the 1930s with its walnut bedside cabinets, fan-shaped headboard and dark brown wooden wardrobe which could easily have led to Narnia. But there was nothing dated about the fat duvet with its crisp cover, the electric kettle and selection of teas or, when he pushed open the door in the corner, the smart bathroom with a huge shower cubicle surrounded by a spotless curved glass screen and fluffy monogrammed towels on the heated rails. When he walked over to the window and pushed aside the net curtain, he had, as Frankie had promised, a perfect view of the Bodleian Library's extraordinary dome. He started to unpack the few things he had brought, and he was hanging up his shirts when there was a knock on the door, which he answered to admit Frankie.

'What do you think?' she said, perching on the side of the bed. 'It's fun here, isn't it?'

'I love it,' he replied. 'I've stayed in a couple of hotels in Italy which haven't been touched for decades but still manage to feel luxurious; this reminds me of one of those.'

'I've never been,' she said. 'But I'd love to – all those extraordinary paintings and sculptures hidden away in little churches. You know you can go into some tiny, dark parish church and there will be a Michelangelo or something casually displayed in the place it was created for, hundreds of years ago.'

Nathan busied himself straightening the already neat shirts on their hangers. Every day Frankie showed him another part of her personality, another part that he liked, and he found it hard, now, to call to mind the petulant rebel he had disdained.

'You'll have to visit at some point,' he said, talking straight into the wardrobe and willing himself not to offer to take her there himself, that very evening. An image of them sitting together at dusk on one of the villa's large balconies, sipping a local *digestivo* as they watched the bats flit about, came to his mind. He shook himself. 'But now we'd better get going to St Delphina's. We don't want to miss the gala opening of the whole garden festival – it might be interesting.'

They stepped out into the early evening light, bidding Walter goodbye, and started on the short walk to the college.

'What time are Juliet and Martha getting here?' asked Nathan, as they dodged a group of slow-moving tourists taking selfies.

'Any time now,' she said, pulling out her phone to check. 'Yes, in fact they're already there. It was a shame that Dad and

Sindhu couldn't come for the opening tonight, but it'll be nice to see them tomorrow. Oh look, there are the girls.'

After saying hello, they showed their invitations at the Porters' Lodge and walked through the ancient flagstone first quad of the college, through an archway that led to a second quad, where there was a large crowd of people milling around near an empty polished wood podium. They didn't have long to wait until a tall woman with iron grey hair in a neat bob stepped up and tapped the microphone.

'As Dean of St Delphina's, it is my pleasure to welcome you all to our inaugural Festival of Gardens. The festival runs for the next three days, and you will find all the information you need about the various exhibitions, talks and activities in this pamphlet or on our website.' She waved a printed booklet at the audience, then went on to speak about the college's gardens, which dated back to the fifteenth century. When her speech had finished, she invited everyone to take a glass of champagne and enjoy the festival. Nathan squeezed through the crowd and came back a few minutes later, giving Martha and Juliet each a glass filled with pale, sparkling fizz, and Frankie one with orange juice.

'Cheers!' they all said, and drank for a moment, taking in the beauty of the buildings surrounding them with their warm honey-coloured stone glowing in the evening sun.

'Come on,' said Frankie. 'Let's go and find our exhibition. I'm sort of dreading seeing my stuff up there with everyone else's, but I don't think I can put it off any longer.'

'It'll be brilliant,' said Martha, linking her arm through her sister's as they started to walk. 'I'm so proud of you, darling, for doing this.'

'It was Nathan who entered it,' said Frankie, nodding at him. 'You can blame him.'

'I might have filled out the application,' he said mildly. 'But it was your work they wanted to show. Look, the Olmsted Room, this is it.'

The room they entered was large and carpeted in rich blue, with a bay window at one end. Pictures of garden design were hung all around, and a screen showed 3D designs from different angles. Thirty or forty people were milling around and, as the Carlisle group paused to get their bearings, a small woman with a high, blonde ponytail came over to them.

'Hello! You *are* Frankie Carlisle, aren't you?'

'Erm, yes,' replied Frankie.

'I was *so* hoping you'd be here. Your designs are so beautiful! We've all been talking about them – we being the organisers, that is – and now, as you can see, they're all anyone wants to look at.'

Looking across the room, Nathan realised that most of the guests were clustered around one small area, clearly looking at something that was generating a lot of interest, and his heart swelled to think that it was Frankie's work causing the ripples.

'Please come and meet them all,' said the blonde woman.

Frankie glanced at Nathan, and he gave her an encouraging nod, then, before either of them could speak, she was borne away to the other side of the room and swallowed up by the group there.

'Do you think she'll be all right?' Nathan asked her sisters. He knew how nervous she had been an hour or two ago, and was worried that she would be overwhelmed by the sudden and unexpected attention, even if the nature of it was the exact opposite of what she had been fretting about.

'Frankie?' said Juliet in surprise. 'She'll be fine! She likes nothing better than being the centre of an adoring crowd. Isn't that right?'

She turned to Martha, who screwed up her face before speaking.

'She *did* used to be like that, but she's changed so much since she's been back.' She hesitated, then continued. 'But you're probably right – she'll get back in the swing of it all, I'm sure.'

Nathan was torn as Juliet and Martha wandered off to look at some of the other pictures on display. He could see Frankie now that a particularly tall man had moved away. She looked excited and animated, chattering away about her design and pointing things out. Every time she spoke, the group around her would burst into laughter. *She doesn't need me*, he thought, trying and failing to glean some sort of relief from that assumption. *I'll go and look at the other pictures and let her do her thing without cramping her style.* He glanced over one more time, to see Frankie look directly at him and give a little jerk of her head. He clocked the empty glass in her hand and went to collect another drink for each of them before heading over, his heart beating fast and his mind at war with itself:

She only wants another drink. Lucky there's a willing lapdog to get it for her.

Maybe she wants me there, not just the drink.

Get real. She's in her element, look at her.

But we've been getting on so well.

In a garden, for a few weeks. She was always going to return to be the star she clearly is.

Neither side had won the argument by the time he reached Frankie and held out the fresh glass.

'Thank you,' she said, then, leaning into him, whispered quickly, 'Please stay and help me talk to these people.'

Ha! You see, she wants me to stay with her, said one side of his brain triumphantly, while the other sneered, *For now, mug, for now.*

THIRTEEN

As she fielded enthusiastic and flattering comments and questions from the other guests at the exhibition – some of them professional garden designers themselves – Frankie was glad of Nathan's quiet and reassuring presence. Her request for him to stay had spilt out almost without her meaning to say it; she would never normally ask someone else for such help, preferring to keep up the 'don't care' image she had cultivated for so long. As they all chatted, an image flicked through her head of what Dylan might have done, had she asked the same of him. Probably have been stroppy that she was wasting his time on her needs, or publicly mocking her. Either that or he would have taken over, answering for her and then swiftly moving the conversation on to himself. Nathan, on the other hand, had given a small nod, then stood calmly, saying little but simply *being* there for her.

'Where did you train?' asked one of the group, taking her glasses off and leaning closer to Frankie's pictures. 'I'm surprised I haven't heard about you – I normally get wind of promising students.'

Frankie's heart sank. Was this when she was to be uncovered as a fraud, not a 'real' garden designer? She glanced at Nathan, who smiled encouragingly.

'I went to art school,' she said. 'I haven't done anything formal yet in garden design, I'm only just starting out. Nathan is training me.'

All eyes immediately swivelled towards him, and he cleared his throat awkwardly.

'Er, yes, that's right. As you can all see, Frankie is very talented. So I'm lucky to be helping her with this new venture.'

The woman put her glasses back on and inspected Nathan with a frown.

'I knew you looked familiar. Nathan Brooks, isn't it?' He nodded. 'Whatever happened to you?' she continued, her voice more inquisitive than rude, although her forthright manner was startling. 'You had promise, Chelsea Gold Medal promise, then you vanished. Gone into teaching, have you?'

Frankie looked at Nathan curiously. What this woman was saying seemed to tally with what Frankie had read online – that Nathan was squandering his talent on municipal projects in Italy. But why?

'Not exactly,' he said calmly. 'I moved to Italy a few years ago, where my brother lives, so I usually work there.'

Much to the admiration of Frankie, who knew she had a tendency to give far too much information away, especially under the scimitar gaze of someone like this woman, Nathan said nothing further, merely smiling pleasantly and with apparently no discomfort. A short silence fell over the group. Eventually, the woman spoke again.

'I see. Well, if your new student is already doing this well, then you're doing something right. Get in touch if you want to do any projects in this country.'

She handed him a business card, nodded briskly and walked away. Frankie was dying to know who she was, especially given the interested looks of the rest of the group, who had been listening to this exchange. But Nathan merely slipped the card into his pocket and said, 'Would you like to look at some of the other exhibits?'

'Very much,' she said with relief, and started over towards Juliet and Martha on the other side of the room. The four of them spent another hour looking at the different designs, captivated by the creativity, imagination and skill on show, demonstrated in so many different ways.

'Can we go and get something to eat now?' said Martha eventually. 'Honestly, I could look at these for another hour, but I'm too hungry.'

'Good idea,' said Frankie. 'And I think at the public opening tomorrow all the exhibitors are given a book or brochure of some sort with every design in it, so you can borrow that. Where shall we go and eat? I bet Oxford is packed; we'll probably end up with sandwiches on a bench.'

'I did actually anticipate that,' said Juliet. 'And much as you might be happy with egg and cress al fresco, I would rather sit at a table for my supper. Things *were* pretty booked up, but Léo knew someone...'

'Of course,' interjected Frankie, grinning.

'...of course,' continued Juliet. 'So we have a table booked.' She glanced at her watch. 'If we walk over now, we'll be in perfect time.'

They left the building and passed back through the two quads, past the Porters' Lodge and out into the street, following Juliet as she led them first through the crowded main area, then down a small side road, flanked by honey-coloured stone walls.

'Are you sure you know where you're going?' grumbled Frankie. 'This doesn't look very promising.'

'Rather depends on your idea of promising,' said Juliet, turning a corner onto a street with several small shops and leading them to the third. It had an exquisite façade: mostly wood and bamboo, with a sort of horizontal split curtain hanging in front of the sliding doors. Panels with Japanese writing flanked the door, along with four white paper lanterns. A lush display of seven or eight green plants of varying heights in shiny ceramic pots stood to one side.

'Oh, it's so pretty!' said Martha. 'And I love Japanese food.'

'We all do,' said Frankie, leaning over to take a photo of the plants. 'You must tell Léo to sharpen up his sushi skills, Jools. Less of the flower quiches and more of the miso ramen.'

'Ha ha,' said her sister, who rarely rose to Frankie's idle jibes. 'Learn how to cook them yourself.' She turned to Nathan. 'Is Japanese food okay with you?'

'Absolutely,' he replied. 'Thank you for arranging this.'

They went inside and were surprised to find that the tranquil, tucked away restaurant was full of diners. A smartly dressed man came over to them, worry creasing his forehead.

'Good evening. Welcome to Tenkū No Teien. Do you have a reservation?'

'Yes,' said Juliet, stepping forward. 'Léo Brodeur rang earlier?'

The man's face relaxed into a smile.

'Of course! We are so glad you are here. Please, follow me.'

They went through the busy restaurant to a section near the back, where there was a sunken floor with four tables, one of which was empty. The man gestured to it, and they slid onto benches. They were surrounded by more plants and there was also a small stone fountain trickling peacefully in one corner.

'It's beautiful here,' said Martha, picking up a menu. 'So tranquil. I must say it was clever of Léo to find somewhere gardeny, given the reason we're in Oxford.'

'He was disgustingly pleased with himself,' said Juliet, smiling. 'He does love it when he can do something like this. Apparently, the name of the restaurant means "Heavenly Garden".'

'I'm tempted to make some sketches,' said Frankie. She

turned to Nathan. 'Wouldn't it be special to have an area like this at Feywood?'

'Japanese-style gardens were very popular at the beginning of the twentieth century,' he said. 'We could have a look and see if there's a suitable spot. I've always wanted to learn how to design one – it's quite an advanced skill.'

There was a brief pause in the conversation as they put in their orders, then Frankie asked, 'Well, why don't you? That woman at the exhibition said you were good enough to earn a gold medal at the Chelsea Flower Show. Who was she, anyway?'

'Her name's Cynthia Bourton-Jones. She's designed some famous gardens, worked with royalty, that sort of thing, and she has a spot presenting from Chelsea each year. She used to take the Gold regularly, but now she judges. I'm surprised she'd heard of me.'

'Well, she obviously thought it was a shame that you weren't still designing at a level she knew about,' said Frankie. 'Or are you very famous in Italy?'

Nathan laughed.

'Not at all. Italy is an amazing place to live, but most of the work I do is pretty boring, I'm afraid, working for the council on public gardens.'

'But why?' persisted Frankie. 'You're obviously amazing, so why don't you do something more creative?'

He shrugged.

'I love living there – wouldn't you like to wake up every morning to golden sunlight and the chirruping of bee-eaters outside your window? The council stuff is steady work. I needed that for a while and now I find it suits me.'

Intrigued, and slightly irked that he wasn't being more forthcoming, Frankie opened her mouth to ask another question, when she was stopped by the gentle but firm voice of her sister, Martha.

'I do the same with my portraits,' she said. 'Almost all my work is commercial and that makes me feel secure, as well as able to help out with Feywood. We're all different and I'm sure the people who use your gardens are very grateful for your expertise. Do you have any tips for reducing water usage? Feywood is a worry in the summer because everything goes so yellow.'

The conversation turned to creating sustainable gardens, and Frankie, half listening, turned her attention to the delicious tempura prawns she had ordered. As Nathan talked, she thought back to the exhibition and how kind he had been – to enter her work in the first place and then to support her with such unobtrusive stolidity. She sneaked a glance at him now, as he earnestly explained to Martha the ideas he had for harvesting rainwater at Feywood, and what a difference it would make not just to their garden but to their bills, if they could install a relatively cheap collection and pumping system.

'It's not my area of expertise,' Nathan was saying. 'But maybe Will would be able to get something working?'

Frankie felt a little jolt as a jokey comment about Will, with whom her eldest sister was hopelessly in love, popped into her head. It was a comment designed, she knew, to make Martha squirm. But looking at Nathan's kind face, and having listened to his patient explanations, she suddenly felt disinclined to go for a cheap laugh, and instead focused her attention on Martha's response.

'You should definitely ask him. He wants to save money for sure, but I know that he has lots of ideas for making Feywood more sustainable. Big houses like that are out of date now, as homes, but we do love it so much.'

'Have you thought about opening up any part of it to the public?' asked Nathan.

The three sisters glanced at each other, and it was Frankie who answered.

'The cookery school is the start of that, but in a very limited way. Our mother would never have countenanced strangers staying in the house, but it's worked well so far. We all think that we could do more, share Feywood more, but there are two problems. First of all, Dad can't be disturbed when he's working, and a lot of people would be keen to come and see his studio and meet him. His work is erratic, so it would be difficult to plan around. And secondly – well, you've seen what a mess the place is in. It's a catch-22. We need money to fix it up, but we can't have people paying to look around when it's in such a state.'

'We're getting there for sure,' added Juliet. 'I think work will start on the roof quite soon, but although that's very important, and hugely expensive, it's the tip of the iceberg.'

'I think...' said Frankie, then hesitated.

'Go on,' said Nathan quietly.

'No, it's probably silly.'

'Even so, it might be the germ of an idea.'

Resisting the sudden urge to lay her head on his shoulder and feel at peace, Frankie took another bite of prawn and continued.

'I think that, if we could fix up the garden okay, there might be some possibility of opening just that for now, and not the house. I mean, I know it would take more than asking for a fiver on the gate – we'd probably have to have loos and a tearoom and insurance...' She rushed on. 'I mean, I know the garden is nowhere near good enough yet and will probably take years, but... it was only an idea. A stupid one.'

'I don't think it's stupid at all,' said Nathan. 'We're working on the disastrous parts at the moment, but we're making good progress. There are plenty of other areas that Will and Sylvia have been maintaining. The rose beds are immaculate, and so is the kitchen garden. And people don't necessarily want perfection. You could set up some tables on the terrace and serve simple teas. It doesn't matter that it's all a bit cracked and mossy – that gives it charm. I think it's a great idea. Although you would need insurance and access to a loo, you're right.'

The wave of pride that rose up in Frankie's chest took her by surprise. Feeling flustered, she turned away quickly and started pouring everyone more green tea in order to hide the unexpected rush of emotion. Nathan continued, a note of excitement coming into his voice.

'And although obviously you don't want to disturb Rousseau, couldn't you display some of his work outside? You could even see if other people would lend you artworks – sculpture gardens are popular and the backdrop of Rousseau and Lilith Carlisle's house would be a massive draw, I'm sure.'

'He's right,' said Juliet. 'We could even get Léo and Sylvia to make some cakes and things to sell, when Sylvia's better, of course...'

'Which she will be soon,' put in Martha firmly.

'Exactly. And we could even have easels or something set up outside with your portraits. And as for facilities, there's that horrible old outside loo that hasn't been used for years. It must have all the plumbing, because we used to use it when we were children. We could smarten that up.'

The four of them looked around at each other eagerly.

'I don't want to pour cold water,' said Nathan, 'but we're looking at quite a long timescale.'

'That's all right,' said Martha. 'The roof will need to be sorted out first anyway, and presuming this is seasonal we wouldn't have time to get it ready for this year. But maybe next? Gosh, I'm glad you came, Nathan.'

'To Nathan!' said Juliet, and they clunked their little stone cups of green tea together.

The man in question smiled around modestly, and Frankie thought about the last time she had been with Dylan when he had been awarded a prize for young artist of the year at yet another gallery who liked to draw in crowds and push up their prices with these ceremonies. Although he had been a shoo-in, being in cahoots with the gallery owner, he had paraded around all night, chest puffed out, posing for photos, showing off and drinking himself into a stupor, of course. In comparison, Nathan's diffidence warmed him to her even further, but when she realised she was gazing at him admiringly, she quickly pulled herself together.

Do stop staring, you only appreciate him so much because he's your teacher. You're learning from him, and he has lots of great ideas and Feywood is going to benefit. That's it.

'Just popping to the loo,' she said abruptly, standing up.

'I'll come with you,' said Juliet, and they headed off together. Once in the loos, Frankie headed quickly to a cubicle; she knew that look on her sister's face and suspected that she was in for a grilling she would rather avoid. But poor Frankie was not to escape. When she emerged, Juliet was waiting for her by the square stone sinks, a slight smile on her face.

'You and Nathan seem to be getting on well,' she said. 'Anything to tell me?'

'Nothing at all,' said Frankie, squirting some bamboo-scented soap onto her hands and rubbing them busily under the tap. 'He's kind, a bit too serious for me, but I'm learning a lot, end of story.'

'Oh, come on,' said Juliet. 'There has to be more to it than that. He's gorgeous, and so nice.'

Frankie shrugged.

'I'm learning a lot,' she repeated. 'The orangery is going to look great, and now he's got some good ideas for opening Feywood up. I wonder if Dad will go for them?'

'Okay, okay, change the subject if you must, but I'm giving you my blessing. Even if I didn't like him as much as I do, he's a definite step up from Dylan.'

'I could hardly take a step down,' said Frankie gloomily,

drying her hands on a fresh, white flannel, then tossing it into a basket. 'But I'm not interested in Nathan, and he most certainly isn't interested in a mess like me. Come on, let's go back.'

Ignoring Juliet's sudden look of concern, she pushed past her and opened the door, moving quickly back to their table before she could ask anything else. She avoided her gaze for the rest of the meal. She hadn't meant to be so revealing about herself and wasn't looking for sympathy or fixing. No, Frankie wanted to be left alone.

After they had finished the meal and paid, Frankie and Nathan walked Juliet and Martha to catch the Park 'n' Ride bus back to collect their car.

'Well done,' said Martha, hugging her youngest sister. 'I think you're amazing to have taken on something new and done so brilliantly.'

'Have a good evening,' said Juliet with another warm hug. Then she murmured so only Frankie could hear, 'Sorry for teasing you. If you're not interested, you're not interested, fair enough. And for what it's worth, I think Nathan would be bloody lucky to have you.'

When they arrived back at the hotel, Nathan asked her if she wanted a coffee in the bar. She shook her head.

'I think I'm going to head to my room, if you don't mind? Today's been great, but I'm tired, and I want to think about some of the things I was asked about today in case they come up again tomorrow.'

'Of course,' he replied. They exchanged a few pleasantries with Walter, then ascended the elegant staircase together, stopping outside Nathan's door.

'Well, good night,' said Frankie, suddenly feeling awkward. What was meant to happen now? She couldn't exactly shake his hand, but it felt odd not to make some friendly gesture. She settled for a small wave, as he leant in to peck her on the cheek. This resulted in her almost hitting him in the face, which she successfully avoided by putting her hand on his shoulder, which made the polite peck feel weirdly intimate. Unusually for her, she felt a blush start creeping up her neck and, desperate to hide it, she turned abruptly and hurried to her own room, almost falling through the door once she had managed to get the key card in a slot that seemed too tiny by far. Once the door was safely closed, she threw her bag on the chair and sat down heavily on the bed.

'What was *that*?' she said aloud, then cringed, wondering whether Nathan might have heard her through the wall.

Best keep it to an internal monologue, or he'll think you're even madder than the box of frogs he probably already has you pegged as. But seriously, Frank, what was that? Blushing? And then a thought crept over her, a thought she knew to be true as much as she wished it wasn't: *you DO fancy him. Yeah, you do. And that is one of the most pointless things you've ever done. What on earth would Nathan ever see in you?*

FOURTEEN

The next morning Nathan awoke early, much earlier than the eight thirty he and Frankie had agreed to meet for breakfast downstairs. After a shower it was still only shortly after half past seven, and he already felt cooped up in the hotel room which, pleasant as it was, had no direct access to the outside. He decided to look over the biographies of the fellow diners he had been invited to join that evening. Although several of them had done work he admired, he found it difficult to focus, until one of them mentioned a garden not far from Oxford that he had heard of but never visited: Rousham. He clicked through to the website to discover that the garden had been designed by William Kent in the eighteenth century and remained virtually unchanged since then. Then he checked out a map and realised it was only half an hour's drive from where they were. So engrossed was he in the photos of the glorious gardens he found online, it was only a knock at the door that reminded him it was time for breakfast.

'Morning!' said Frankie when he opened it. 'The breakfasts here are legendary – are you ready to go down?'

Nathan grabbed his key card and followed her to the dining

room, another art deco masterpiece with a shining parquet floor, towering palm trees and a circular glass ceiling that allowed the morning light to pour in. Once they were equipped with flaking, buttery croissants, porridge and coffee, Nathan cleared his throat, feeling the nerves he was so good at hiding from others making his stomach muscles ball up and rendering him unable to eat a thing.

'Frankie, I know you were planning to go straight back to Feywood after this morning's opening, but I was looking at a garden not far from here and wondered if you'd like to visit it this afternoon.'

He went on to explain about the design and history of the place, his body relaxing as she nodded eagerly and took out her phone to look up some pictures.

'It looks amazing, and we've got the weather for it. Are you sure you'll be back in time for the dinner tonight?'

'I think so,' he said, finally able to start on the delicious breakfast, and not adding that he would far rather be wandering around a beautiful garden with her, anyway, than at a stuffy dinner with a lot of people he didn't know.

The morning opening of the exhibition was busier than either of them had expected.

'Can't we skip it?' said Frankie to Nathan when they arrived and saw four times as many people as had been there yesterday.

'I don't think we can,' he replied. 'You've promised to do that interview and they're going to present everyone with their exhibition catalogues. Can you bear it for a bit longer?'

She nodded and he hoped that she could keep going; what he hadn't told her was that there were going to be prizes awarded, one of which he was optimistic might be given to her.

'Look, they're getting stuff ready on the podium, so it won't be much longer.'

Indeed, within five minutes the woman who had spoken to him and Frankie the previous day, Cynthia Bourton-Jones, was standing tapping the microphone and looking around confidently, as if she expected everyone to realise she was there and turn their attention to her which, to Nathan's impressed amazement, they did. He couldn't imagine wanting to command a room like that, and he admired her confidence.

'Welcome, everyone, to the opening of Garden Design in Action,' she said, pausing for the smattering of polite applause that followed. 'We hope you enjoy all it has to offer, starting here with an exhibition of sketches and computer designs by professionals who have been working in this sphere for fewer than five years.' More applause. *When was she going to get on to the prizes?*

Frankie wondered how much longer she was going to talk for, and how long it would be before she could go with Nathan to see this garden; it felt infinitely more appealing than being in a stuffy room full of people she didn't know. 'We also have three prizes to award to our up-and-coming designers.'

Now, Frankie turned to Nathan and raised an inquisitive eyebrow, but he merely smiled and turned back to listen to Cynthia. Infuriating.

'The first prize we wish to award is for Innovative Use of a Computer Model and it goes to Nina Edgbaston.'

Everyone clapped again as Nina went up to the podium to receive her prize. *I'll have to look her work up in the catalogue,* thought Frankie. *I might learn something.*

'The next prize is for Incorporation of Sustainable Elements, something that each one of our exhibitors can be commended for. The prize goes to Jack Swann.'

A willowy young man, beaming with pride, went up to collect his prize. Frankie checked her watch. If this hurried up a bit, they'd be able to spend longer in the other parts of the festival before everyone had finished in here and it got too crowded.

'Frankie?'

Nathan put his hand on her arm and she jumped.

'What?'

Nathan, who seemed to be wearing the most enormous smile for some reason, nodded towards the woman at the podium, who was holding an award and looking amused. She leant back into her microphone.

'Once again, the prize for Most Promising Designer goes to Frankie Carlisle.'

'Me?' squeaked Frankie, and Nathan, laughing now, nodded.

'Yes! Go and collect it!'

Muttering apologies, she scuttled through the crowd and took the award.

'Well deserved,' said Cynthia, shaking her hand. 'I hope to see more of your work in the future.'

Frankie stammered out her thanks and went back to Nathan. She didn't hear Cynthia's closing words, but when the audience applauded for the final time then started to disperse into the room, she turned to Nathan.

'I can't believe I won a prize! Did you know about this?'

'I knew there were prizes. I'm sorry I didn't tell you, but I knew you were nervous about the exhibition, anyway, and I didn't want to add to it. And I'm not remotely surprised that you won.'

She gazed at the stylish Perspex trophy in her hand, then back up at Nathan.

'I'm in shock! Do you think everyone will be annoyed with

me because I'm such a newcomer and I haven't had any proper training?'

Nathan frowned, although a smile still crinkled the sides of his eyes.

'By "proper", I assume you mean "formal"?'

'Oh gosh, sorry, of course I do. Your teaching has been brilliant. But you know what I mean.'

'I do and no, they won't be annoyed. They'll all want to work with you. And you could do a diploma, if you were thinking of pursuing this.'

As they had been talking, people walked past them, clapping her on the back and offering their congratulations. She smiled at and thanked the last of these, then said, 'I don't have the faintest idea what I want to do next, but I'm so happy with this. Thank you. Can we go and see the rest of the festival now?'

'You don't want to stay and entertain your adoring public?'

She pulled a face at him.

'Certainly not. Think how much you'd hate it if you were me.'

He laughed.

'Fair enough. Come on, pick up your catalogue and let's go.'

An hour and a half later, they were in the car and heading up the Banbury Road to Rousham.

'So, tell me about these gardens,' said Frankie, and as Nathan explained about the designer and the historical value of the gardens, she listened intently, whilst still letting a part of her mind wander around her emotions for him. She had become used to working with him in the orangery and garden at Feywood, but seeing him in this new context had stirred up feelings she wasn't too happy about. When she added supportiveness, understanding and the undoubted admiration Cynthia Bourton-Jones had for him to the patience, kindness, intelligence and good humour – not to mention the handsomeness – he had already shown, Frankie couldn't deny that *not* fancying him would be odd. But it was as if the more she found to like about him, the more confused she was. She had never had any problems in the past with approaching – and yes, seducing – men she was attracted to, and had thrown herself into a string of love affairs with joy, abandon and not much thought beyond. But with Nathan, it felt different. Although he never lorded it over her, told her what to do or criticised her – things she had grown used to putting up with or shrugging off in the past – she felt, and she hated to admit it, intimidated by him. *He doesn't mean you to feel that way, though. You've met plenty of intimidating men before and had them eating out of your hand within half an hour. So, what's different?* She knew what it was, and she had no idea how to handle it. It was the little kernel of shame she felt deep inside, a sense of her own unworthiness, that she was lightweight. The Frankie she had been – and enjoyed being – for so many years wasn't, she was sure, someone that Nathan would be remotely interested in being with. No, he must find someone better suited to him: an elegant, understated woman who could be the partner he deserved. And anyway, since Dylan the last thing she needed was any other man in her life, for a while at least.

She pulled into the car park and they paid at the machine for a ticket, then wandered into the grounds, which opened up magically before them.

'Which way do you want to go?' asked Nathan.

'I don't know, it all looks so glorious. Shall we wander?'

They set off along a gravelled path, overflowing rose beds flanking them as the scent of the blooms filled the air, making Frankie feel quite heady. Each time they turned a corner, a new delight awaited, from quiet shady corners to rolling lawns to little stone follies, romantic bridges and enticing iron gates set into high hedges. It was through one of these that they discovered an immaculate knot garden.

'Is this what we're going to do at Feywood?' asked Frankie, a note of doubt in her voice as she thought of the overgrown and patchy yews they were slowly taming.

'Keep the faith,' said Nathan, taking photo after photo with his phone. 'We have all the raw materials, it's the patience and time that have to go in.'

A nearby squawk took Frankie's attention from the garden, and she laughed.

'Sounds as if they have peacocks too. I hope Holmes and Watson aren't missing us too much.'

'Those peacocks!' said Nathan, shaking his head. 'I can still hardly believe you got them.'

Frankie turned from him, feeling her happiness ebb. The peacocks were a typical example of her silly, childishly spontaneous behaviour. She loved them, but it had been a mad and quite unnecessary venture. She shrugged.

'It was stupid of me,' she said, her voice catching. 'I know we should be focusing on more important things at Feywood.'

'Frankie?'

Nathan put his hand on her shoulder and she turned back towards him, the look of concern on his face making her stomach flip.

'What?' she mumbled. 'It was stupid.'

'I'm sorry,' he said. 'I didn't mean it like that at all. I can't believe you did it because I don't know anyone else who would have such a madcap idea and then follow it through, but I don't think it's stupid, I think it's great.'

For a moment, they stared at each other. Frankie could feel Nathan's hand on her shoulder, her awareness of his touch making it feel as though her skin was burning. Looking into his eyes, she saw a maelstrom of feelings. They matched those tumbling around her own mind: attraction for sure, but also confusion. If it had been anyone else, she would have known exactly what to do, gone through the routine seamlessly. She would have offered a small smile. Blinked slowly. Taken a tiny step towards him. And the rest would have fallen into place. But with Nathan, she couldn't. She didn't want to play the game she'd played before, however much she longed for him to kiss her. Another cantankerous cry from the peacock gave her the opportunity. She stepped back slightly, hiding her disappointment as Nathan's hand fell from her shoulder.

'He's louder than either of ours,' she said, her voice shaky. 'I wonder if anyone has remembered to feed them. I should probably get back. Spontaneous peacock purchasing is one thing, not looking after them properly another altogether.'

'Of course,' replied Nathan. 'And I need to get ready for this dinner.'

'Will it be fun?' asked Frankie, as they walked back up the enormous, immaculately striped lawn.

'Not really,' he replied, 'but probably interesting.'

See? said that unkind inner voice again. *Proper adults don't need things to be 'fun', they can have an 'interesting' night out instead.*

The atmosphere between them felt awkward now. Frankie had mixed feelings when she dropped him off back in Oxford and headed for Feywood. On the one hand, she was relieved not to have to think any more about the moment that had passed between them. But on the other hand, the empty space beside her in the car affected her more than she ever would have imagined. She felt almost bereft, aware how much she already missed him.

FIFTEEN

Frankie turned the car into the gates of Feywood, trying not to take off a wing mirror, as she had done before on more than one occasion. As she straightened up and bumped over the cattle grid, she looked ahead and let out a little exclamation of surprise. More than a year after their father had first raised the issue of the serious problems at Feywood – problems with both the finances and the structure of the old house – scaffolding had finally gone up all around. Frankie could see two figures standing at the top taking photographs. As she pulled the car up, hoping it was a safe distance from any falling debris, she gazed out of the window at her beloved family home. Seeing it swathed in poles and planks like some sort of external skeleton, she smiled. It was good to see the old lady getting the help she needed.

It's a bit like you and Nathan. He's propping you up like that scaffolding while all the old, broken bits get thrown away or mended. And I wonder if you'll be able to stand on your own when he goes? The thought of him leaving gave her an unpleasant jolt, and she climbed quickly out of the car, grabbing her bag. Then she paused and looked up again at the great house before her. *If Feywood can survive for five hundred years through all the transformations, trials and neglect she has endured, then I reckon I'll be able to manage too.* She found this inspiring, and was smiling as she ran into the house, almost straight into Martha, who was carrying a tray into the living room.

'Frankie! You're later than we expected you. Do you want some tea? I put on extra mugs and made a pot because someone always wanders in.'

'Yes, please, good timing.'

The sisters went into the sitting room and Frankie sat in one corner of the large, high-backed sofa, while Martha poured.

'I didn't know the scaffolding was going up today, but I'm glad it's finally happening,' said Frankie, leaning forward to take a couple of biscuits, which she perched on the faded chintz arm of the sofa.

'None of us did,' said Martha. 'Dad and Will have kept their cards very close to their chest, but I don't know what the big secret is.'

'No secret,' said a voice behind them, and Frankie turned to see Will, who had come in through another door. 'Rousseau hasn't been talking about it much because he didn't want Sylvia to start getting worried.'

'Would you like some tea?' asked Martha.

'Yes, please.'

He's got pretty good timing too. I wonder how often he casually wanders in when Martha's here at this time?

But her musings were cut short as he continued.

'It took ages to sort it all out. You can't get in a normal roofing company for a job like this. We needed a historic building architect and a specialist company to be available at the same time as well as an almost cast-iron guarantee of good weather. It was helpful you finding those plans for the orangery, Frankie – there were other documents in that map chest that have given us a good idea of what we'll find underneath the tiles.'

'I'm glad,' she replied, then tutted as the biscuit she had been dunking for too long plopped into her tea. 'How long will it take?'

'That's anybody's guess – it depends on what they find when they start looking at the supporting structure, which we think is original. If it's sound which, believe it or not, it still could be, then we're looking at weeks. They'll still have to reset all those clay tiles, have some new ones made for the worst patches and check the chimneys, not to mention the waterproofing. If not, then it could run into months.'

'Can we afford it if it does?' asked Martha, looking worried.

Frankie saw the look on Will's face as he tried to ease her concern and wished, for the millionth time, that the pair of them would get together.

'It will be okay,' he said soothingly. 'As long as we keep on with the changes we've made, and push on with some others, then the bank is happy.'

'We had a good idea when Martha and Juliet came to Oxford,' said Frankie, changing the subject.

'To open a sculpture garden?' said Will. 'Yes, Martha told me. I think it's inspired.'

So they'd already caught up about that? Cosy! But I must not tease her. Really, Nathan is having a good influence!

She was about to reply when the door from the hall opened, and Rousseau entered.

'Ah, Frankie, you're back. Good. Will you go and find Juliet and Léo? I'll track Sylvia down if she's not with them in the cookery school. I have something to tell you all.'

'Not another dire announcement about Feywood?' said Frankie. 'Don't tell me Mum sold it out from under you and we've got twenty-four hours to leave?'

In an unusually coquettish way for him, Rousseau beamed and wagged a finger at her.

'Now, now, none of that. This is *good* news. Go on!'

Frankie sauntered deliberately slowly from the room, but broke into a faster pace once she was out of the door, intrigued as to what her father could want to tell them. She crossed the lawn, waving at Holmes and Watson as she passed their cage.

'I'll come and see you later, boys, I promise!'

Then she burst slightly breathlessly into the cookery school, where she found Juliet, Léo and Sylvia all sitting around the middle island, mugs in hand.

'Oh, good, you're all here. You need to come up to the house, Dad's looking very pleased about something and says he has good news for us all. Do any of you know what it is?'

They all shook their heads.

'He probably thinks we haven't noticed the scaffolding,' said Juliet. 'And he's delighted at springing such a nice surprise on us.'

Frankie grinned.

'Well, I wouldn't put it past most of us to be so absorbed in something else that we didn't realise it was there. Do you remember the time I dyed my hair pink and when Martha saw me for the first time, she asked me if I knew anything about Hans Holbein? When I said I didn't and waited for her to notice my barnet, she just looked vexed and wandered off to the library.'

Sylvia laughed.

'You may have a point, Frankie, but I think I can probably guess what his news is.'

'What?' said Juliet and Frankie in unison, but Sylvia glanced at Léo, who raised his eyebrows and also refused to say anything.

'Come on then, if you're both going to be so infuriatingly

smug about it, let's get up there and find out,' said Frankie. 'You might as well bring your tea. I'll carry yours, Aunt Sylvia.'

A few minutes later, they were back in the sitting room, where Sindhu had also arrived, and awaiting their father's news. He stood up.

'Thank you, all of you, for gathering here. I know that last time we all got together it was to impart the news that Feywood was in some trouble. Happily, I have no such thing to tell you today. Rather, she is doing well – most of you have probably noticed, have you? – that the scaffolding has finally gone up and the roof is on its way to full restoration. Thanks go to all of you for your help in making this happen. But today's news is happy news.' He paused, and reached out a hand to Sindhu, who took it and moved to stand next to him. 'I – *we* – are delighted to tell you that, this afternoon, I asked Sindhu if she would marry me, and she said yes.'

There was a collective intake of breath at this, although Frankie wasn't sure why they were all so surprised. It was swiftly followed by a round of applause, chatter of excited congratulations and a flurry as everyone stood up to hug and kiss the fiancés.

'I hope none of you will find it too early to join us in a toast?' asked Rousseau, and when everyone responded eagerly, he went behind one of the curtains and produced a champagne bucket complete with two bottles. Will disappeared to find some glasses while Rousseau eased out the corks. When Will returned, Rousseau started filling glasses, and when it came to Frankie, he put a hand on her shoulder.

'The second bottle is for you, my dear, if you prefer?'

He turned it so that she could see the label, which showed it was non-alcoholic kombucha. She stepped forward and hugged him again.

'Thanks, Dad, I do prefer for now. You don't mind me not toasting you with champagne?'

He handed her the glass.

'All I mind is that you are well and happy. You are, aren't you? You *look* happier, these days.'

'I am, and it's down to you. You were right about Nathan – he's a great teacher and a nice guy, and I love doing the garden and the orangery.'

'I'm thrilled, just thrilled.' He dropped his voice a little. 'And I wonder if you can be happy for Sindhu and me? Not too soon after your mother for you?'

Frankie smiled.

'I was a bit of a spoiled brat about that before; I'm sorry. I'm happy for both of you, Dad.' She could see his eyes start filling, and she elbowed him. 'Come on, none of that. Make your toast before everyone's bubbles go flat.'

He delved into his pocket and pulled out a small marble sculpting chisel, which he tapped delicately against the side of his glass until everyone had stopped talking.

'Thank you. We have thought carefully about what we should raise a toast to on this occasion and, while of course we toast to love, we also wanted to choose something that everyone here might be able to find relevance to in their own lives. So, with that in mind, please raise your glasses – to new beginnings.'

'To new beginnings,' they all repeated, and clinked their glasses.

'Do you know where and when yet?' asked Léo. 'Or is it too soon for that?'

Rousseau and Sindhu glanced at each other, and Frankie wondered whether she detected a slight discomfort. It was Sindhu who spoke.

'Rousseau – that is, *we* – would like to use Feywood, of course...'

He squeezed her hand.

'We can talk about all that later, darling. It certainly doesn't have to be here.'

Why not? Mum's ghost haunting too loudly, maybe.

No more was said on the subject and the next half hour passed in a pleasant hubbub of conversation. As glasses emptied so, too, did the room as people slowly drifted back to their work, until it was just the three sisters left.

'Why don't you come and see the orangery?' suggested Frankie. 'It's nowhere near finished, but I think you'll love what we've done so far – and I've got an idea.'

When they walked in, Juliet and Martha looked round in amazement.

'I can hardly believe it,' said Martha. 'You said you hadn't done much, but you've worked wonders. Look at the beautiful brickwork – I never even knew that was there! And some of these look like real plants, not weeds.'

'That's right,' said Frankie proudly. 'We've uncovered some amazing plants that are actually supposed to be here – that's a clematis and this is called a sensitive plant, look.'

She stroked the tiny leaves gently and they instantly folded up together.

'It's stunning,' said Juliet, sitting down and looking around her. 'I'm seriously impressed, Frank.'

'Thank you. Now you've seen it, I hope you'll like my idea. I was thinking that Dad and Sindhu might like to use it for the wedding in some way. I don't know, it's probably silly and they won't want to, but if they're going to do something here at Feywood, the orangery is sort of new. If that makes sense.'

She petered out and kicked at the ground, annoyed with herself for not articulating her idea better and sure that her sisters would have something more special in mind. It was Martha who spoke first.

'I think that's a *lovely* idea.' Frankie looked up, feeling a little spark of pleasure inside. Martha continued. 'You're so clever, Frankie. It must feel odd for both of them with so much history here, especially of Mum, but the house is undeniably special. The orangery would be the perfect compromise.'

'I agree,' said Juliet. 'You should definitely mention it. You get on much better with Sindhu now, don't you?'

Frankie nodded.

'Yeah, she's nice and I'm happy for Dad. When she first came on the scene, it was a shock. Childish of me, but the thought hadn't crossed my mind that Dad would meet someone else; the family was the five of us, then four when Mum died, and Aunt Sylvia, of course. But Sindhu hasn't tried to replace Mum or be a mother to us; she's who she is, and I realised that she was going to be there whether I accepted her or not. The choice I had wasn't whether she stayed or not, but how I reacted to her.'

Juliet stared at Frankie.

'You've put it perfectly, Frank. Bloody hell, if you're this mature now, that must make me and Martha ancient. I feel the same.'

'Well, I'm glad that you two have *finally* caught up with your big sister,' said Martha, a twinkle in her eye. 'Maybe some of my wisdom is finally rubbing off.'

'Ha,' said Frankie. 'Maybe in this case, but you need to take notes from us about not acting like a lovesick thirteen-year-old around *you know who.*'

'Leave it,' said Juliet, warningly, as Martha's smile faded. 'What sort of space will be in here once it's finished – enough for the actual ceremony?'

'Sorry, M,' said Frankie, reaching over to squeeze her sister's hand. *Oh, when would she learn to curb her tongue?* 'I suppose it will depend on how many people they invite. You never know with Dad – he could randomly insist on ten or five hundred. I think, when it's finished, you could probably fit in about twenty people for the ceremony. Or we could use it for a drinks reception and fit in more.'

'We'd better ask them,' said Martha. 'Why don't we speak to Sindhu separately first, and find out if she minds having all or part of the wedding here? If she doesn't want to, then that's that. I think you should speak to her, Frankie; it was your idea and it's such a good one.'

'Okay,' replied Frankie. 'I'll find a good time to ask her. Shall I suggest at the same time that we're all bridesmaids? I'd look charming in lemon taffeta – you have to admit, we all would.'

Juliet stuck her tongue out.

'Don't you dare, or if Léo and I ever tie the knot, I'll make you organise the hen night – no, sorry, hen *weekend* – as well.'

God forbid, thought Frankie. But deep inside, no matter how hard she squashed it down, there was a tiny feeling that romance and all its associated paraphernalia, wasn't *quite* as bad as she had once believed.

SIXTEEN

Nathan had found the speakers interesting at the dinner he had been to. Even so, he hadn't been able to help wishing that Frankie had been there too, with her witty asides and down to earth dissection of people and situations. He had made a couple of useful contacts and spent a great deal of time talking to a designer he had long admired, who was thinking of spending some time in Italy, which had been useful. But he had also found himself stuck for nearly half an hour with a man he had known at college, who seemed determined to put Nathan firmly in his place, as if Nathan cared what that was, or wasn't happy to be there, anyway.

'*Municipal* work,' the man, Jonty, had said, 'is useful, isn't it, if one is looking to stay in one's comfort zone and simply take home a salary at the end of the month? It does suit a certain genre of designer – like you, I suppose. Personally, I find that I like to be challenged by diverse and artistic projects. I'm sure you remember the work I did for Lord Snaresborough?'

'I do,' said Nathan mildly. 'Twenty years ago, wasn't it?'

'Indeed, indeed,' Jonty had replied, nodding in what he no

doubt thought was a sage way. 'Start as you mean to go on, that's what I say. What *did* make you change your path into *municipal* work?'

Not easily riled, Nathan felt that if this odious man said the word 'municipal' one more time, especially in such a way that implied it was sullying his lips even to utter it, he would say something he regretted. Maybe something along the lines of how he was fully aware that Jonty's career had more or less hit the skids after college, and he relied on family money and a few cushy jobs for friends to maintain any kind of profile in the industry. But that wasn't Nathan's style.

'My parents left chaos behind when they died and it became more important to have steady work,' he replied bluntly. 'Living in Italy suits me and working to deadlines and strict client requirements has honed my discipline and skills for if I ever do decide to take on more creative projects again.'

Damned if he was going to tell Jonty about Feywood. If he knew the man, he'd be there like a shot, inveigling his way into the house and claiming all the credit for the garden and orangery. *Mind you,* he smiled as the thought crossed his mind, *Frankie would make short work of you.*

'If you ever do, give me a call,' said Jonty graciously. 'I'm sure I could help get you started.'

Nathan shoved the proffered card into his pocket, said something bland about the time and made his exit. Back early to the hotel, but not fancying a drink alone in the bar, he picked up the phone to ring his brother. Henry answered after a couple of rings.

'Nathan, good to hear from you!'

They chatted briefly about what they had been up to, then Nathan put forward the idea he had been turning over for a few weeks.

'Do you think it would be all right with Antonio and Carla

if I came back for a visit – and brought Frankie with me? Just for a few days. I'd like her to see some of the projects I've worked on as well as the gardens of their villa.'

'I'll double-check with them, but you already know that the answer is yes. They'd love to see you and to meet her as well. How's it going with the *enfant terrible?*'

Nathan laughed.

'Not terrible at all. The opposite, in fact. She's hard-working and very inspired. I'm there to help her, but it's been good for me as well.'

'I'm glad. Let me know your dates and I'll confirm.'

They chatted for a few minutes more before saying goodbye, and Nathan went to bed that night glad that he would be back at Feywood soon and hoping that Frankie would be pleased at his idea of a trip to Italy.

When the taxi from the station deposited him at the house the next morning, he was surprised and pleased to see that the scaffolding was finally up. Workpeople were clambering around on the roof. He went in and was immediately reminded of the day he had arrived at Feywood, to an empty house with music blaring. He remembered Frankie's sudden appearance bringing colour and light to the scene and to his life in a way he could never have anticipated. Unsure where the family was, but knowing better than to go haring around the myriad rooms looking for them, he instead put down his bag and listened. At first, apparent silence, broken only by the occasional cooing of a collared dove outside. But, as he waited, he heard voices and laughter – very faint, but unmistakeable. *The family must be at the back of the house.* He set off through the sitting room and out into the passage by the dining room. The voices were louder now, coming from the left. *Maybe Rousseau's studio?* Although it was usually such a peaceful place. He headed in that direction, before realising that the family was behind a closed door he had always passed by until now. Pushing it open, he found a painting party in full swing. The room was bare of furniture, although he could see that it had been piled outside the open French doors, except for a single armchair and small table in the middle of the room where Sylvia sat, laughing at something her brother had said. The floor was swathed in white cloth dustsheets and the other members of the household were busy in various ways. Frankie was lying on the floor apparently inspecting the bottom of the panelling. Martha was standing by the window, engrossed in a highly illustrated book. Rousseau and Sindhu were sitting on the floor, poring over a large sketchbook and Juliet and Léo had been painting little patches of paint in different parts of the room, which they were now inspecting. Will was up a stepladder, scraping carefully at some discoloured paint where there had been a leak. Not one of them noticed him come in, until he said, 'Hello.'

Frankie rolled over on to her back.

'Nathan! You're back! Good timing, we're having a painting party to sort out the back parlour so that Aunt Sylvia can use it.'

'I can see you're hard at work,' said Nathan, grinning. 'Lying down on the job?'

'I'm assessing the panelling,' said Frankie with dignity. 'Will said it was important, didn't you?'

Will raised an amused eyebrow and continued scraping.

'I'm afraid I did get rather distracted by this incredible book I found,' said Martha, closing it gently. 'But I can finish looking at it another time. What are you two up to?'

She directed this last comment at Rousseau and Sindhu.

'We were wondering if a mural would look good,' said Sindhu, looking up from the sketchbook. 'With this beautiful view of the gardens, we could do a sort of 'bringing the outside in' theme, and we could all contribute. What do you think, Sylvia? After all, it's you who will spend time looking at it all, and if you'd prefer us to do the whole lot magnolia, then that's your call.'

Sylvia laughed gently.

'I can't remember the last time a Carlisle opted for magnolia in paint or in life,' she said. 'Everything all of you are planning sounds super – I'm so grateful to you for doing it for me.'

'Well, of course,' said Frankie, sitting up, her face suddenly so serious that it made Nathan want to go over and wrap his arms around her. 'We'll all do everything we can to make you comfortable while you get better.'

Everyone nodded sombrely, then Nathan said, 'Now that I'm back, I'd like to help too. What can I do?'

'I think we're decided on this pale green for the walls that aren't panelled,' said Juliet. 'If Léo and I go and buy some, could you go over the patches of other colours with some white so that they don't show through?'

Gladly, he picked up a brush and started work, soon joined by Frankie.

'I thought you were looking at the panelling?' asked Nathan. 'Or have you finished your survey?'

'Ha ha,' she said, waving her paintbrush threateningly at him. 'Actually, I have good news for Will.' She turned to speak to him. 'It's all in good shape, so I don't think that Gulliver can have come in here much.'

'Good,' chipped in Rousseau. 'I don't know why we all found that monstrous rabbit so charming – he wreaked havoc. I hope you're not planning to let those peacocks into the house once they're released from confinement, I can't imagine what harm they could do.'

As the family started an apparently serious discussion about the pros and cons of having peacocks indoors, Nathan painted over the sample patches and listened in amusement, reflecting as he did on what his reaction would have been a few weeks ago. *You would have been horrified, and tight-lipped about the whole thing. You would have written the whole lot of them off as frivolous and irresponsible and look at you now!* He smiled to himself as the thought crossed his mind. *You're wondering whether anyone has considered how hard it would be to see the TV if a peacock opened his tail in front of it! Looks like the Carlisles are rubbing off on you, and maybe that's not such a bad thing.*

Juliet and Léo returned shortly, and everyone put down what they had been doing and rushed to find a brush.

'Not so fast, I'm afraid,' said Will. 'I hate to dampen everyone's enthusiasm, but we can't start painting until we've taped off all the panelling.' The assorted company groaned in disappointment, and he grinned. 'Sorry, children, work before play. I've got a few rolls of masking tape; it won't take long if we all help.'

Nathan took a roll and started to do his bit, noticing how much the family seemed to like and respect Will, and how easy the relationship was between them. Will had struck him as a serious and quiet man, not unlike himself, and for a moment, before he sharply pulled himself back to reality, he let a thought wander across his mind: *Maybe I could find my niche here, too, with Frankie...*

For a few moments, there was relative quiet in the room as everyone measured and stuck tape along the panelling. It was broken, suddenly, by a shout of laughter from Frankie.

'Look what I've found! Jools, Martha, do come and see!'

Everyone instantly downed tools and went over to see what Frankie was pointing at. Nathan peered over Rousseau's shoulder, but couldn't work out what first Frankie, and now her sisters, were finding so funny.

'When did we do that?' said Juliet. 'Must have been at least fifteen years ago. Did you know about it, Dad?'

'I didn't,' said Rousseau. 'But my daughters' awful behaviour has ceased to shock me.'

As he turned away, Nathan saw that his smile belied the strict words. He moved to look again, able to get closer now, and saw that there were various letters carved haphazardly into the five-hundred-year-old panelling.

'Did you three do that?' he asked, trying to keep his voice from sounding schoolmarmish, but slightly taken aback by the vandalism, nevertheless.

'Years ago,' said Frankie. 'We were in our teens and all lovelorn, although it was a different boy every week, so I'm not sure what made these three so special that we decided to immortalise them in the woodwork.'

'Might have been something to do with that Drambuie you found in the kitchen,' said Juliet drily.

'I'd forgotten that,' said Martha. 'Completely disgusting and it made us all terribly depressed.'

'So we came in here and scratched our initials in – well, I think they were supposed to be hearts but they're a bit wonky,' spluttered Frankie, dissolving into giggles.

'Using the compass from your pencil case!' shrieked Juliet, and the three sisters were once again incapacitated by mirth.

Nathan felt a bubble of laughter rising up in his own chest, so infectious was their hilarity, and when he looked around, he saw that everyone was smiling at the memory. His own parents, he thought, wouldn't have cared if he'd painted the house neon green, but only because they barely noticed anything he'd done, anyway. They had been monumentally selfish and chaotic and embroiled in their own hedonistic dramas for most of his life. With the Carlisles, it seemed different. The air of benign neglect pervading Feywood had a mantle of warmth and love over it that he had only ever dreamt of in his own childhood. He had found something similar in his brother's new family, but he knew he couldn't live there forever, however much he loved it: it was temporary, if not so much so as Feywood. He picked up his roll of masking tape to resume the task. Would he ever have the life he was beginning to realise he craved, or was he destined instead for his safe, boring job and merely being a tourist in other people's families?

SEVENTEEN

A week or so later, Frankie opened her eyes to a glorious spring morning that was in direct contrast with the way she was feeling inside. While sunshine poured in through windows and birds sang with lusty good cheer, she felt a shrinking darkness inside that was cold and hard in her stomach. She dressed quickly, ran a brush through her hair without looking in the mirror – she felt too anxious, even, to meet her own eyes – and trudged down to breakfast. Soon, the whole household was there, helping themselves to the food that Rousseau had prepared, as he always did.

'I very rarely dare attempt a Continental breakfast,' he was saying as she tore off a piece of her flaky, golden croissant. 'I have to confess that even I am somewhat intimidated by the presence of a bona fide French chef in our midst, at times.' He nodded at Léo, who gave a little bow in return. 'But today I was carried away by this glorious weather. So... *bon appétit!*'

For a few minutes, the chatter was about Sylvia's surgery, which she now had a date for, and their collective success in redecorating the back parlour in which she would spend her convalescence. After some discussion when they had been working there, they had decided to leave the carved initials as they were, with the sisters insisting it was for posterity, while Sylvia teased them that it was nothing more than nostalgia. This morning, it was all Frankie could do to force down some food, let alone join in the conversation, and it wasn't long before her silence was noticed.

'Are you okay, Frankie?' asked Sindhu, who was sitting next to her. 'You're very quiet this morning. Do you feel unwell?'

Frankie turned to look at her soon-to-be stepmother's kind face, and suddenly longed to rest her head on her shoulder and sob out everything. Either that or to make some quip before leaving as soon as possible. Instead, she took a shaky breath and said, 'It's Dylan's retrospective today and I said I'd go. To be honest, I'm dreading it.'

'Is that today?' asked Martha with distress in her voice. 'Oh, Frank, I wish you'd said – I would have come with you. I've got a sitting I can't possibly get out of, I'm so sorry.'

Frankie shrugged.

'It's okay. I'll get on with it and not stay long. I promised Fabian, the gallery owner, that I'd take a few bits with me, and I can't let him down. They're in the catalogue and have spaces in the exhibition waiting ready for them.'

'What are you taking?' asked Juliet.

'I've got a preparation sketch for that massive thing he did for the investment bank a few years ago, with a note from him to me about it. And there's a maquette for that ugly piece that went into the exhibition at Tate Modern.'

'Fall For Me?' asked Rousseau.

'That's the one,' she replied. Then she grinned. 'I put aside all my artistic integrity to help him assemble the thing, and he gave me the maquette.'

'What's a maquette?' asked Nathan, frowning.

'It's a small model sculptors make to practise before they make something full size,' explained Frankie. 'Although I don't know why he bothered with "Fall For Me" because it looks like a junk heap from any angle. Luckily for him, he had a very flowery explanation for why it had artistic merit, which everyone seemed to agree with, and it's one of his biggest successes, so the maquette should make good money. It's money for Feywood, Dad,' she added.

'No, Frankie, I can't let you do that,' replied her father immediately. 'You're making enough of a contribution as it is.'

'Not at the moment, I'm not,' she said baldly. 'And I want to do more. Let me give it to you, Dad. I don't want it myself, anyway. I'd much rather it helped everyone. And if you refuse to take it, I shall buy one of Dylan's monstrosities and hang it in the hallway.'

Everyone laughed and the momentary tension was relieved. Rousseau half stood and gave a bow.

'Very well, you have outmanoeuvred me once again. Feywood gratefully accepts.'

After breakfast, Frankie headed to the orangery, where she found Nathan staring into space in a way that was unusual for him.

'Boo!' she said, coming up behind him. 'What are you looking all spaced out for?'

A blush came to his face in the way that she was beginning to find adorable.

'I was thinking about today actually, the retrospective.'

'Ugh, I don't want to think about that. I don't have to leave for two hours, so I was going to spend it cleaning the windows on the south side.'

'Really?' A teasing tone came into his voice. 'That's a job that's been on the list for a while – I thought it was going to be one for me.'

'Hmm, well, today I feel like doing something straightforward and mindless. If you get me fussing around with little potting trays, or trying to think about in which direction ferns might possibly decide to grow their fronds, I'm only going to mess it up.'

'Good honest labour?' he asked.

'Exactly.'

'Okay.' He paused. 'Look, Frankie, not to talk about it anymore, but this retrospective...'

She gave a small sigh.

'Yes?'

'I'll go with you. I know you'll be fine on your own, but you know, in case you'd like, I don't know, company...'

His words petered out and he blushed again, the red stain reaching his ears this time. Frankie's heart skipped a beat, and she resisted the urge to reach out and take his hand to reassure him that his kindness was not something to be embarrassed by, but something she appreciated greatly.

'Wouldn't you hate it?' she asked. 'It's in a grungy, hip part of London and will be stuffed with all manner of awful people. Wouldn't you rather stay and talk to the peacocks?'

He grinned now.

'Yes, of course I would, but so would you, and you're going.'

'I wish I wasn't,' she confessed. 'Fabian is so nice – a rose among the thorns that are the rest of those addled sycophants.'

Nathan looked half-amused, and she raised an eyebrow.

'You think I'm exaggerating? Wait and see,' she said darkly.

'So I *can* come with you!' he said triumphantly. 'Even if only to wade in the cesspit you describe.'

'You'll hate it,' she said warningly, 'but yes, and thank you.'

She started work on the grimy windows, saying little more, but inwardly filled with a swelling feeling of hope and gratitude. With Nathan coming, the hours ahead in London didn't feel so intimidating. Rather, a cocoon of safety had wrapped itself around her: safety from the unpleasant people she knew would attend the retrospective but also safety from herself, who she still didn't entirely trust. With Nathan there, she wouldn't feel the drag of temptation towards the self-destructive hedonism that had nearly swallowed her up a few months before. Or, if she did feel it, she wouldn't give in.

A few hours later, they were walking along a street in Walthamstow, east London, towards Fabian's gallery.

'This is it,' said Frankie, stopping outside a black-painted brick building with huge windows, in which hung two of Dylan's typical splashy, lumpy canvases. Amongst the nail bars, fabric warehouses and bookies, it looked smart and sleek. The 'closed' sign was up on the door, but she knocked on the glass and a tall man, completely bald and wearing large, dark-rimmed glasses and a very natty suit, appeared and unlocked.

'Frankie!' he said, in a deep, resonant voice, and drew her into an embrace before holding her at arm's length to inspect her. 'You look *wonderful*, my darling. I am beyond thrilled to see you. And who is your companion?'

'This is Nathan,' said Frankie, and the two men shook hands. 'I've been working with him at Feywood.'

'Another artist?' enquired Fabian, as they stepped inside and he locked the door again.

'Of sorts,' said Frankie. 'Garden design.'

'I see, I see,' said Fabian, smiling broadly but, Frankie knew, probably totally bemused, both by the concept of garden design – the nearest anyone he knew came to it was probably growing hydroponic weed in the cupboard under the stairs – and by the thought that this could be what Frankie was now spending her time on. He soon changed the subject. 'So, have you brought me some goodies? These' – he gestured dramatically towards an empty white plinth and a space on the wall, both labelled – 'await your contribution.'

'Here they are,' said Frankie, opening the enormous bag she carried and taking out two boxes. 'I hope they do well.'

'And you're *sure* you want to part with them?' asked Fabian, opening the larger of the boxes and removing the maquette. 'This is magnificent.'

'One hundred per cent sure,' said Frankie, taking the framed sketch out of the other box and handing it to her friend, who tilted it towards the light and breathed out in pleasure. 'The documents are all here too,' she said, pulling out a large, white envelope.

'Perfect,' said Fabian, taking it from her and placing the maquette carefully on the plinth. She jumped when he suddenly shrieked, without turning around: 'Diana!'

A very young, pale woman, with light brown hair pulled back into a neat ponytail and wearing a huge, chunky, bobbly greige sweater that looked as if it could have belonged to her grandfather and should have been consigned to the charity shop in 1984, appeared instantly from a back room.

'Ah, Diana – Frankie Carlisle and Nathan... er, Nathan.'

Diana's enormous blue eyes widened.

'Frilled to meet ya,' she said with a south London accent Frankie found to be at odds with the girl's frail, esoteric appearance. 'Luv yer werk as much as Dylan's, 'ope to see more of it, shime yer've stopped.'

'Thanks,' replied Frankie. 'I'm, er, trying other things at the moment.'

The girl nodded and turned to Fabian, who gave her swift instructions for displaying the two pieces. He then swept Frankie and Nathan away into the back room.

'I have the paperwork ready,' he said, gesturing them towards two uncomfortable-looking metal chairs, and sitting down behind his desk on a large, padded, leather club chair. 'Just a few signatures and we'll be good to go.'

Frankie signed gladly, feeling that she was unburdening herself of another piece of her past.

'Thank you,' said Fabian, taking the papers and putting them in a file. 'I would say "let's hope they sell", but there's little doubt of that. Dylan is hot property right now. You do know, don't you, my dear, that everyone here tonight is going to want to know about your sudden departure?'

'I know,' said Frankie, glancing at Nathan, who smiled at her encouragingly. 'And I'll stick to the truth – I couldn't stand the heat of the hot property, so I got out of the fire.' Now, it was her turn to change the subject. 'Which are the pieces you said I was his muse for? I would like to see them.'

'Then come now. I need to check that everything is taking shape out front, anyway. Having said that, Diana may look like she's either about to faint clean away or ask for help with her RE homework, but she's tough as old boots and splendid at organising things. Come on.'

They went back into the gallery to find that much had changed in the short time they had been away. A table was set up with drinks, and waiters in black T-shirts and jeans milled around filling glasses and polishing trays, while Diana watched them with an eagle eye to make sure they didn't spill anything on the artworks. Frankie's pieces had been displayed, and she only felt a momentary pang as she looked at them.

'Are you all right?' asked Nathan. 'You can still decide against selling.'

'Absolutely not,' said Frankie firmly. 'I want them to go. It's just odd, being thrown back into all of this. Some of the pieces are new, but of course as this is a retrospective, there are a lot which are familiar. It's bringing back memories, but I'm okay.'

'Champagne?' said a waiter, suddenly materialising.

For a moment, the pull in Frankie's stomach almost winded her, the urge to grab a glass and neck it, knowing that it would give her some much-needed courage; hell, she could probably even make herself enjoy the evening. She could feel both Nathan and the waiter looking at her, awaiting her answer, and she raised her eyes from the glasses to look at each of them in turn. The blandly handsome waiter smiled, and she moved on from him quickly. Nathan's face was concerned, but he smiled, too, and said, 'What would you like to drink?'

His calm voice, devoid of judgement, had the effect she had been craving, and her shoulders dropped. She turned back to the patient waiter.

'Actually, do you have anything non-alcoholic?'

She tried to keep an apologetic note out of her voice, but the waiter's polite smile, rather than faltering, broke into a beam.

'Oh, absolutely. My friend has started an AF artisan distillery – not far from here actually – and his spirits are to die for. I'm going to make you a cocktail you'll never forget. Would you like one as well, sir?'

'Yes, please,' said Nathan, and the man beamed again before walking briskly away.

'Are you sure?' asked Frankie. 'Don't you need a drink to get through this evening? Look, people are starting to come in.'

'I'll be fine,' said Nathan. 'If we can get through this sober, we deserve a reward, and I've got something in mind.'

No matter how much Frankie badgered him, he wouldn't divulge what it was, and she had to give up as more people came in, some of them barely glancing at the art on display and instead making a beeline for her. Clutching her cocktail – which, with its delicate flavours of lemon and basil, was as delicious as she had been promised – she tried to fend them off by scrutinising pictures closely and talking to Nathan, but it was a fool's errand.

'Hey, Frank,' said an insistent voice at her shoulder. 'Didn't expect to see you here. Thought you'd dropped us all to go and be lady of the manor.'

Frankie turned slowly, knowing who was speaking: Tara

Bradbury, heir to a company that sold niche but very costly stationery to people who still had time to write things by hand and couldn't understand why everyone else was so *déclassé*. Tara was tall, impossibly groomed and beautiful, and was the owner of a bottomless trust fund. She had had a long and expensive education and been expected to go into the family business. She did dabble – it was useful these days to be able to say you had a job that exhausted you, so that you could get out of things you didn't want to do – but had mostly adhered herself to the east London artistic community and to Dylan in particular. Frankie wasn't unaware that she, too, came from a privileged background, but at least she actually *was* an artist, not a hanger-on. *Mind you, that doesn't make much difference to the way Tara Bradbury makes me feel: inferior.*

'Hello, Tara,' she said, her heart racing as she tried to calm it inconspicuously with slow breathing. *Don't give too much information. Be like Nathan: no babbling.* 'Yes, Fabian invited me and I'm selling a couple of pieces.'

'Dylan didn't say you were coming,' said Tara peevishly.

'He probably didn't know,' said Frankie with a shrug. 'We won't be staying long, anyway.'

'Ah yes, *we*,' said Tara, running her hand through her short, glossy hair and turning to Nathan. 'And you are?'

His face impassive, he replied, 'Nathan Brooks.'

Her perfect face creased momentarily, then cleared as she said, 'The bankers?'

'Sorry?'

She spoke slowly, as if explaining something to a particularly dim toddler, 'The Brooks? Banking family? Chelsea, Cotswolds and the Highlands?'

Frankie could tell that, as far as Nathan was concerned, Tara was stringing random words together, and she came to his rescue.

'No, Tara, not those Brooks.'

'Oh.' She looked disappointed, but resigned. 'Oh well. So, Frankie, everyone said you had a breakdown – is it true?'

Frankie knew Tara reasonably well, but even she was taken aback by the bluntness of the question. For a moment, she floundered, different answers running through her head and the desire to grab a glass of champagne from a nearby waiter almost overwhelming her. *What to say?* It was then that she felt Nathan's warm hand calmly take hers and she turned to him as if he had rescued her from drowning. He didn't speak, but gave her hand a gentle squeeze and looked at her steadily. Drawing strength from him, she turned back to Tara.

'No, I didn't. I realised that the life I was living wasn't working for me, none of it.' She shrugged with a nonchalance she didn't feel. 'So I went home. No biggie.'

Once again, disappointment crossed Tara's face. She had been denied the drama she craved and had nothing left to talk about.

'I see.' Her eyes raked Frankie from head to foot. 'Enjoy the exhibition, anyway.'

She left and Frankie exhaled.

'You see. *That's* the kind of person I'm talking about. And Tara may be an emotional vampire, feeding off people's misery to make herself feel better, but she's not the worst of them.'

'I can't believe you stayed for as long as you did,' said Nathan. 'I can't imagine you fitting in with people like that at all.'

'I didn't, not really,' replied Frankie, suddenly hyper aware that he was still holding her hand. 'It worked for a while because of the art and because Dylan and I – well, until it started going wrong, we got on well and worked brilliantly together.'

Like I work brilliantly with you, she wanted to add. *But with you, it's different, never stultifying or panicky, more meaningful because you believe in me wholly and give me space to make mistakes and grow*. But she couldn't say it out loud, didn't want to embarrass him, didn't want to risk her growing feelings for him spilling over.

'Let's go and look at those pictures over there,' she said instead, pointing to some smaller canvases grouped together. 'They might be the ones Fabian was talking about, that I'm supposed to have inspired.'

As they walked, Nathan dropped her hand to weave through the crowd, many of whom greeted Frankie with curiosity but, she was relieved to note, no further intrusive questions. When they were in front of the artworks, Nathan put his head on one side, then the other, then looked at her.

'I don't want to be rude, or a philistine, but I'm struggling to see exactly *how* you inspired these. They look to me more like they were inspired by a plate of spaghetti Bolognese somebody dropped.'

Frankie dissolved into laughter, and soon the tears were streaming down both their faces as they whispered to each other about various components of the dish they found in the pictures.

'Look, there's a piece of chopped onion,' Frankie would say with a snort, and:

'I think I've found a pea, although it could be a bit of green bean,' Nathan would add with an exaggerated frown.

It was thus that Dylan found them, his appearance putting an abrupt halt to their hilarity.

'Glad to see you're enjoying yourself, Frank,' he said, clashing his face against hers in an awkward air kiss. 'Didn't know you were coming, although Fabian said you were selling stuff.'

'Yeah, I hope you don't mind,' said Frankie, feeling cold as all the laughter drained out of her. She wished Nathan would take her hand again; she didn't dare reach for his.

'Nah,' he replied, his eyes struggling to focus on her in a

way she found chillingly familiar. He probably wouldn't even remember seeing her by tomorrow. 'All art is trade, it's good, it's good.'

'Are you doing okay?' she asked, noticing the long sleeves covering his scarred arms, his hollow cheeks and the dark smudges beneath his eyes.

'Me? Yeah, never better, darlin'. Got this, haven't I?' He spun round to gesture at the exhibition, lost his balance and would have fallen if Nathan hadn't caught him. 'Thanks, guv,' he said, nodding at him but not enquiring as to who he was. 'Yeah, got this, the Americans love me, I'm on the up, babe.' Tara came over then, and he slung his arm around her shoulder. 'Well, better go and let my adoring public meet me,' he said. 'Good to see you, Frank.'

Frankie nodded and watched as he left, her nose wrinkling slightly at the sour, sweaty smell he left in his wake. For a moment, she could barely look at Nathan. *What must he think of me, to have been with Dylan for so long, to have loved him?* She felt once again as she had when she had first gone back to Feywood: tarnished, ashamed, complicit. And then she felt Nathan's hand take hers again, and pulled her eyes up to look at him, where she saw only warmth and compassion in his face.

'I'm sorry he's so unwell,' he said quietly. 'It must be hard for you to see.'

She nodded, swallowing.

'And it's – it's – oh, I can't explain. I feel so bad.'

'Frankie, I don't want to put words in your mouth, but I think I understand.'

She frowned. *How could dignified, civilised Nathan possibly understand this?* But she was willing to hear him out; he had never disappointed her yet.

'Please, tell me.'

The hubbub of the room seemed to fall away as he spoke.

'My parents – they weren't unlike Dylan. I won't go into it

here, but let's just say that they made a lot of poor choices. I helped them as much as I could, but, like you, I got away. I left them to it. They're both dead now.'

Frankie gasped.

'I'm so sorry.'

'So am I. But not that surprised. And I know how it feels, to be the one who left. It's a sort of survivor's guilt – could I have done more? Did I give up too quickly? But I left to save myself, as I think you did, and there's no reason to feel guilty about that. Believe me when I say, there are certain people you cannot save, and the only thing you *can* do is to stop yourself going down with them.'

Frankie took a step closer to him.

'That's exactly it. Everyone at home has been so kind, but no one has understood that.'

She glanced around at the chattering crowd, still necking champagne and barely looking at the art, in the hope that someone might be looking at them. 'Shall we go? I think I've seen enough here.'

He nodded and they went to say a quick goodbye to Fabian. He told Frankie that her pieces had sold instantly, and for higher prices than had been placed on them, due to warring buyers. Then they pushed open the door and were back in the street, even more scruffy-looking now that most of the businesses they walked past on their way to the Tube were closed for the night, their shutters pulled down. *Why had Nathan gone so quiet again? Was he mulling over their conversation?*

'Frankie, I've been thinking about going back to Italy, just for a few days.'

'Oh, right.' Her heart shocked her by plummeting at the thought of not seeing him.

'And I was wondering if you'd like to come with me. There's plenty of space at my brother's in-laws' villa,' he went on. 'And they'd be glad to put us both up. There are some outstanding

Italian gardens we could visit, and I'd like to show you some of the work I've done.'

Her heart returned to its normal position – or maybe floating a little higher – and Frankie nearly laughed for pleasure.

'I'd love to, Nathan, really love to!'

His face relaxed and he smiled back.

'I'm glad. I'll get it sorted out, then.'

And they continued their journey back to Feywood talking excitedly about this new adventure ahead, Dylan and the gallery forgotten.

EIGHTEEN

They arrived back late at Feywood from the exhibition but found a few of the family still up in the sitting room. Martha jumped out of her chair as soon as they came in, turning off the TV programme she had been watching.

'Frankie! How was it? Are you all right?'

She swept her sister over to sit on the sofa, and Nathan flopped into a chair. It had been a long day and he felt exhausted. Even so, he surprised himself by being happy to spend a little time in the company of the Carlisles, rather than rushing straight to his room, craving time alone. He smiled now as Rousseau put down his book and Sylvia shut her laptop, both also eager to find out how Frankie had fared in London.

'It was okay in the end,' said Frankie, accepting a large glass of tonic water from her father, who then also presented one to Nathan, which touched him immeasurably. 'Fabian was nice, as he always is, and he sold both the things I took for good prices.'

'Was Dylan there?' asked Martha, then added hastily, 'Obviously you don't have to talk about it if you don't want to.'

'He was,' said Frankie. 'He was a mess, but it was all right seeing him. Nathan stuck by me the whole time and helped me out.'

Everyone beamed at him, and he felt that beastly red flush leap to his face, as usual.

'I didn't do anything,' he said shortly, wishing they would look away again.

'You were *there*,' said Sylvia in her soft voice. 'And that counts for everything.'

'The worst person was Tara Bradbury. She was trying to make me feel bad and is obviously Dylan's girlfriend now.'

'Well, then we must feel sorry for her,' said Rousseau. '*Did* she make you feel bad?'

Frankie thought for a moment, then replied, surprise in her voice, 'No, she didn't. I was so busy being annoyed about it that I hadn't noticed till now. No, I felt good, if anything.' She suddenly flung her head back and let out a dramatic groan. 'Oh God, that means I've grown up, doesn't it? Oh man, I'm all mature now, look at me!'

Everyone laughed and Nathan thought how, a few weeks ago, he would have found her silly, even superficial – but how wrong he would have been. She tended not to take herself too seriously, and didn't ask anyone else to either, although she was perfectly capable of *being* serious – even about herself, but certainly about her work – if the occasion demanded it.

'Good for you, darling,' said Sylvia, 'but you'll know you're *really* old when eleven p.m. is two hours past your bedtime. I'm going up – goodnight, everyone.'

She stood up carefully and Rousseau also yawned and declared he was tired. Knowing that the artist was renowned for staying up until the early hours, Nathan looked at him curiously, then quickly realised that tiredness was a cover story: he was going to help his sister, who was increasingly weak and breathless, upstairs. She was still sleeping in her old bedroom until her operation.

'I'm going to check on Holmes and Watson,' announced Frankie, also standing up.

'I'll come with you.' The words were out of Nathan's mouth before he had a chance to think about them. Frankie looked mildly surprised, but nodded and smiled, and soon they were crossing the lawn in the sweet-scented night air.

'Do you think they'll still be awake?' asked Nathan.

'Probably not,' replied Frankie. 'But I like to make sure everything is secure. I know Will has done it perfectly, but they're my responsibility.'

When they reached the pen, all was indeed quiet, and Frankie carefully checked the door. Her hand rested on the lock for a moment and then she turned to Nathan.

'Sylvia's seriously ill, isn't she?'

He hesitated for a moment before answering. His first instinct was to comfort her, to help clear the worry that had crossed her face, but he knew he must be honest with her, now and always.

'She does seem weak, yes. Does she have a date for the operation?'

'She did, but it was cancelled and now she's waiting again. The doctors seem to think that with all the medication she'll be okay in the short term, but it's awful to see her like this.'

He put his hand briefly on her shoulder, longing to hug her and hold her, but didn't want to be inappropriate, or to take advantage, in the circumstances. So he was surprised when she stepped closer, wrapped her arms around his waist and laid her head on his shoulder. He slipped his arms around her back and rested his cheek on her hair, hoping she couldn't feel his treacherous heart pounding, giving away how strongly he felt about the woman he had to admit he was falling in love with. And then, as quickly as she had moved towards him, Frankie stepped back and turned away, starting to walk back up towards the house. He quickened his step to join her. Had he upset her further? But she suddenly stopped and when she spoke, she sounded normal.

'Well, I'm sure she'll get a date soon and then she'll start feeling better. Until then I think we all need to carry on, and try not to treat her as an invalid – she'd hate that more than anything.'

'Yes,' said Nathan, then caught at her hand. Frankie turned to face him, and for a moment, they gazed at one another. How easy it would have been to drop his head, just a little, and kiss her as he longed to. But it wasn't the right time. 'Yes, that sounds like a good idea. Shall I go ahead and book Italy? We could go soon – next weekend, maybe?'

'Yes, I'd like that very much. Thank you.'

And before he could even smile, she set off towards the house again, and this time she didn't stop.

The next morning, after breakfast, Nathan rang his brother. Italy was an hour ahead, so he knew he wouldn't be waking anyone up, or disturbing their morning meal.

'Henry?'

'Nathan, good to hear from you!'

'I'm not interrupting anything, am I?'

'Not at all, I was having a coffee on the balcony before starting work. How are things in England?'

Nathan had a vivid picture of Henry sitting looking over the immaculate gardens and the hills beyond, listening to the birds, and had a powerful longing to be back there himself.

'It's going well, very well. Rousseau is an incredible teacher and Frankie's an absolute natural with gardens. Because she's an artist, her designs are amazing. Well, you saw the one I sent you that was in the exhibition.'

'Did it go down well?'

'Very, it caught the attention of a lot of people.'

'And what's she like to work with? You haven't said much in your messages since we last spoke.'

Where the brother he was so close to was concerned, Nathan's tiny hesitation was like getting out a megaphone and proclaiming his innermost feelings at top volume.

'Nathan? There's a reason you haven't said much! What's going on?'

'Nothing, nothing at all. It's just that she's not what I was expecting. Not at all. She's... Well, she's great. Fun and lively and a bit unpredictable, yes, but also hard-working and sensitive and kind, and so talented.'

'Do I detect quite a bit of affection there?'

Nathan paused again, but this time his brother didn't cut in. Eventually, Nathan spoke.

'I'd be lying if I said there wasn't.'

'Well, this *is* exciting!' said Henry. 'Allegra will be thrilled – you know how she wants you to meet someone.'

'Don't let her get too excited,' replied Nathan, his voice serious. 'There's no way in a million years that Frankie would be interested in me, so there isn't anything to say.'

'Why not?'

'Oh, just *look* at me,' said Nathan, a sudden force in his voice. 'I'm under no illusions. I'm dull, I design municipal gardens for the council, and I don't even live in my own place. Hardly a draw for Frankie Carlisle, even if she has left her life with Dylan Madison behind.'

'Nathan,' said Henry seriously. 'You are a man any woman would be proud to be with. Don't put yourself down.'

'Anyway,' continued Nathan abruptly, 'I didn't ring to talk about this. I know you said Antonio and Carla would be happy for us to visit – do you think next weekend would be okay?'

'Of course!' said Henry. 'It'd be good to see you, and we're all dying to meet Frankie, even if she's not as decadent and wild as we've been led to believe. I'll double-check with them and text you later, but you know that you and your friends are always welcome here.'

'I know,' said Nathan with gratitude. 'Allegra's family has been amazing. A bit different from our own parents.'

'Thank God,' replied his brother. 'Poor Mum and Dad, I always felt sorry for them, however much they seemed to enjoy throwing their lives away.'

'I know. But I think it's done us *some* good – we both recognise a happy family when we see one. It's not just Frankie – I like all the Carlisles.'

'I'm glad,' replied Henry, warmth in his voice. 'All right, well, I'll be in touch later – and see you next weekend.'

After a few more words, Nathan rang off and started walking to the orangery. He thought how lucky he was that, despite their own fractured and unstable background, both he and Henry were managing to find new families – families that were very different from their own. Could he yet dare to dream that the Carlisles might become a more permanent fixture in his life?

NINETEEN

They arrived at Pisa airport midmorning on Friday and were soon in a hire car heading towards the Fosdinovo area, where Henry and his in-laws lived.

'It only takes about an hour to drive from here,' said Nathan. 'And it might be useful to have the car when we're there.'

'It's breathtaking,' said Frankie, gazing out of her open window as the miles of rolling green countryside flashed past. 'And the air is glorious. Thank you for bringing me.'

After the stress of Dylan's exhibition and the ongoing worries over Feywood and, in particular, Sylvia's health, Frankie hadn't expected to feel such an overwhelming sense of well-being so quickly. And yet, sitting in the car with Nathan, gazing out at the Tuscan scenery, she was suffused with relaxation and joy. The unbidden thought popped into her head: *it feels like home*. There wasn't the familiarity, of course, but the ease and comfort she was experiencing brought about a strong sense of *rightness* that she had only ever felt before at Feywood. She sneaked a look at Nathan, who must have sensed her gaze because he flicked his eyes towards her for a moment and then smiled. *Maybe home is where the heart is?* whispered the voice, but Frankie quickly silenced it. *Nonsense! It's good to be on holiday and not to have made any of the plans. Anyone would find it relaxing,* she added firmly. *It's nothing more than that.*

'So, remind me who's who,' she said out loud as she realised that they had already been travelling for nearly an hour, and hoping a change of subject would silence the irritating little inner know-it-all.

'Henry's my brother, of course,' replied Nathan. 'And his wife is Allegra. Her parents are Antonio and Carla, and she has a younger sister, Lucia. Donata is Antonio's mother, ninety if she's a day and an amazing advertisement for the Mediterranean lifestyle. The final member of the household is Giorgia, who's the housekeeper but like one of the family. She's been there since she was a girl, stayed throughout her marriage and children, and is still running the place now that she's widowed and her children have left home. They're all great; I do hope you like them.'

And I hope they like me. Frankie glanced down at her uniform of ripped jeans and a black band T-shirt. She felt an uncomfortable and unaccustomed sensation grip her and turned shyly to Nathan.

'Are they all terribly chic and beautiful?' she asked, trying to keep her voice light and carefree.

'Of course they are, they're Italian,' he replied, grinning. 'But you are chic and beautiful yourself, so don't worry on that score.'

Frankie flushed with pleasure and surprise. Pushing down her first instinct, which was to deflect the compliment with a joke, she simply said, 'Thank you. They all sound terrific – I can't wait to meet them.'

'Well, you don't have to wait any longer,' said Nathan as he turned the car off the main road and navigated it between two stone gateposts. 'We're here!'

Peering out of the window, for a moment all Frankie could

see were thick trees on either side as the car pulled up the steep, winding road. Nathan had not even shown her a picture of the house, saying that he preferred her to wait for her own first glimpse. All he would teasingly say was, 'You're used to living at Feywood, so I'm sure you'll take the Villa Torre in your stride.' When the trees finally parted, they swept into an immaculate, thickly gravelled drive with a central circular garden of pristine grass and severely clipped box hedges, around an elegant fountain. It was so different from the drive of her own home, with its balding patches and weeds and she knew that he had been right. Seeing a photo in advance would have spoiled the impact of her first sight of the magnificent building that stood before her. It was stone built and in two, joined parts. One was a classically proportioned villa with three arched, glazed doors positioned centrally and shuttered windows to the sides and above. An immaculate tiled roof sat atop, and two grand stone lions sat either side of the doors. This part of the building was rendered in smooth, cream stucco as if it had been iced to perfection by a royal baker. The second part was a massive, square tower which rose two or three storeys above the house. Its stone was unrendered, there was a scattering of small windows and the very top of the tower was open, with castellated walls. Frankie sat, open-mouthed, speechless, until Nathan said:

'Quite something, isn't it?'

She turned to him.

'It's spectacular. What a beautiful home. It makes me feel even sadder than usual that Feywood is in the state it is.'

'You'll all get Feywood back on her feet again. When Allegra's parents moved here, it was almost uninhabitable, and they've spent years restoring it. The tower dates back to the tenth century, and the house to the sixteenth, so it was worth saving.'

'I'll say,' said Frankie. 'I wonder if they had as many sleepless nights over their roof?'

Nathan laughed.

'More! Navigating the Italian buildings regulations is no fun at all. I'm sure they'll tell you all about it. Come on, let's put the car away and go inside.'

He drove down a small, paved track at the side of the drive, which led to a yard with a couple of other cars and some garages, then turned off the engine. Getting out, Frankie stretched in the warm air and sighed with pleasure before taking her bag and walking with Nathan back to the front of the house. When they arrived, the door was already being opened and a smiling man with Nathan's auburn hair and kind eyes emerged.

'Nathan! I thought I heard a car!'

They embraced warmly, then turned to Frankie.

'This is my brother, Henry,' said Nathan. She went to shake hands with him, but he hugged her as well.

'Welcome to Villa Torre – it's great to meet you, Frankie. Let me take your bag.'

They followed him inside to a terracotta tiled hallway with a vast, faded pink and cream rug and high, vaulted ceilings. An enormous, gilt-framed mirror hung on one wall, and a framed tapestry opposite. Frankie could have spent half an hour looking around this space alone, but Henry had now put her bag down at the bottom of a sweeping staircase and indicated to Nathan to do the same with his. He strode briskly on down a long, light-filled passageway, tiled in gleaming black and white hexagons, through a grand dining room in which stood a walnut table so highly polished you could see your reflection in it, and out through French windows onto a terrace. He paused here so that they had a moment to admire the view of the Tuscan countryside, before swiftly descending a stone staircase to the right, chattering as he did so, asking about their journey and explaining a little about the history of the house.

He's so different from Nathan, thought Frankie, as they

neared the bottom of the stairs. *Just as nice, but in a different way. I wonder if he's more like their parents?*

But she didn't have time to ponder further as Henry came to an abrupt halt. They were on another, larger terrace, with the same incredible view, but here there were chairs and tables and what looked like, at a quick count, the entire family that Nathan had described, all of whom leapt up when they saw them coming. For a moment, there was a whirlwind of hugs, kisses and quick Italian before a beautiful woman of around Martha's age took Frankie's hand and led her to a seat.

'Please, sit down,' she said in English. 'Let me get you a drink, what would you like? We have, of course, exquisite wine here, or there is tea and coffee, or lemonade?'

'Lemonade would be delicious, thank you,' said Frankie, an unusual feeling of shyness creeping over her as everyone else also came to sit down and she felt her shoulder squeezed warmly by each one as they passed by her. Goodness knows she was used to getting along with all sorts of people, but the confidence of Nathan's extended family made her feel tongue-tied, not to mention the fact that her Italian didn't stretch beyond *buongiorno* and *buonasera*, and she wasn't a hundred per cent sure of those.

Time you got out a bit more. She sipped her delicious drink. *You've spent too long cooped up at Feywood, scared of the world outside. That's not you, Frankie.*

'I'm Allegra,' said the woman who had given her the drink. 'I'm married to Henry. It's lovely to have you here! Nathan said that you are an amazing student.'

'He's an amazing teacher,' said Frankie, smiling over at him. 'I don't think I've ever met anyone so patient.'

'Certainly not me,' put in Henry with a laugh, and his wife pulled an amused face and said something to him in Italian. Everyone else also laughed, and Frankie looked into her drink, smiling anxiously. *Was it too late to download one of those language apps? Four days probably isn't long enough to learn how to make jokes, anyway.*

'So, what are you planning to do while you're here?' asked one of the other women at the table who, Frankie deduced, must be Carla, Allegra's mother.

'I want to show Frankie some of my work,' said Nathan. 'I know the things I've done in town aren't hugely inspiring, but I want to explain about soil drainage and longevity of design.'

'Sounds like you're in for a fascinating holiday,' said Henry, arching an eyebrow at Frankie. She gave him a nervous grin in return, whilst privately thinking how much she was looking forward to learning the nuts and bolts of design. She might have said as much out loud, but didn't get a chance, as the other young woman at the table, the only one who had shaken her hand on arrival rather than embracing her, spoke up while looking straight at Frankie, her face disapproving.

'I'm sure it is extremely interesting, if you are serious about learning what Nathan has to teach.'

'I am,' replied Frankie, stung.

'It was me who made the joke, Lucia,' put in Henry. 'Not a very good one, I admit.'

Lucia who, Frankie remembered, was Allegra's younger sister, merely shrugged.

'You laugh at your brother, but his work is good.' She glared at Frankie again. 'He should not have his time or expertise wasted.'

Deep inside, Frankie felt something of her old fire flicker into life. Why was she being judged by this woman who had never met her, judged and apparently found wanting? She was about to snap back, defending herself, when she felt Nathan looking at her and let her eyes turn to him. He smiled gently, and she was brought back, not to the present, which felt hot and irritating, but to the cool green of the orangery at Feywood, and the sense of calm it brought her, especially when they were working there together. She took a breath and looked directly back at Lucia, keeping her gaze soft.

'You're right,' she said levelly. 'Nathan has already taught me so much and I can't wait to learn some of the more technical stuff so that I can apply what I have been learning practically.' She relaxed her face into its old, wicked grin and glanced around the table, her eyes resting on Henry, who looked abashed, but still merry. 'Besides which, I don't like to think where any one of us would be without drainage – up a proverbial creek with no paddle, I suppose.'

Henry laughed again, then explained the saying in Italian. Even Lucia smiled, and nodded with what Frankie hoped was some sort of approval. The last thing she wanted was to get on the wrong side of anyone in the family.

After drinks she had been shown her room, which was large and light filled. It had been decorated simply, but by someone with very good taste, having cream walls, floor-length blue silk curtains and a smooth stone floor. This minimal backdrop showed off the magnificent furniture, which outstripped even Feywood's pieces for sheer size and grandeur. There was a gigantic, gleaming, carved mahogany wardrobe, complete with a tasselled key and antique ivory plaques on each shelf to denote what should go where. *Shame there's no 'ripped jeans' option,* thought Frankie, grinning to herself as she shut the doors again. Between two of the windows stood an elegant, curved sofa, freshly upholstered in navy blue and cream striped silk; the bed had a matching headboard and was dressed with crisp, white sheets, with a bedspread embroidered with leaves and flowers, also in white. It was all so beautiful that she hardly dared touch it. She took several photographs from different angles, then perched on the edge of the sofa to WhatsApp them to her sisters, and a couple of other friends from home, who she was trying to reacquaint herself with, having lost touch when she was living in London with Dylan. The squalid studio couldn't have seemed further away as she looked around her new, luxurious quarters and felt the warm breeze through the open windows, making her feel drowsy after the long journey. Pushing off her shoes, she went to the bed and lay down, planning to close her eyes for just a few minutes.

'Frankie?'

'Mmm?'

She turned over, feeling deliciously comfortable and relaxed, then stirred awake as someone cleared their throat and the realisation slowly came back to her of where she was. She opened her eyes to see Nathan standing at the end of the bed.

'Sorry to wake you, but supper's in about half an hour. I thought you might like some time to get ready.'

She pulled herself up to sitting.

'I do, thank you. I didn't mean to fall asleep for so long. It's very quiet here.'

'It won't be soon,' said Nathan with a grin. 'The family have got some cousins coming over, so expect the peace to be shattered.'

'Do I need to dress up?' asked Frankie, running her mental eye over the contents of her bag, still unpacked.

'No,' said Nathan. 'Just wear whatever you're comfortable in. Do you know the way down, or do you want me to come back for you?'

Frankie paused. Really, she would have loved to ask him to come back, but she didn't feel she could say it. She had always been famously good at going into any party on her own, no matter how few people there she knew. She opened her mouth to give her usual confident dismissal, but Nathan spoke first.

'I'll come back. You don't need me to, I know, but I will.'

She nodded her thanks, and he left her alone to change.

. . .

Half an hour later, a knock came at the door.

'Ready!' called Frankie, giving herself one final glance in the mirror. Even though she only had to walk downstairs, it was the first time in weeks that she felt she was going 'out out' and the idea had put her on edge with both nerves and excitement. She had delved into her bag, knowing exactly what she was going to wear: a dress she had stuffed in at the last moment 'just in case'. It was made of mesh with wide sequinned stripes and had the silhouette of an oversized T-shirt, falling to just above her knees. Under it, she wore a simple black satin slip, and she finished the look with her customary boots. The finished look struck a fine balance between edgy and casual, and it was extremely comfortable.

'Wow,' said Nathan, stepping into the room.

'I take it that's a good wow?' asked Frankie, striking a pose. 'Not, "wow, what a mistake"?'

'Definitely a good wow,' replied Nathan. 'Although I'm feeling that I should have chosen something more dramatic myself.'

Frankie grinned.

'You can borrow some eyeliner, if you like, and rip your shirt in a few places – we could funk up your look pretty easily.'

'Sadly, I don't think there's time,' said Nathan. 'Maybe tomorrow.'

Laughing, Frankie walked past him, out of the room to the landing, catching as she did a waft of his lemony aftershave that set her head spinning in a more pleasurable way than any drink had ever done. For a breathtaking second, she thought she was going to push him back into the room, slam the door shut and kiss him with all her pent-up passion, trusting that he would kiss her back, his body telling her everything he didn't have the words for.

'Frankie?'

She shook herself and pulled out a cheeky grin to cover the thoughts she assumed must be written across her face.

'Sorry, just imagining you in ripped jeans and leather – you could totally pull that off.'

He held her gaze just long enough for her to start losing her breath again, then raised an eyebrow and, saying nothing more, ushered her in front of him towards the stairs.

It was a glorious evening. Seven cousins arrived, between the ages of about three and ninety-three, as far as Frankie could tell. She never managed to catch all their names, and didn't understand a word they were saying, but this didn't stop her joining in with the laughter and feeling drawn in and accepted. Nathan stayed by her side all evening and, whereas once she would have felt that this cramped her style, tonight she felt proud to be with him, cared for by him as he translated snippets of the conversation and made sure she had a full glass. Despite the incredible wines on offer, she had felt no temptation to drink any and stuck happily to the unusual fruit cordials. The children were drinking them as well, watching her curiously.

'Look,' she said to a little girl of around nine years old, who had huge dark eyes and long, glossy hair caught up in neat plaits. 'Why don't we mix them? We can make a cocktail!'

Nathan said something in Italian to the child and she beamed, nodding.

'What do you fancy?' asked Frankie. 'I'm going to try passion fruit and raspberry, yum.'

She poured in the two syrups and added ice and sparkling water, then offered the glass to the little girl, who grabbed it then ran over to her mother; she smiled and waved and said something Frankie didn't understand. She turned to Nathan.

'Is her mum okay with it?'

'Yes, she says thank you, it looks delicious.'

'As long as she doesn't mind me introducing her daughter to cocktails. Mind you, that was a different matter from the ones I used to make... those would have floored a rhinoceros.'

'Do you mind not drinking?' asked Nathan curiously.

'Not really,' replied Frankie. 'I don't think it's forever, anyway. I just needed to "find myself" and be braver about not having to rely on it to get me through events. Endless cordial does dampen the old sparkling personality somewhat, but it doesn't seem to matter as much when the company's as nice as this.'

'I don't think your personality is at all dampened,' said Nathan. 'It seems perfectly sparkling to me at a party or knee deep in box clippings and peacocks.'

Frankie looked up at him through her lashes. Was he *flirting* with her?

'You're not doing too badly yourself, you know. All that strong, silent stuff is working for you.'

And for me, she thought. *Big time.*

He snorted.

'I can't say that's deliberate, but I'll take the unintended consequences.'

They grinned at each other, and he shifted his leg slightly so that it touched hers under the table, making her feel so heady that she was doubly glad she hadn't had any wine. She glanced across at the rest of the family, who had mostly moved to the more comfortable seating area, where large wicker sofas and chairs with padded cushions were placed in a U shape around a low table. Two of the children were fast asleep, oblivious to the chatter around them.

'It's lovely here,' said Frankie, turning to face Nathan. 'It reminds me of Feywood in the summer.'

'Yes, beautiful,' he murmured, not taking his eyes off her face. And then his fingers were lacing with hers and she closed her eyes in anticipation of his kiss, the kiss she had longed for.

'Ciao ragazzi!'
Hi, guys!

Frankie's eyes opened again and she saw Lucia standing behind them, a glass of wine in one hand and the half-empty bottle in the other. Nathan's fingers slid away from hers and she forced a smile to her face to hide her feelings of disappointment and irritation.

'Come and sit with the rest of us,' went on Lucia, in English. 'You're being very antisocial over here. Come on!'

They had little choice but to pick up their glasses and follow her to the sofas to join the rest of the family and settle for casting each other regretful glances in place of the passionate kisses Frankie was sure would have followed.

The next day, Frankie woke early, pulling aside the drapes in her beautiful room to let the sunlight pour in. She opened the long, narrow windows and stepped out onto the small balcony, which overlooked the front of the house. The views this way were as stunning as those they had enjoyed the day before, this time of tall, thick trees and the tiniest glint of sea in the far distance. She snapped another photo with her phone to send home and put on social media, then switched the device off and threw it back inside onto the bed in order to luxuriate uninterrupted in the sun's rays and the memories of last night's almost kiss. A few moments later, she heard feet crunching on the gravel below and opened her eyes to see Nathan.

'Buongiorno!' she called down, and he turned and looked up, shielding his eyes with his hand, then waving when he spotted her.

'Buongiorno! You're up early. Do you want to come and see something?' She nodded vehemently. 'Okay, I'm grabbing my sunglasses from the car – meet you in the hall in fifteen minutes?'

She went inside and into the bathroom, which was decorated in green and black marble and better equipped than she imagined the smartest of hotels to be, with giant, fluffy towels and floral toiletries in fluted glass bottles. There was a moment's regret that she couldn't spend longer there, but she was excited to see Nathan and find out what he wanted to show her.

Beats waking up to yet another hangover, doesn't it? said the small voice in her head. She had to agree, although the sense she had had last night that her life at Feywood had become rather small was still nagging at the back of her mind. But she shook it off – after all, she was in another country now, even if she was still safely living in luxury in a spectacular family home – and opened the bag she hadn't got around to unpacking last night. Automatically, she reached for her jeans and another T-shirt, then a flash of colour gave her pause, and she pulled out the entire contents of the bag onto the bed. Lilith, Frankie's mother, had been well known for her exquisite taste, not to mention the vast sums of money she spent on clothing. As she was packing, Frankie had realised, not for the first time, that her entire wardrobe consisted of the same sorts of garments: clothes that served her well most of the time, and that she was comfortable in, but nothing that felt fun or summery or, well, holidayish. Even last night's dress had been black. She had gone to her mother's walk-in wardrobe, which had lain undisturbed since her death over a year before, and run her hands over the riot of colours and fabrics. Many were too formal, but she had found some wide-legged trousers, silk blouses and light dresses that could be perfect for an Italian break. Trying them on had given her violently mixed feelings: memories both good and bad of her mother, with whom she had fought regularly but adored, and confusion about herself. For so long she had projected a certain image of herself, an image which appeared to have an edge of danger but which, in fact, was solidly her comfort zone. Rainbow silk and palazzo pants felt terrifying but, nevertheless, she had packed a few items. And now, standing in the opulent bedroom of this glorious villa, she was glad she had. Not quite ready for the full transformation, she chose a pair of cropped jeans she knew suited her, then shook out one of the tops. It was a radiant shade of burnt orange, scattered with pale pink and vivid green flowers, and when she put it on, it skimmed and floated over her body, making her feel glamorous and sensual. It was a little too large, so she tied the front up in a knot at her waist and looked in the mirror again.

'That's better: Frankie, but not Frankie,' she said aloud. 'Today's Frankie.'

And she went downstairs to meet Nathan.

'The grounds are amazing,' she said as they walked down wide stone steps, flanked by scented shrubs.

'Just wait,' said Nathan. 'You are not going to believe what I'm going to show you.'

'Is it something you've done?' asked Frankie, and he laughed.

'Definitely not! And not something that will give you much inspiration for garden design, I'm afraid, but too amazing to miss.'

He wouldn't give her a single clue and, although she was suffused with curiosity, she also enjoyed the suspense and the pleasure he was taking in surprising her. At the bottom of the steps, he took a right turn, and they found themselves beside a turquoise swimming pool with wide, stone edges and elegant carvings of what Frankie guessed to be water gods. A small structure with showers and changing cubicles stood at one end, and white metal loungers with pale green cushions were set out around the pool.

'Oh, my goodness,' she said. 'It's insane, like a scene from some nineteen fifties Hollywood movie. What a stunning pool.'

'Superb, isn't it?' he said. 'And we should have a dip later. But that isn't what I wanted to show you. Come on!'

He set off again, Frankie following.

'So the out-of-this-world swimming pool would have been plenty, you know. I'm not sure how much more I can take of this dream house...'

She broke off as they passed through some trees and emerged in a clearing where a small, ruined building stood. It was built of brick and stone, and the roof was long gone, but you could see where the window openings had been. Nathan stopped.

'*This* is what I wanted to show you,' he said.

Frankie turned a full circle, looking at her surroundings, then returning her gaze to him.

'Please tell me this isn't what I think it is,' she said, feeling chills run up and down her arms.

'What do you think it is?' he asked, a teasing look in his eyes.

'Obviously I'm no expert, but it looks—'

She paused, not wanting to look silly if she expounded her current theory to him.

'Go on,' he said, and Frankie looked into his kind eyes, knowing he would never laugh at her, or make her feel stupid. Nathan could be trusted.

'It looks Roman,' she said finally. 'But it has to be a modern folly, surely?'

Nathan shook his head.

'Nope. What you are looking at is a bona fide Roman ruin. Come inside.'

It was natural as they stepped over the uneven ground into the interior for him to take her hand, and she was disappointed when he dropped it again once inside. But she was soon distracted.

'Nathan, is it a bath house? It can't be.'

She looked at the unmistakeable round shape with stepped edges, cracked and uneven now, and could hardly believe what she was seeing. Nathan stood close to her and for a moment, they could do nothing but stare, then he said, 'Yes, we are looking at a second-century BC Roman bath house – well, part of one, anyway. This was the frigidarium, the cold bath, and you can see on the other side, next to those alcoves, some of the original wall painting.'

Frankie was feeling anything but cold, with Nathan standing so close to her and knowing that she could turn her head, just a little, and maybe... But he was talking now about the remains of the hypocaust system that could be seen outside, and she followed him slowly, torn between relief and disappointment that he was far too engrossed in the ancient ruins to notice her new outfit or, indeed, her growing desire. And that, of course, made him even more attractive. Frankie had never had any trouble getting boyfriends – her own or anyone else's. Even Dylan had been easy to hook; she simply played the games she knew he would respond to. It was only later that she found that she was the one who was losing. But Nathan, for all that he was straightforward, confused her more than anyone she had ever met. She knew she was falling for him, but couldn't fathom how he felt about her, even after last night. She still didn't know if acting on her feelings would be a huge mistake. She could ruin the friendship, ruin the working partnership, ruin the progress she had made in her own life, because no matter how well they got on, the fact was still staring her in the face that they had led very different lives. But was it a case of 'never the twain shall meet' or 'opposites attract'?

Once Frankie had learnt more about Roman hypocaust systems than she had ever expected to, they walked back up to the house for breakfast. As they approached the curving staircase which led directly to the terrace where the family seemed to gather, Nathan stopped and reached for her hand.

'I should have said it when I first saw you today, I thought it then, but you know...'

'What?' she asked. Was she going to hear about another architectural gem hidden in the grounds of this remarkable house? She would have been interested, but her stomach was beginning to rumble.

'Just that, well, I noticed your top, I mean, your blouse, shirt, that is. It's different. For you. It looks nice.'

He squeezed her hand before dropping it, turning and continuing up the stairs, not looking back, as Frankie smiled and hugged herself. It may not have been the most elegant of compliments, but to her it meant the world.

TWENTY

Nathan jogged up the steps, knowing his face was burning. He didn't look back, fearing that Frankie would be laughing at him. *You absolute idiot. Different – for you? Nice? And why did you call it a blouse? Jeez, she's not your grandmother. It was bad enough wittering on about that bloody Roman bath, especially after things went so well yesterday. She's probably glad Lucia turned up and interrupted.*

He was grateful when he saw that the rest of the family was already at breakfast, chattering away, and he could busy himself getting orange juice and coffee while the hateful blush subsided. Frankie came and got herself a drink as well, but Nathan didn't say anything else, keeping his lips pressed together until he was sitting at the table.

'Where have you two been so early?' asked Antonio. 'Not gardening?'

'No,' said Frankie. 'Nathan took me to see the Roman bath, it was amazing!'

Nathan raised his eyes from his plate. Was she teasing? No, she looked sincere. She continued.

'I couldn't believe what I was seeing at first, but that almost complete cold pool and the remains of the hypocaust system were fascinating.'

'You have an interest in Roman history?' asked Carla, taking a sip of her coffee.

'Only in a very amateur way,' replied Frankie. 'But I studied classical sculpture as one of my modules at art school and I've had an interest ever since then. I often think I could have been tempted into archaeology if it hadn't been for the art. Actually, I'd like to go and look at it again – we didn't spend very long there.'

'Of course,' stumbled out Nathan, stunned that this woman had managed to surprise him yet again, and rather ashamed that he had prejudged her yet again. 'There are other sites near here we can visit as well, if you like?'

'But then how will you impart all your scintillating knowledge of drainage systems?' cut in Henry with a twinkle in his eye. 'There's only room for so much fun in a few days.'

Nathan felt the familiar burn starting in his neck, but pushed down the automatic feeling of self-reproach, knowing that there was nothing more to his brother's words than a gentle tease. Instead, he smiled and said, 'Very true, and I do have some studies on earthworms and their different casts that I'd love to discuss.'

'Worm poo and plumbing,' said Frankie, batting her eyelashes exaggeratedly and letting out a loud sigh. 'I knew Italy was romantic, but I wasn't expecting this level.'

Everyone laughed and the breakfast continued in the same light-hearted and friendly manner, but Nathan noticed that Lucia was much quieter than normal and didn't join in the talk or jokes. When he went up to his rooms afterwards, he wasn't surprised when she followed him, and he ushered her inside.

'Is everything all right?' he asked in Italian.

'Not really. I am very worried about this girl you have brought here.'

'Frankie? Why?'

'I looked her up online and she seems like trouble to me. I know that part of what you were doing in England was having her work with you and learn from you, but you are obviously more friends now than mentor and student, or colleagues. She seems very happy, which is good, of course, but leopards don't change their spots. I don't want to see you hurt, knowing what you went through with your parents.'

Nathan sat down on the chair at his desk and frowned.

'I appreciate your looking out for me, and I know what you're talking about – I looked them up as well, before I went. But I've got to know Frankie, and her family, well over the past few weeks and I honestly don't think you have anything to worry about. I can't see her going back to that way of life. And besides,' he added, feeling a heaviness in his chest, 'how could she hurt me? Friends we might be, but that's all.'

Lucia let out a loud snort.

'Oh, come off it, Nathan! You're both perfectly doe-eyed around each other, haven't you noticed? No, I suppose you haven't.'

'Wh-what?'

Lucia clicked her tongue impatiently.

'Surely Frankie can't be as clueless about it as you are? Even to the casual observer you two are clearly *infatuati*.'

Nathan stared for a moment. *Infatuati? Besotted?* Well, yes, if he was being honest, then that did describe his feelings about Frankie, but was Lucia suggesting that Frankie felt the same?

'I don't know what you mean,' he said feebly, hoping that Lucia would elaborate. She did.

'Oh, Nathan, neither of you can stop sneaking glances at the other, you jump to defend each other and you're practically finishing each other's sentences. I'd be thrilled for you if it wasn't...'

She stopped and bit her lip.

'If it wasn't Frankie?' supplied Nathan.

'Well, yes. In fact, I like her, very much, but what if she decides in a week or a month that she feels better now, thank you very much, and disappears back off to her old life?'

Nathan sighed.

'I'd be lying if I said I haven't thought the same thing myself, but the fact is...' It was time to admit it to himself, as much as to anyone else. 'The fact is that I do have feelings for Frankie – strong ones. And I've not felt like this about anyone else. I've tried ignoring it, talking myself out of it, but feelings like that don't just go away. The one thing that was holding me back was the assumption that she wouldn't look twice at me in that way, but if what you're saying is true...'

'It's true,' said Lucia, a smile touching her lips now. 'She's crazy about you.'

'Well then, how can I let worry about something that might not happen stop me?'

'You're right,' said Lucia. 'And it's good to see you so happy.'

She stood up and left the room, but Nathan stepped onto the landing after her.

'Lucia?'

'Yes?'

'Is everyone worried – Henry and Allegra too?'

'Henry is over the moon and planning the wedding flowers as we speak.' They grinned at each other, both hugely fond of Nathan's exuberant brother. 'Allegra is more circumspect, of course, but wouldn't dream of interfering.'

'Thank you,' said Nathan, hugging her briefly. 'I won't say for interfering, but for being brave enough and caring enough to check in with me.'

Back in the hire car, Nathan drove him and Frankie the short distance into the nearby town, where he stopped in a large square.

'A bit easier than parking at home,' said Frankie, getting out and looking around at the sparse scattering of cars parked neatly in front of the shuttered buildings.

Nathan laughed.

'Absolutely, although you might have more trouble in Rome. Would you like to have coffee before we go to the park?'

'Sure,' said Frankie, stretching in the sunshine. 'It's such a treat not to be busy, but I hope that Holmes and Watson are all right.'

Nathan led the way to a tiny café that Frankie hadn't even noticed and took a seat outside. The waiter greeted him warmly and they exchanged a few friendly words before Nathan turned to Frankie.

'What would you like?'

'What do Italians drink in the morning?' she asked.

'Cappuccino, usually,' he replied. 'But have whatever you want.'

'Black for me then, please,' she said, and he delivered the message to the waiter, who disappeared. Soon a hissing and clattering could be heard inside the dark interior of the café.

Nathan noticed that Frankie was looking a bit agitated. His initial concern was that she was, maybe, bored, bored of him, but he pushed down the thought with some irritation. *Time to have a bit more confidence. Remember what Lucia said?*

'Are you all right?' he asked, touching her hand briefly.

She gave him a small smile.

'Everything's wonderful,' she replied. 'It's just that...'

She tailed off, looking embarrassed.

'Please, tell me.'

'Well, I'm worried about Holmes and Watson. I know Will and Martha will look after them beautifully, but even so.'

Nathan felt his heart swell. He was relieved, yes, that her

unease was nothing to do with him, but he was also unbearably touched by the concern she had for those peacocks, who would doubtless be being spoilt rotten in her absence.

'Haven't you heard from Martha? Why don't you give her a ring?'

'I think I will, if you don't mind?'

'Of course not!'

Frankie stood up and walked a little way off to make her call and Nathan took this opportunity to luxuriate in watching her. He longed to go and hug her, first because of her worried face as she waited for Martha to answer, and then as the clouds cleared at what was obviously good news. She came back to the table as the coffees arrived.

'They're doing brilliantly,' she said with a grin. 'Martha said that she and Will have discovered that they love scrambled eggs, so Dad's been making them every day for her to take down. I shouldn't have worried; it sounds like they're better off than they would have been with me there.'

'That's great news,' said Nathan as she sat down again. 'And I'm sure they'll be pleased to see you back.'

'I won't hold my breath, but you never know. So, tell me about this park we're visiting today: did you design it?'

Nathan shook his head.

'Absolutely not. The gardens themselves were laid out in the sixteenth century, but there was an area which had spoiled badly – it was derelict with nothing growing there or able to grow. I was asked to create a garden that would be simple but beautiful and fairly low maintenance, also with various sensory elements so that anyone who visited it might enjoy it.'

'Was it difficult?'

'Very. The main problem was preparing the land and, yes, sorting out the drainage. But the results prove that a bit of boring engineering is worth it.'

'Well, I don't think it's boring at all.' Frankie drained her coffee. 'Let's go.'

They left the square and walked along some narrow streets, quiet and shady, before the road opened out. A short way down, there was a large, rugged stone arch with open iron gates. They went through and walked past several fountains and statues. All were well known to Nathan, but Frankie stopped at each, wondering at them, taking photos and jokingly discussing how feasible it would be to create something similar for Feywood. Nathan felt no impatience as they meandered along. Instead, he remembered the occasions when their hands had met, how natural it had felt and how much he would like to do the same again. It was when he saw one of his favourite fountains, created from the dramatic form of Hercules killing the hydra and with the words *Audentes Fortuna Iuvat* inscribed on a tablet on the base, that he was inspired. *Fortune Favours the Brave*. He edged slightly closer to Frankie, extended his hand a tiny bit to touch hers. He felt her jump, but she didn't turn. Instead, she let her fingers move towards his, so that soon they were entwined as they stood looking at the water.

'Let's go and see this garden then,' said Frankie, her voice sounding slightly hoarse, and they moved on down some sandy pathways and past a couple of formal, Italianate gardens. It was when they had passed the second of these that Frankie suddenly said, 'Oh! I can smell it!'

Indeed, the scents of rosemary and lavender were wafting towards them on the warm breeze, and Nathan was glad that his sensory garden was still working exactly the way he had designed it: first, smell and next, hopefully, sound. And, indeed, that was the next thing that Frankie noticed.

'Is that running water?' He nodded. 'How on earth do you manage that out here?'

'I'll show you exactly how it works when we're closer, but

it's a combination of an underground spring and solar powered pumps.'

They had reached the garden now, and Frankie stepped onto the path that meandered through the space, her face full of delight, her hand remaining in his.

'Well, sight's an easy one – it's beautiful. So many different greens and the purples and whites... Do things flower all year?'

'Almost,' he said, pride rising in his chest as he saw how much she loved it. 'In the winter the emphasis for sight is more on shadows and light, as well as the different heights.'

She gazed around.

'Yes, I can see that now,' she said quietly. 'It's not just about colour. Oh! And Nathan, there's another sound – the bees. I don't think I've ever heard so much buzzing.'

'Yup, that's because everything flowering here is super attractive to our little pollinating friends. There's a sort of nod to honey for taste, but can you see what else?'

She continued through the garden as it developed into different spaces.

'Oh, my goodness, I was going to say the lavender and rosemary again, but I wasn't expecting a whole vegetable garden! Tomatoes, basil, chives – and I love the different coloured chillies. This isn't what I was expecting from your prescribed commissions! I thought they'd be boring.'

'Some of them are. I got lucky with this one. There's a reason it's the first one I'm showing you. I'm so glad the veg here are thriving. The garden is maintained on behalf of the *comune* – the equivalent of our local council, that is – by an amazing organisation called ILM, which stands for *insegnamelo, te lo mostrerò*. It more or less means "teach me and I'll show you". They provide workplace-based education for adults with learning needs, with a view to them becoming qualified then finding work.'

'That's wonderful,' said Frankie. She turned to him with shining eyes, which suddenly clouded over.

'What's wrong?' asked Nathan. They were standing face to face now, their fingers still entwined. He had never wanted anything more than he wanted to kiss her then, but he could see that she was upset.

'It's just...' Now, it was Frankie's turn to redden. She continued almost in a whisper. 'It's just that I've wasted so much time. I've spent years mucking about, playing around with people like Dylan.' Nathan couldn't help being pleased by the way she spat out her ex-boyfriend's name. 'I could have been doing things that were so much more worthwhile. I'm– I'm rather ashamed of myself.'

Her head dropped, but Nathan put his hand gently under her chin and lifted it until she was looking at him.

'Frankie, please. You're a very special artist, you've created more in a few years than most people manage in a lifetime. That's something to be proud of, not ashamed.'

'Yes, but it was all for me, for pomp, showing off. It wasn't meaningful.'

Nathan didn't want to deny her feelings, but he couldn't let her go unchallenged.

'I've seen your work, and I don't know much about sculpture, but even I could see the power of it. And the work you've done while we've been together... You're inspirational. Maybe, in the past, you've had fun, done whatever, but don't you see that you are moving forward?'

She gave a small nod.

'I know, but I still feel so *lightweight*. These people running – ILM, did you say?' He nodded. 'They're doing something that matters, that makes a difference. And not only to a couple of peacocks.'

He laughed.

'Well, Holmes and Watson are doubtless grateful. And

don't you see, *that's* who you are! Someone who cares, someone who *does* make a difference. You've got plenty of time to expand that in whatever way you want. I think you could change the world, Frankie, but you don't have to. Just one or two lives is enough, if we all did it. And after those daft birds, well...' *Audentes Fortuna Iuvat, Nathan!* '...well, I make it up to three, so you're over your quota.'

'You?' murmured Frankie.

He nodded, then moved forward the short distance that had felt like miles, to touch his lips to hers and find, miraculously, that she was returning his kiss.

After several minutes, they parted and smiled shyly at each other. Nathan knew that he had a daft expression on his face, but didn't care, especially as he could see it was exactly mirrored by the one on Frankie's. But it was she who regained the power of speech first.

'Talk about a sensory experience,' she said, a slight wobble in her voice. 'We hadn't even got on to touch.'

Nathan laughed.

'Not every visitor to the garden gets the full package, you understand? For touch, most people have to make do with the different grasses I've planted, over there somewhere...'

He waved his hand loosely over his shoulder, not taking his eyes from her face.

'I rather prefer this version,' said Frankie, and stepped towards him again.

They floated around the rest of the garden, barely taking it in, only noticing other people when they went to have some lunch. Dusk was nudging the horizon when they drove back to the Villa Torre.

'Everyone will be out the back having a drink before supper,' said Nathan. 'I want to send the ILM a quick email to tell them how pleased I am that the garden's looking so beautiful still, so why don't you go out and I'll join you in a few minutes?'

He walked slowly up the stairs, casting occasional glances behind him so that he could see Frankie until the very last moment, reflecting hazily on the developments of the day. He remembered how it had started, with Lucia's concern, and tried to push down the little worry that was picking away at him, despite his happiness – the worry that she might be right. He opened his laptop and went to his email, always preferring to do it this way rather than use his phone. He quickly wrote out a message to the ILM, congratulating them on their fantastic maintenance of the garden, then ran his eye down his inbox. Spotting an email from the *comune*, he clicked to open it and quickly read:

Dear Mr Brooks,

We are writing to open a discussion with you concerning a public space project with our neighbouring comune. Some of their streets and squares require the planting to be redesigned in order to maximise aesthetics but keep costs and maintenance at a minimum.

Nathan chewed on his lip as he read the rest of the message, which detailed exactly how predetermined and dull this project would be. Then he clicked on the attached document, which laid out the timescales and financials. Six months' work, commencing at his convenience, for a very healthy fee. He shut the laptop, pushed his chair back and ran his hand through his hair. That sort of money would help a lot towards the deposit he wanted to put down on a house, and he had already started looking online, enchanted by dwellings that were far more modest than the splendour he had become used to at the Villa Torre, but were nearly within his price range.

And what about Frankie? You know you're falling in love with her, and that wasn't part of the plan.

Ah, the plan, the plan that offered such security, but was also a millstone around his neck, holding him down and restricting him to a line of work that rarely offered an outlet for his talent and creativity. He rose and went to stand by the open balcony window, where he could see the family but they were unlikely to spot him. Frankie was laughing at something that Donata had said, which had been translated for her by Allegra, and now she reached out and took the old woman's hand. Donata, who could be difficult to please, was beaming and gabbling so fast that the rest of the family were shouting at her to slow down so that they could translate.

What would pursuing a relationship with Frankie mean? Staying in that crumbling house with the family who, although warm and wonderful, were outrageously irresponsible at times? The family who said they wanted to save Feywood but thought it was hilarious to find some childhood vandalism of the Tudor panelling and would spend money on champagne before setting it aside for some boring house job. Was she truly his future – or he hers? Maybe Lucia was right, and now that Frankie was feeling better, she would revert to her old self, the woman who he wouldn't have got on with at all – nor she with him. Being brutally honest with himself, he knew that the Frankie of a year ago would have found him boring. Or should he trust that this Frankie, the one he knew, was who she was and who she was going to stay? He took a step forward, almost involuntarily, and the movement must have caught her eye as she looked up and waved and beckoned to him. Joy rose again in his heart, banishing doubts for now at least, and he turned to run downstairs and be with her.

TWENTY-ONE

The following day was spent looking at some of Nathan's less inspiring commissions.

'You've obviously done them beautifully,' said Frankie, looking at what felt like her thousandth box hedge. 'But they're a world away from that awesome sensory garden, and from what you're creating at Feywood.'

'What *we're* creating,' he replied with a smile. 'I know they are, but they pay well and have been steady work.'

'Maybe so, but I'm glad you're doing something more creative now. Perhaps we could even submit an application to create a garden at one of the RHS shows next year!' Nathan didn't reply, but looked down at his feet, which he was shuffling on the dusty ground. *Had she overstepped in some way?* 'Or maybe that's a bit too ambitious right now. But we could do *something*, couldn't we?'

He looked up.

'There's nothing I'd like more than to create beautiful gardens with you, but these commissions are my livelihood. I can't give them up.'

Frankie's mental image of herself proudly displaying her Chelsea gold medal melted away.

'Oh, right, I see. Sorry. I assumed, with being at Feywood and everything, that you would be able to focus on the stuff you haven't been able to do. I thought you'd be glad to leave the council stuff behind you.'

He took her hand, which she let lie limply in his.

'But Frankie, what would I live on? My job at Feywood – the one your father employed me to do – is going to be finished soon. It's you who will need to explore your next steps as a garden designer – if that's what you want to do.'

'I thought you had lots of savings,' she said in a small voice, knowing as she did so how ridiculously privileged she sounded. Of course, Nathan wanted to ensure stability in his life: he didn't have a family with a stately home for him to live in while he messed around exploring his creativity. Well, other than his brother's in-laws' house, of course, but even she understood why he didn't feel comfortable to go on living there, fabulous though it was.

'They're being saved for a reason,' he said gently, squeezing her hand. 'And maybe now is a good time to tell you that the *comune* has just offered me a new commission, which I'm going to take.'

Tears filled Frankie's eyes.

'So it's real? You're going to keep pushing down all your talent in order to plant a few' – she batted a nearby unsuspecting bush in irritation – 'box trees?'

She was desperate to ask *and what about me?* but couldn't bring herself to utter the words, fearing the answer too much. But, as usual, kind Nathan understood.

'Frankie, don't take it out on the poor box. I know it's frustrating and disappointing – it is for me, too, but it won't be forever. I've worked too hard to stop when I'm nearly there, nearly able to move out of the Villa Torre and buy my own place. And I don't believe it means the end for us either. I hope it doesn't. I hope— I hope you feel the same.'

She looked at his dear face, worried but at the same time calm and strong, and she flung her arms around his neck.

'I do! Oh, Nathan, I do! We can make it all work out, can't we?'

'Of course we can,' he said firmly. 'Who knows? You, too, might end up doing grounds maintenance for the council, so satisfying...'

She frowned, then saw his amused eyes and kissed him.

'Maybe I will. Although they might be cross when I went off brief.'

And Frankie knew that would be inevitable. When had she ever done what anyone else had told her to do?

After lunch, they spent a leisurely afternoon wandering around two more of Nathan's commissioned projects, as well as the exquisitely manicured garden of a private villa. It was open only occasionally for visitors and Nathan had been delighted to obtain tickets. Captivating though the visits were, Frankie found it hard to concentrate. Despite Nathan's assurances, she was worried. Could they develop and maintain a relationship living in different countries? Her heart sang out 'yes!' and urged her to embrace the uncertainty. Her head, which she had only started paying proper attention to since things had ended so sourly with Dylan, told a different story. On the one hand, it took a sensible approach: *do you think long distance would work?* But on the other, it asked difficult questions: *Is he right for you? What is security compared to art? Maybe, Frankie, maybe you were right and he is a bore?* She tried telling this voice a firm 'no', but it persisted. *Okay, maybe 'a bore' is unfair, but is he enough to hold your interest? Aren't you just going to revert to form?*

As they walked around the different gardens, Frankie's internal battle raged until she felt exhausted with it. When they eventually ended up at a beautiful *trattoria*, its terrace draped with vines, its view across the countryside second to none, she was relieved when Nathan went to talk to the owner about the specials and she was left by herself for a few minutes. Not wanting to address her churning thoughts anymore, she took out her phone and tapped through to Facebook to check her garden design forums. However, it was not one of these threads at the top of her feed that evening, but an invitation from a group she had forgotten she was part of, a group whose members were usually too busy living life to the full to have time for social media. The title of the invitation read '*Summer Solstice Gathering*' and she tapped on it.

Come and join us to welcome the Summer Solstice together. Come alone and embrace new friendships or bring your loved ones. We will dance, we will feast, we will create art for art's sake, opening our bodies and minds to this powerful, glorious event. Communal creation is our theme, whatever that means to you.

Normally, Frankie would have rolled her eyes at what she considered to be 'woo', but the final line of the invitation stopped her in her tracks. The gathering was to be held in a small village which – a quick search on Google Maps informed her – was a couple of miles away from the Villa Torre. She ran her eye down the guest list and realised that one of her old art school friends had moved there, a friend who had been gentle, funny but distinctly avant-garde in her approach to art, particularly in her use of colour and materials. One piece, created with jagged remnants of car accidents found at the side of the road, had won her a prize; another, sculpted from different animal faeces found on a country walk, had cleared the room. A vision of this friend, who went only by the name Fable, came into Frankie's head, and as Nathan came back to the table, she looked up at him with shining eyes.

'Look!' she said, holding out the phone to him. He took it as he sat down.

'This isn't far from the villa,' he said. 'Tomorrow night.'

'I'd love to go,' said Frankie. 'I was at art school with Fable. She's lovely – completely bonkers, of course, but lovely nonetheless, and she always has such interesting people around her. I'm not into the whole summer solstice thing, but shall we go?'

Nathan handed the phone back.

'Er, yes, if you'd like to. I'm not sure that it sounds like my sort of thing, though.'

Frankie laughed.

'No, probably not, but you might be surprised. Good, I'll tell her we're coming.' She tapped the screen a few times, then put the phone in her pocket. 'So, what are the specials?'

He listed them, then reached for her hand.

'You look happier than you've looked all day. You're excited about this party, aren't you?'

'Only because of you. It's not long ago that I would have gone, but dreaded it. Now, I feel open to getting out there again. We should probably drink to Dad. He couldn't have known how well we'd get on, but he was right that you'd be good for me. I hope I'm good for you too.'

As they clinked glasses and started on the plump olives that had been brought to their table, she fervently hoped it was true. Was she the right person to draw Nathan along in life, offer him new opportunities for growth, as he had done for her? Or would the risk that she was a backward step towards a life that he had rejected be too much? Only time would tell and for tonight, at least, Frankie was determined to enjoy the view, the food and the man with whom she knew she was falling in love.

TWENTY-TWO

The next evening, Nathan stood in front of his wardrobe in despair. He had only brought a handful of clothes with him for the short stay in Italy, and the garments he had left behind when he went to Feywood were all either ill-fitting or things he hated. He had no idea what to wear for a summer solstice party full of artists. When he had asked Frankie for advice, she had waved her hand airily and told him to pick something he was comfortable in. He hadn't wanted to say that he was comfortable in any of his clothes, if the setting was right, because he didn't want to look resistant or churlish. Sighing, he pulled on some jeans and a dark green polo shirt. *You'll probably look like Fable's dad, but at least you'll feel like yourself.* Whether or not these people would like him as himself remained to be seen. He ran a comb through his hair and went downstairs to meet Frankie, who was back in her old uniform of a black band T-shirt with cut-off jeans and chunky boots.

'Ready?' she asked, and he nodded.

'As I'll ever be.'

'It'll be fine! Fun! If I know Fable, she will have gathered a good group together; she's always had interesting friends.' She paused. 'Look, they're nothing like the people Dylan hangs out with, if that's what you're thinking.'

That was exactly what I had been thinking.

'No, of course not. I didn't expect you'd want to spend the evening with people like that.' *Oh God, was he going to sound like a disapproving Victorian every time he opened his mouth tonight?* 'I mean... I'm sure it will be fine. Great. Shall we go?'

They went and collected the car and drove the short distance to the party. Nathan could feel Frankie's pent-up excitement as they got closer. Though he wanted to match it, longed to share it with her, the more she chattered about her friend and her art college days, the more he found himself drawing inwards. It wasn't that he was scared; he was good at meeting new people. It was more that he dreaded the sense of chaos that might exist at such a gathering, the sort of atmosphere that had always prevailed at his parents' house parties and made him deeply uncomfortable. He was happy in his own skin, he always had been, and unpredictability and decadence made him uncomfortable. He felt no shame about that, had no sense or need to be any different, but he had been criticised and mocked for it by his own parents for years, and had no desire to see that replayed. *Frankie wouldn't.* He parked the car outside a large, square house, lights shining from every window and the faint sound of music coming from around the back. *You can trust her.* He truly believed he could, but was on edge as they walked around the side of the villa.

There were probably fifty people already at the party. Some stood around talking, some sat with their feet in the swimming pool and others lay on sun loungers or sat on the floor. A couple of large easels had been set up with canvases, one of which was already daubed with bright colours, and a huge white sheet had been strung between two of the upstairs windows, with the words 'come and make me beautiful' scrawled across it in jagged black writing. Several tables held food, drinks and artists' materials. There was a strong smell of marijuana in the air. Strings of lights were suspended across the entire space and more lights hung from trees. A large fire burnt in a metal firepit just below the patio, where it became lawn. Nathan found the scene at once beautiful and intimidating but, taking a breath, went to step forward into it. It was Frankie who hesitated, pulling slightly on the hand he was holding. He turned to her.

'Are you okay?'

She laughed nervously.

'Yes, I think so. It's been such a long time since I've been to anything like this, I feel weirdly nervous. I'm glad you're here with me.'

'Can you see your friend anywhere?'

Frankie's eyes roamed over the people, then she gave a little yelp.

'There she is! Fable!'

She let go of Nathan's hand to wave. The moment Fable saw her, she broke away from the group she was talking to, smiled widely, and dashed over towards Frankie. Nathan was left standing alone as the two women hugged each other tightly, then began talking rapidly. Unsure as to whether he should go and join them or wait and let them catch up on the years since they had last met, he took out his phone and started looking at some photos he had taken of his projects, pleased with how well they had endured since their design and implementation.

'Nathan?'

He looked up to see Frankie and Fable standing by him. Frankie looked faintly annoyed, and her friend was gazing at him with open curiosity.

'Oh, sorry, I was just, erm...'

He pushed his phone back in his pocket guiltily.

'How divine to meet you,' said Fable, throwing her arms

around him and squeezing him tightly to her. He found his face pressed into her long, thick hair, which smelt of woodsmoke, and felt her body pressing against him. When she finally released him, he knew the hated blush had surged up his face again, but at least Frankie was now looking at him with more amusement than irritation. 'I'm so glad you join our simple gathering, and I feel that you have brought a beautiful, calming energy. Thank you.' She seized him again, drawing him to herself as if he was a child. 'Bless you, Nathan, for the joy you bring Frankie, and all of us,' she murmured into the side of his head. 'Now, let your spirit be free and your creativity reign!'

She let him go again and it was all he could do not to straighten his clothes and hair, feeling that it might appear rude, or somehow not Bohemian enough. Instead, he smiled rather stiffly and said, 'Thank you, you have a beautiful home.'

With a tinkling laugh, Fable threw her arms out wide. Nathan almost ducked, fearing that he might be enfolded by her once again, but she spun around a couple of times, then kissed Frankie on the cheek.

'Get a drink, make some art, find new friends,' she trilled, then skipped away to launch herself at another new arrival.

Frankie's eyes danced as she looked at Nathan, her lips pressed together with suppressed mirth.

'Sorry about that. She's a bit exuberant, but isn't she sweet? She hasn't changed a bit. Oh, I'm so glad we came! I think there might be a few other people here I know. Shall we get a drink and mingle?'

Nathan nodded, taking the opportunity to pull his shirt straight and run his hand through his hair as he followed Frankie to the drinks table. Fable *did* seem nice, but he hadn't known what to say to her. He would sound flat next to someone so otherworldly, and didn't want to embarrass Frankie with his dullness in such sparkling company. No, it had been better to remain silent; at least that way there was a chance people might think he was excitingly mysterious, rather than pondering drainage.

They both took some sparkling elderflower, then turned back to the party. Frankie's initial reticence had disappeared, and she was peering eagerly into the soft duskiness of the night to see if she recognised anyone.

'Oh!' she suddenly said. 'I think that's Laura! Come on!'

She darted off. Nathan watched as she went up to a small group standing near the pool and put her hand on one of the women's shoulders, who turned then shrieked and flung her arms around Frankie. They started chattering to each other and Frankie was drawn into the group. Nathan moved back a little so that he was leaning on the wall of the house and sipped his drink. He felt content there, watching Frankie so happy and animated and feeling the warm brick on his back. Maybe he should ask Frankie if she would drive home, as he had spotted a couple of special bottles of Italian red wine left casually on the drinks table; a glass of that would complement his mellow mood perfectly. He felt it might be rather boorish to interrupt the group to ask, so he stayed where he was, letting the party wash over him, and was rather disappointed when a man wearing a loose white linen shirt and matching trousers, with bare feet, started walking purposefully towards him. Nathan tried to look interested in the contents of his glass, but there was clearly going to be no putting him off.

'Hey, man, welcome to the gathering. I'm Orion, it's very cool to meet you.'

Nathan automatically went to shake hands, but Orion ignored that and, instead, enveloped Nathan in his second hug of the evening. He wouldn't naturally have embraced a stranger in any situation, but this went on for longer than he felt most people would be comfortable with.

'Mmm *hmm!*' said Orion with a final squeeze, letting Nathan up for air. '*So* good to meet you, man.'

'Er, likewise. I'm Nathan. I'm here with Frankie.'

He gestured over to where she was now sitting on the floor with the group, which had been joined by Fable and another man with a bottle of sparkling white wine, which he was splashing into glasses.

'Oh wow,' said Orion, gazing over. 'She's Fable's friend, right? So beautiful that they've reconnected after all this time, and at the solstice.'

Nathan nodded and took another sip of his elderflower.

'How do you know Fable?'

Orion gave a gentle laugh.

'We believe our souls have lived in tandem throughout time, but our first physical meeting was about four years ago, at a shamanic retreat in Peru. We held our handfasting ceremony about six months ago.'

Nathan nodded again, not sure how to answer. When his father had died, he and Henry only then discovered that their parents had not had a legal marriage. No will had been made and Nathan was seventeen at the time, so there had been a horrific tangle of inheritance law to work through as the brothers had tried to do right by their mother, protect what money there was left and abide by the law, through a lens of grief and pain for all of them. For a moment, the memory of that difficult time suffused his body. He didn't know what to say, not wanting to look disapproving when he wasn't. Truly he believed that people should be free – and legally protected – to love and unite and celebrate and commit however they wanted to, but he didn't know how to say all of that to this stranger, no matter how well he expected it would be received. He was grateful when the music was suddenly turned up and Orion sprang forward.

'Time to dance together – will you join?'

Nathan shook his head and indicated his half-full glass, but Orion had already gone to melt into the throng that had formed on the lawn below the fire. There were more people at the party now, and there must have been more than seventy of them swaying and leaping. Frankie came rushing over to him, her face flushed.

'Are you having fun? Are you coming to dance?'

Nathan shook his head again.

'No, I'll stay here. You go, though.'

'Oh, please come!' said Frankie, taking his hand and lifting it to spin herself around. 'It's been ages since I've had a dance.'

'No, really, it's fine. I'm happy watching.'

'Oh, suit yourself.'

She flitted across the patio, past the flames, and disappeared into the morass of bodies, until he could no longer discern which she was. He knew she was disappointed that he wouldn't relax and let himself go, but this wasn't a place he felt comfortable, no matter how kind and friendly everyone was. Watching them, they looked beautiful: free and happy. A part of him longed to join in, to see how it felt. *God, I must look boring, next to these creative, glittering people.* He felt paralysed, tucked in against the comforting wall. *It's like your commissions. You're not able to leave their safety, however much you know it could mean growth.* A wave of sadness flowed through him and the wall that had felt so warm and sturdy suddenly became hard, unwelcoming brick. *If you can't find the courage to try, things will never work out with Frankie.* Rather than being inspired to step out, the realisation that he would not – or could not – change settled over him like a dank blanket of fog.

TWENTY-THREE

Dancing in the group of people, Frankie felt a rush of energy and happiness course through her body. It was as though her hibernation was over, and she had burst out into the world again, refreshed and revived. Fable shimmied over to her and, grabbing both her hands, spun her around as they laughed for joy.

'Where's that dishy man you came with?' asked her friend, shouting to be heard over the music.

'I don't know,' said Frankie, stopping still and moving closer to Fable to speak in her ear. 'I tried to get him to come and dance, but he wouldn't. Oh, I *wish* he would!'

'Are you together?'

'Only very recently. He's wonderful; I don't think he realises just how wonderful.'

Too wonderful for you, whispered the nasty little voice in her head. *He probably can't wait to go home. It's like waiting for your child to finish playing musical bumps and eat sweets so you can leave.*

'He has an amazing aura,' said Fable, drawing Frankie into a warm hug. 'And he loves you.'

Frankie gave a small smile and hugged her friend back.

Oh, I hope so, I hope that's true.

'And look!' Fable suddenly shouted. 'He's talking to Orion. So he's all right. Come on, Frank, let's dance!'

Frankie glanced over to see the two men talking. Her heart swelled as she saw Nathan's face, serious as Orion spoke to him, the two men looking very different but clearly in conversation.

Maybe he's okay. The music beat through her, almost lifting her feet off the floor in its insistence to her that she let it sweep her away. *He looks okay. I'll dance for a little longer, then I'll go over.*

And she set off again, dancing alone, with others, wherever she found herself, giddy with the pleasurable overload to her senses. The loud music, the crowd around her, the sweetness of the Italian night air mixed with the scents of bodies, perfumes, cigarette smoke, marijuana. The ache in her legs was enjoyable and the heat of her body as she danced made her feel alive, in the same way it did after an arduous session working the garden with Nathan. This abandon wasn't what she had felt when she was with Dylan. Then she had been caught up as if in a tsunami, unable to touch her feet to the ground or make decisions about where she was and what was happening. That had an uncomfortable feeling of chaos and unpredictability, whereas tonight she felt safe and in control. Now here was Fable again, doing silly dance moves, not caring if she looked daft, simply enjoying herself.

A tall man, his hair caught back in a bun, wearing only loose linen trousers and leather thongs, came up behind Fable and slipped his arms around her waist, lifting her off the floor. She shrieked in delight, then snuggled into his side and said, 'Frankie, this is Orion, my husband.'

He grabbed Frankie with his spare arm and drew her in so that the three of them were hugging.

'So good to meet you,' he said, when he finally released her.

'So amazing how yours and Fable's souls found each other after so many years.'

Frankie nodded, trying not to giggle.

'And what of Nathan?' the man continued. 'I felt an urge to connect flow between us when we spoke together, but he resisted it. What is his story? He may benefit from a sage burning ritual to enhance and release his intuition.'

'I'm not sure Nathan is quite ready for that,' said Frankie hastily, realising that if Orion was talking to them, then Nathan may well be on his own again. 'I'll go and find him, though, see how he's doing. See you later.'

She started pushing through the dancers, getting caught up once or twice but eventually emerging near the fire. It was still burning strongly. She waved the smoke away and saw that Nathan was standing where she had left him, looking at his phone again.

'Nathan?'

'Oh, hello. Are you having a good time?'

His face creased into that familiar smile and she stepped closer to him. He put his arm around her shoulder as she leant into him.

'I'm having *such* a good time. It's ages since I danced, far too long.'

'I'm glad.'

'But you're not enjoying yourself at all. Do you want to go?'

'I'm fine. I don't want to dance, but you go on.'

'I saw you talking to Orion earlier.'

'Yes, he seems nice.'

'I don't know him at all, but he and Fable look very happy together.'

'That's good.'

He smiled again, but for the first time since they very first met, conversation felt stilted, although Nathan looked relaxed and was still smiling.

'Do you truly not mind if I go and dance again?'

'Of course not, you enjoy yourself.'

'I'm going to get something to drink first, I'm so hot. Would you like something? Look, there's a nice red here, do you want some of that? It might make the party a bit easier. I can drive back.'

'Can you?'

For a moment, Frankie was confused. *He knows I can drive.* And then, with a jolt, she realised what he meant.

'Do you think I've been drinking?'

She knew that the hurt she felt was evident in her voice, but she didn't want to hide her feelings. How *could* he? How *could* he think that she had been drinking, when he knew how important it was to her not to right now?

'No, no, of course not,' he said quickly, then paused. 'Look, I saw that man in the group you were in earlier – he was pouring prosecco into everyone's glasses. It would have been kind of difficult to avoid.'

'Well, I did avoid it,' said Frankie, her pleasure in the party draining from her. 'You're right, he tipped some in, but I threw it away. You *know* I've decided not to drink for a while.'

'I'm sorry,' said Nathan, taking her hand. She allowed this, but didn't return any pressure.

She shrugged.

'Okay, it doesn't matter.' *But it does.* 'As I said, I'm happy – and sober – to drive home, so get some of that wine if you want to. I'm going to go and find Fable.'

She slipped away quickly and was soon cocooned back in the throng of dancers. But she couldn't regain the feelings of happiness that had suffused her mere moments before. *This is exactly when a drink would bloody help.* She waved her arms listlessly to a song that everyone had been screaming for. She snatched a glance at Nathan, who was looking very anxious, although he was now holding a glass of red wine in his hand.

Despite everything, this cheered Frankie up. *At least he believes that I haven't been drinking and can drive home.* Her spirits lifted and she joined in the dancing more enthusiastically. It was then that the crowd parted to reveal Fable standing on a chair. The music turned down and she raised her voice.

'Beautiful people! I love to see you dance, but I am going to create some art now! I invite you all to join me so that we can come together to produce something lasting, or something fleeting, but relish the experience together!'

There was a cheer, and the music was turned up again. People surged up towards the patio, heading for the different materials on offer. One man stripped off all his clothing and offered himself as a living canvas, a suggestion leapt on eagerly by several others, who began daubing him with paint. Frankie headed back over to Nathan, who smiled as she approached. He had not taken his phone out again.

'Fancy making some art?' she said. 'I don't think anyone minds how good it is, it's just for fun.'

She had expected him to refuse as he seemed glued to his piece of wall, but he surprised her.

'Sure, I'll give it a try. It's a shame no one's set up a nice computer program to help me, but hey.'

'What do you want to do?'

He grinned.

'I've been showing you garden design for weeks, so maybe it's your turn to show me something now.'

Delighted, she led him over to a large pile of items, which a couple of people were already rooting through.

'This might look to you like a random load of junk,' she said, 'and you'd be right. But it's what you can do with it that counts.'

'What *do* I do with it?'

'Try looking at the different forms and materials, which ones work in harmony, belong together, and which jar. Think about which ones you like – it doesn't matter why, there's no need to explain. Place them against each other and move them around, then see what images your mind produces. Do the arrangements make you think of rage, or heaven, or neglect, or injustice? Find the theme that clicks and focus on that. The rest will start to come.'

Nathan opened his mouth to answer, but Frankie never heard his reply, for a small, blonde woman next to her caught her arm, looked up at her with starry eyes and said:

'You're Frankie Carlisle, aren't you?' Frankie nodded. 'It's an absolute honour to meet you,' gushed the woman. 'And to hear you explain your process – I can't believe this is happening. I've followed your career and I was devastated when you stopped. Does this mean you've started working again?'

Frankie looked at Nathan, who was puzzling over a piece of driftwood and an old tin can, then back at the woman. She didn't know what to say in reply, but felt her ears buzzing as she realised what had happened. For the first time in months, she had approached sculpture without fear, without shame, without ugly memories forcing their way out.

'Do you know what?' she said slowly. 'I think it might mean exactly that.'

TWENTY-FOUR

Nathan stood looking at the pile of things in front of him. Frankie had certainly described it accurately – it was junk, and he had no idea how to begin turning it into art. He understood in principle what she meant. When he was presented with a derelict garden, he didn't see it as rubbish; rather, he was able to envisage what it *could* look like, what changes he would make, how everything would come together in a coherent way to be beautiful. But, staring sadly at the bit of wood and old can in his hands, he had no idea how to even start thinking about uniting these objects so they became something meaningful. He looked now at Frankie, who had clearly found a fan and was talking away animatedly to the girl about her process.

God, she's beautiful. Can't you try, for her?

He put down the tin can and looked determinedly at the piece of driftwood. *Come on, help me out here*, he silently urged it. But the only images that came to mind were childish and superficial: beach holidays, pirate ships, lolloping dogs. *Let's face it, you're never going to find deeper meaning in that stick: love, beauty, truth. You'd be better off throwing it on the fire.* He dropped it back on the pile and picked up his wine glass.

'What's wrong?' asked Frankie. 'Aren't you going to make something?'

'I've tried, but it's not for me.'

'What about some painting? Look what they're doing to that sheet – you could join in.'

He nodded, but knew he would feel silly dabbing at the sheet with a paintbrush while everyone else expressed themselves so confidently. He was saved from answering when Fable came over, holding hands with Orion, who was stark naked and partially covered in paint.

'Hey, you guys,' she screamed, and Nathan noticed that her eyes were slightly unfocused. 'Do you want to contribute to this beautiful living canvas?'

Frankie and the girl she had been discussing sculpture with both laughed and took brushes from Fable. Frankie went around behind the man and started painting something on his back, while the girl crouched down and began to decorate his foot.

'Help yourself, man,' said Orion, grinning. 'Transitory art. I'll be washing it off in the pool later, so you can go mad.'

I've never gone mad in my life. And now that I wish I could, even a little, it turns out that I can't.

'I think I'll get another drink,' he said, holding up his empty glass. 'Can I get anyone anything?'

But they were too engrossed in what they were doing even to hear him.

Nathan took up his position by the wall again, sipping his wine, which was now making him feel sleepy, and watching as the party became wilder. He caught the occasional glimpse of Frankie as she danced and painted and sculpted, chatting to and laughing with the other guests as if they were all old friends. There were fewer people there now and no wonder, he thought, looking at his watch: it was getting on for two in the morning. He would have liked to find Frankie and suggest going home, but he didn't want to look like even more of a miserable killjoy than he was sure he already did, so he garnered all his patience and stayed put.

Suddenly a shout went up, first from one voice and then echoed by many others: skinny dip!

And people were swiftly shedding their clothes – those of them still wearing them – and leaping into the swimming pool with shrieks of joy. Despite being glad he was far away enough not to risk being caught up in this particular activity, Nathan grinned. Everyone looked so happy and carefree as they frolicked in the water, playing like merry children. There was a split second when it crossed his mind to cast away his clothing and join them, but the idea was gone almost as soon as it came. It left him feeling slightly breathless, as if there was a danger he might have actually acted on the fleeting whim. It was then that he saw Frankie, standing at the side of the pool, naked, her arms stretched wide before diving into the water and joining the seething throng of bodies.

Nathan had never felt so torn. Part of him longed to watch her, admire her beauty and radiance, allow all those feelings he had for her to wash over him and carry him away. But another part cringed from this, worried he would look creepy and voyeuristic, pictured his embarrassment the next day if he participated in any way. For a moment, the two sides of him wrestled, but the fear that penetrated when he realised that he genuinely didn't know which side might win, superseded everything. *If in doubt, do nothing.* It was a phrase that had kept him safe for years now, a phrase that his parents would never have uttered. But he had used it time and again to protect himself and build a career and life that he knew were dull and predictable, but which offered him the security he craved.

So there he stood, awkwardly, waiting for the revelry to end, resigned to the fact that he would not join in. When Frankie came over to him, dressed again, her face flushed with fun and her hair slicked back, he could only summon up a small smile. Their differences had been so starkly highlighted to him, and he knew that she could never give herself over to someone as hidebound as he was.

'Are you ready to head off?'

'Yes, I feel suddenly tired. I'm so sorry, I just looked at my phone: I hadn't realised how late it was.'

'It's okay. Here are the keys.'

She took them and they got in the car and drove the short distance back to the Villa Torre in silence. It was a beautiful night, but Nathan barely noticed it as he stared out of the window. Now, all he wanted was to get the conversation Frankie was bound to want to have with him over and done with, the conversation where she told him sorry, but this wasn't going to work out.

TWENTY-FIVE

Frankie pulled the car up outside the garages and they got out, still in silence.

Oh God, he's properly angry with me. I shouldn't have stayed so long; I didn't realise the time. Better have it out, I suppose.

They stepped inside and Frankie said, 'I know it's late, but I could do with a cup of tea. Would you put the kettle on while I run to the loo?'

'Of course,' said Nathan with that same small smile, and they went in opposite directions. Once inside the cavernous bathroom behind the stairs, she sat on the side of the marble bath and stared at herself in the huge, gilded mirror that hung opposite.

'Well done,' she said out loud, her voice heavy with sarcasm. 'Classic Frankie move. Look at you, bedraggled from that ridiculous skinny dipping, exhausted and you've made a complete fool of yourself. I don't know why you ever thought you could have a proper relationship with someone as lovely and mature as Nathan.' *It was fun, though, wasn't it?* whispered a little voice in her head. She smiled. 'I will concede that it *was* fun, yes, and without having a drink. But it looks like this is going to be life for you for now: fun, but you can't expect anything more meaningful, you're not cut out for it.'

Tears sprang into her eyes as she realised what she was saying: however much she loved Nathan, and she knew without a doubt that she did, however young their relationship was, he would never choose to make a life with someone like her. No, she had shown her true colours and ruined everything. Fed up though he had been that evening, he might not want to be the one to bring the axe down. It was going to be painful to see the relief in his face, but it was better to make the cut clean and quickly, and she was going to have to be the one to do it.

She found Nathan in the kitchen with two steaming mugs of herbal tea and some toast just popping up.

'I thought we could both do with something to eat,' he said, putting it on plates and buttering it lavishly. 'Do you want anything else on it?'

'Amazing idea,' replied Frankie. 'No, thanks, that local butter is too delicious to have jam or anything. I should take some back to Feywood, they'd love it.'

They crunched and sipped for a few minutes, then Frankie cleared her throat and swallowed down her dread.

'Look, Nathan, I'm sorry about tonight, I know it wasn't your scene at all. We should have left sooner.'

'No, no. I kept saying I was all right and I meant it. You were enjoying yourself, it's all good.'

She shook her head.

'It's not.' *Come on, girl, say it so that he doesn't have to.* 'Look, I know we're due to stay here a few more days, but I think I'm going to go home tomorrow. I think you know as well as I do that... *this* isn't going to work out.'

She wasn't sure exactly what she had been expecting to see in his face: relief, shock or maybe even anger. But what she had not anticipated was his look of absolute resignation.

'Okay, I understand. Of course. I'll drive you to the airport.'

'Oh, right. So that's it then?'

He frowned.

'What do you mean? You just told me we were over, didn't you?'

She could feel those stupid tears again and she quickly swallowed some tea to try to help her regain some semblance of composure. Wasn't he going to argue with her, even out of manners?

'Well, yes, but don't you want to say anything else?'

He stood up and turned away, looking out of the window into the dark garden.

'What else can I say? You're probably right. We're very different, you and I, and I guess that tonight threw a pretty strong light on that.' He turned halfway back towards her and her heart leapt, then huddled away again as he seemed to change his mind, resuming his gaze into the night. 'You were so at home with those people tonight, Frankie, whereas I couldn't fit in with the best will in the world. I'm better left to my mortgage and boring box trees; you don't fit in there either.'

Suddenly, a mortgage and box trees seemed to Frankie like the most wonderful things in the world, if they came with Nathan.

'I think I could. Tonight was fun, but it's not how I want to live.'

'And council commissions are?'

Frankie bit her lip. He clearly didn't believe that she was able to settle down and leave her past behind her, and she could hardly blame him, after tonight. She didn't like much of what she'd seen in herself that evening either. Why did she join in that bloody skinny dipping? She'd known the minute she'd launched herself into it that it was a mistake, but of course she'd kept going, same old Frankie, have the fun no matter what the consequences. Well, she was reaping them now.

'Don't worry about taking me to the airport, I can get a car,' she said stiffly. 'And maybe I'll see you around here sometime: Fable and Orion have given me an open invitation, and it's probably time I moved on from Feywood again, anyway.' Now, it was bravado doing the talking, but she couldn't seem to stop the words streaming out of her mouth. 'Yes, that sculpting I did at the party was kind of regenerative for me as an artist.' *What on earth are you talking about?* 'I could feel my creative spirit awakening, and I don't want to let it lie dormant again now,' she lied. 'I know I have you to thank for the huge part you played in it all.'

Nathan nodded, his face expressionless.

'I understand,' he said. 'Of course you want more. I would never hold you back, Frankie.'

She nodded, unable to speak. So that confirmed it.

Once upstairs, she thought the tears might come, but her regret and self-hatred made her feel more destructive than sad.

Maybe I should just have a bloody drink. It's not like I can do any harm. I've managed to do enough of that sober.

She sat down abruptly on the bed and, for a moment, her head spun with the longing not to sit with her feelings but to blot them out, or at least soften them around the edges.

Yes, the worst that will happen is a hangover, nobody else involved, and this will all feel much more manageable.

She stood up and headed for the door. She knew that there was wine in the kitchen and a plan started rapidly forming in her head: if Nathan was still there, she could pretend she had lost her phone; if he wasn't, she could take a bottle, stick it under her jacket and get back upstairs without being seen.

She was halfway down the stairs when a tiny, quiet voice in her head began to whisper to her.

Frankie?

Shut up.

A step further and the voice was a little louder, more insistent.

Frankie, a drink is not the answer. You're actually going to have to think about this stuff sooner or later.

And this time, she listened. Furiously, she turned around, stamped back up the stairs and flung herself into her room.

Fine! I won't have a drink! Bloody smug annoying voice!

But the voice was her own, and it was herself she had stopped for: not Nathan, not her sisters, but herself. As the realisation hit her, the desire to have a drink ebbed away, the space it had left filled with a crushing tiredness and not a little pride. She grabbed her suitcase and stuffed in her clothes, then collapsed on the bed with her phone to book her journey back to Feywood.

The first flight out of Pisa to Heathrow which didn't involve changing three times and take ten hours wasn't until midday. Frankie had no intention of hanging around the next morning, so she booked a car for seven a.m. and left before she saw anyone. She wrote a letter to her hosts thanking them for having her to stay and apologising for her dawn flit. She left nothing for Nathan, fearing that if she tried to write something down, it would either be stiff and anodyne or she wouldn't be able to stop herself from begging him to forgive her and try again.

The airport was comforting in its anonymity and lack of a sense of time. She spent the first hour trundling her small case around the duty-free shops, spraying on perfumes and buying giant chocolate bars for everyone at Feywood. When she had tired of that, and with a couple of hours still to wait, she bought some magazines and went to sit in a restaurant, where she ordered a huge breakfast and tried to eat away her exhaustion. Two hours of sleep definitely wasn't enough. But she found it hard to concentrate on what she was reading and kept picking up her phone to reply to a message or two from friends, then flick through it impatiently, swiping away any notifications that popped up in disappointment that they weren't from Nathan. Eventually, she rang Martha.

'Hi, Frank! How's bella Italia?'

'Not so bella in the end, so I'm on my way home. I should be back midafternoon, so make sure you've put the kettle on, will you?'

'Yes, of course. But why are you coming back early? Is Nathan with you?'

'No, I'm coming on my own.'

'Why? Is everything all right? You both seemed so happy when you left. We...'

She broke off.

'You what?' asked Frankie. 'Had our happily ever after all planned out?'

'Well, sort of, I suppose. I mean, it did look promising.'

Frankie emitted a laugh that was meant to be carefree but sounded manic.

'Ha! Well, any promise fizzled out before we'd even spent the night together. Come on, Martha, even you have to admit that we're hardly a match made in heaven, me and Nathan. We couldn't be more incompatible if we tried. Can you imagine him putting up with me?'

'Yes, of course I can.'

Damn, she wasn't meant to say that. I should have rung Juliet – she would have been much more critical.

Martha continued.

'You always have a downer on yourself, but you're incredible.' She sounded genuinely confused. 'Of course, Nathan would want to be with you. He always looked at you like you were the cat's pyjamas.'

In spite of herself, Frankie smiled at the old-fashioned expression.

'Well, the cat forgot to do its laundry. Don't worry, M, it's all good. How are Holmes and Watson?' she ploughed on, hoping to change the subject.

'You've been away a matter of hours, they're fine. I'm more worried about you.'

'You don't need to be,' replied Frankie firmly. 'I just wanted to let you know. Oh, they're announcing something, I'd better go. See you soon, don't forget the kettle!'

She rang off before her sister could say anything else. There had been nothing over the tannoy, but she didn't want Martha to probe anymore, especially if she was going to insist there was nothing wrong with her, Frankie.

I'll have to show them when I get home that the old Frankie is back in town and can't have her style cramped by Nathan.

But when she picked her phone up again, she knocked the photos icon by mistake and was presented with a picture of him standing by the Roman ruins at Villa Torre and looking so sweet and handsome that her throat constricted violently. It was going to be hard to brazen her way through this one, even to herself.

TWENTY-SIX

Nathan stepped away from the window, from where he had watched Frankie get into the taxi, his heart breaking. He dropped heavily down into a chair and pushed his hands into his hair. He hadn't had a choice – had he? – in agreeing, even pushing her further away, when she had ended things. He stood up, his head feeling fuzzy from the wine and lack of sleep and went to the bathroom, where he stepped under a cool shower. No, what else could he have done? He had seen how free and happy Frankie had been last night and had loved seeing her that way. The refreshing water rained down on his face and he remembered how nearly he had joined in, feeling his frustration rise again at his inability to be spontaneous, to step into the unknown. Well, maybe today he would make it matter.

As he turned off the taps and dried himself, he made a decision that felt as right to him as pushing Frankie away had felt wrong: he would turn down that commission. Yes, he would turn it down and, instead, work on a project that had been tempting him for years, but he had never been willing to step in to. And, to make sure it happened, he wasn't going to keep this decision to himself.

. . .

When Nathan came down to breakfast, a little late, the whole family was there. *Good. Now, he would have more witnesses, and he wouldn't be able to back out.*

'Are you all right?' asked Henry in Italian. 'You look very serious. And where's Frankie?'

Nathan took a large sip of strong coffee and cleared his throat.

'Frankie has gone home.'

It came out louder than he had intended, and he had sounded unprecedentedly dramatic: no wonder there was a sudden hubbub of chatter and questions.

'Gone home, why?'

'Is everything all right?'

'It's not her aunt, is it?'

'Is she coming back?'

'Everything's fine,' he said firmly. The questions stopped, but he could see everyone looking at each other in confusion. He ploughed on. 'She – we – realised that things weren't going to work between us, and she didn't want to stay.'

Amongst the concerned faces, he noticed that Lucia's wore a look of satisfaction. *Well, she was right, so fair enough.*

'So, what are you going to do now?' asked Henry. 'Are you going to go back to Feywood and get your things?'

'I'm not sure,' answered Nathan. 'Probably, or I might ask them to pack them up and send them, although it would be a shame not to put the finishing touches to the gardens and orangery myself. It depends how busy I am here.'

'With the *comune* commission?'

'No. I'm going to turn that down. It's time I did something I genuinely want to do.' He turned to Antonio and Carla. 'I know I have been living here for a long time, saving for a deposit on a house, and this will slow that down again. I cannot take advantage of your hospitality any longer, so I will move out and rent somewhere.'

'No, you will not!' Nathan was shocked at the force behind Antonio's words. 'You are family, Nathan, and you can live here as long as you want to or need to. This is your *home* – we hope that's how you feel about it, anyway.'

He turned to his wife, and she nodded vigorously.

'Yes. Of course, if you want to live somewhere else, then you must, but if you are happy here, then please stay, we insist.'

Nathan's face relaxed into a smile for the first time that day.

'I would love to, thank you.'

'What are you going to do?' asked Henry again. 'If not the commission?'

'After creating that sensory garden, which as you know is now run by ILM, I have wanted to create more, similar, projects. But instead of being tucked away in the grounds of a villa, I would like them to be in more publicly accessible spaces: hospitals, schools and so on. Each one would be tailored to meet the needs of the people who would be using them. Flat, wide paths for wheelchair or even hospital bed access, soothing or vibrant colours, plants with culinary or medicinal uses, shady trees, running water or Japanese-inspired dry gardens.'

'It sounds marvellous,' said Allegra, reaching over and squeezing his hand. 'Just marvellous and totally inspired. How will you go about it? It sounds like a huge undertaking...'

'It will be,' admitted Nathan. He felt a surge of courage – or was it recklessness? For once he didn't care. 'The truth is, I don't know how I'm going to do it. But I am. It will need research – into the gardens themselves, of course, but also where the need will be and how to fund it all. I'll have to publicise it, set up a proper business. I was thinking about applying for a space at garden festivals to get my ideas and name back out there. There are the big Royal Horticultural Society ones in England, but some here in Italy too.'

'Oh yes!' said Carla. 'I've been to the Radicepura Garden Festival in Sicily – it's amazing.'

Nathan nodded.

'The competition to display there is fierce and it's only held every other year, but I'm going to try. There's another one near Lake Como in the autumn, which I'm going to look into as well – for next year.'

A sudden peal of laughter came from the end of the table where Donata had, so far, been sitting in silence. Every head turned towards the old lady.

'Finally!' she shouted, banging her coffee cup down into its saucer. 'Finally, you are doing what you should be doing! And about time. I *liked* Frankie, she had some life about her. You shouldn't have let her go, of course, but...' She lifted her small shoulders in a shrug. 'Men do stupid things all the time, but at least she gave you the *boccata d'ossigeno* you needed.'

Unsure of what the idiom meant, Nathan turned to his brother, who grinned.

'She means that Frankie was a shot in the arm, and I'm inclined to agree, but...' He mirrored Donata's shrug. 'Men do stupid things.'

Stung, Nathan pushed back his chair.

'She was the one who ended it. What was I supposed to do? She made her decision, and I listened.'

Allegra spoke up in a calm voice.

'No one is criticising you for being respectful. I think we could all see how much you liked each other, that's all. We're disappointed.'

'As am I. But I'm trying to move on and do something positive.' He stood up. 'In fact, I think I'll go and get started.'

He strode upstairs, hating himself even more now for

having been so abrupt with the family who had always been so kind to him. Back in his room, he opened his laptop and tried to push aside thoughts of whether he had, indeed, done a stupid thing in letting Frankie go without a fight. Sighing, he got down to work.

TWENTY-SEVEN

Frankie fell asleep as soon as the plane took off, but didn't feel remotely refreshed when they landed at Heathrow. Her onward journey by train and bus did nothing to improve her mood or energy. When she finally found herself trudging up the drive she could only hope to get inside and up to her room before anyone spotted her. But, of course, this being Feywood, she knew the chances were slim and this was proved to be the case when, as she approached the front door, it opened and out came Rousseau, Sindhu and Martha, all talking at the tops of their voices. She looked furtively from side to side in case there was any chance of making a dash for it, but she was spotted.

'Frankie!' exclaimed her sister. 'You're back! I wish you'd told me the exact time, I would have come and picked you up.'

'It's fine,' she muttered, trying to edge past the little group, avoiding their concerned eyes. Sindhu put a hand on her arm.

'Are you okay? Martha told us you were coming home early – alone.'

'I'm all right. Are you going out?'

'Yes,' replied her father. 'Just into Oxford to do some wedding stuff.'

Frankie nodded, not trusting herself to speak, and Rousseau seized her in one of his big, sudden hugs.

'Okay, I hope it goes well,' she said, disentangling herself. 'See you later.'

She slipped inside before anyone else could speak, dropped her bag and went straight through the house and into the garden, where she made a beeline for the peacocks' cage.

'Hello, you two,' she said, relieved that they couldn't answer back and start questioning her about why she had been so idiotic. 'Have you missed me? Probably not. That's okay, as long as Martha looked after you.'

'She did,' came a voice from behind, and Frankie turned to see her eldest sister there, a half-smile on her face which didn't hide her worry.

'It's all right,' said Frankie, speaking more roughly than she had meant to. 'I'm not going to lose it again like I did after Dylan.'

Martha nodded.

'Okay, good. But you'll need to talk about it. Shall I see you in the orangery in ten minutes? I'll bring that tea you wanted.'

Unaccustomed to hearing such firmness in Martha's voice, and overwhelmed by tiredness and sadness, Frankie acquiesced.

'All right. Bring some biscuits or something too.'

As her sister went back up towards the house, she returned to the peacocks, who were now squabbling over some invisible treasure in the grass.

'Not long until we can let you two out to roam around,' she said. 'I hope you'll enjoy your freedom – it's a mixed blessing.'

She watched them for a few more minutes, then trudged to the orangery. When she opened the door, the smell of wet soil and warm greenery filled her nostrils, and she staggered back as if she had been punched. With the earthy, evocative smell of the space came a rush of memory so vivid it was shocking. Her and Nathan digging, planting, watering, deciding together what went where, excited over each new discovery as choking weeds were removed and revealed things that had lain hidden for decades. A sensation of her own happiness there with him, the way she had felt relaxed and authentic, yet invigorated and inspired, crashed into her like a tidal wave. Her hand flew to her mouth to suppress a sudden gasping sob as she was hit by the full impact of what she had lost, the potential their burgeoning relationship had.

It was here that Martha found her a couple of minutes later. She hurriedly put down her tray and rushed over to Frankie. Wordlessly, she put her arm around her shoulder and guided her to sit down. She handed her a mug of tea and pushed the plate of biscuits towards her.

'Thanks, M,' Frankie whispered, taking one. 'Sorry, I promise I'm not cracking up. It was that coming in here reminded me so much of Nathan. Oh God, M, I've been phenomenally stupid.'

Martha went to reply when the door through to the house opened again, and Juliet came in.

'Frank! What's going on? Martha said you were coming back without Nathan, and...' She broke off. 'Oh, what have you done?'

'You see,' croaked Frankie, finally finding her voice. 'She knows it's my fault without even asking.'

Martha shot a furious look at Juliet, who quickly sat down.

'No, I'm sorry, ignore me. You look awful, what's happened?'

'Thanks,' said Frankie drily. 'I haven't had much sleep and the last twenty-four hours have been a complete mess.' She took another biscuit. 'My fault, as you have already concluded. Things were going well, then I made Nathan go to a party – it was being thrown by Fable, do you remember her?' The sisters both nodded, but didn't speak. 'It turns out she lives up the road from Nathan's brother's in-laws. Anyway, it was my sort of thing – loads of arty types dancing and talking nonsense, then creating group artworks, you know the routine.'

Martha and Juliet nodded again.

'The sort of thing Mum and Dad used to have here, back in the day,' said Juliet.

'Exactly. Well, I was throwing myself into it, but I *knew* Nathan hated every second. I did ask him if he wanted to go home, but he kept saying no. I thought he was getting into it at one point, talking to people and so on, but then I'd see him on his own again.'

'Maybe he was happy watching,' suggested Martha. 'You know I'm more like that. I don't mind at all.'

'I know, and he kept saying that, so I kept going,' said Frankie. 'But of course, as usual, I went too far, throwing all my clothes off and chucking myself in the pool.'

At this declaration, Martha and Juliet both screamed with surprised laughter.

'Oh, Frank, you didn't!' said her eldest sister.

'I did,' replied Frankie miserably. 'I don't know what came over me.'

'Look,' said Juliet, sounding uncertain. 'I hope you don't mind me asking, and I'm not judging, but...'

'Was I drinking?' supplied Frankie. Juliet nodded. 'No, I don't mind you asking, it's a fair question, and no, I wasn't. I don't know if that makes it worse.'

Martha giggled.

'I'm sorry, it sounds so funny, you casting off your kit and poor Nathan standing there not knowing which way to look.'

Frankie gave a small smile.

'It does sound funny, I suppose, but then I realised how ridiculous I must look and how I haven't changed after all that stuff with Dylan.'

'Well, that's not true,' said Martha. 'But the changes you're talking about aren't the ones that matter. There was never anything *wrong* with you – I wish you could see that. What's changed is your self-respect, your confidence, your courage. If anything, you're *more* yourself since you left Dylan and started up the gardening stuff with Nathan.'

Frankie shrugged.

'Thanks, M, but the point still stands. There's no way someone as grown up and lovely as Nathan wants to be with me.'

'Did he say that?' demanded Juliet.

'Not in so many words, but he was incredibly quiet and obviously horrified and then when I said I was going home and we weren't going to work out, he agreed and said I didn't fit into his life.'

'He didn't mean it!' exploded Juliet. 'This is Nathan we're talking about. He probably thought he was being all noble and respectful, and I'd put money on him thinking that *he's* the problem, not you.'

'Why on earth would he think that?'

'I bet he saw you at the party all happy and believes that you think he's boring for not joining in. Then you dumped him and confirmed it.'

Frankie dropped her head into her hands and moaned.

'I did dump him, didn't I? I didn't mean to; I was kind of trying to make things easier for him.'

'So, why don't you call him, then?' said sensible Martha. 'Tell him you made a mistake.'

'But I'm not sure I did,' said Frankie, lifting her head and looking at her sisters. 'He said himself that he didn't think I was cut out for the sensible sort of life he wants to lead. No, he'll be breathing a sigh of relief and enjoying the peace of that amazing villa. I'm a hot mess, girls, he doesn't need me complicating his life. He was about to accept another one of those boring commissions, anyway, so that he can keep saving for a deposit.

Even if I hadn't made a fool of myself at the party, he doesn't want anyone mucking up his careful plans.'

'Now you're putting words in his mouth,' said Juliet, sounding exasperated.

'Maybe, but he's had a pretty tough time and he's trying to get his life sorted out. I'm sure that doesn't involve some delinquent English girl who doesn't know what to do with her life and has nothing to offer but a couple of squabbling peacocks and a knack for drawing pretty pictures of gardens.'

'Now you're being ridiculous,' said Juliet crossly. 'Why can't you take anything seriously? Maybe you haven't changed, after all.'

Martha laid a calming hand on her sister's arm.

'What Juliet means is that you've got masses to offer. You know that and so does Nathan. Are you sure you won't call him?'

'No,' said Frankie stubbornly. 'I'm going to sign up for that garden design diploma and get a dog. I'm going to be perfectly happy, you'll see. Now, what about this wedding? Are they going to have it here at Feywood?'

'I think so,' said Martha. 'Did you ever speak to them about using the orangery?'

'Yes, and they loved the idea, but now Nathan's gone, I'm worried about getting it finished.'

'Is there much more to do?' asked Juliet, looking around. 'It looks amazing, transformed from before.'

'It's about halfway there,' said Frankie. 'I suppose it depends when they get married – have they come up with a date yet?'

'Not a firm one,' said Martha, 'but I know they want it to be sooner rather than later, and it's not going to be huge. Maybe you'll need to get Nathan back to help you finish.'

Frankie stuck her tongue out at her sister.

'Nice try.'

. . .

The next day, after a long night's sleep and still no word from Nathan, Frankie went to find her aunt, who was in the kitchen staring at her phone as a cup of coffee rapidly cooled on the table in front of her.

'Morning,' said Frankie. 'Is everything okay?'

Sylvia looked up, her face so thin and drawn that it clutched at Frankie's heart.

'It is and it isn't,' she replied. 'I've just had the email through from the hospital with the date of my surgery. It's in three weeks' time.'

Frankie sat down and took her aunt's cold hand in her own.

'We're all here for you,' she said. 'And we're so sorry you're going through this. But we're here for you as much as we possibly can be.'

'I know,' said Sylvia. 'And it makes the world of difference. But I'm frightened.'

'So am I, we all are. But it's good you've got a date.'

'I know. Now come on,' said Sylvia with a rather forced smile. 'You are the perfect person to take my mind off things, if you haven't got anything better to do?'

'I can't think of anything better than spending some time with you,' said Frankie. 'And I've got the perfect activity to keep us both busy.'

Half an hour later, they were in the car. Twenty minutes after that, they pulled up at the Belminster animal sanctuary.

'Isn't this where you got those peacocks?' asked Sylvia. 'Don't tell me you're rehoming some more?'

'Nope,' said Frankie, grinning. 'Not peacocks this time, guess again.'

'Oh Lord,' said Sylvia. 'With you it could be anything. Hens? Lizards? A monkey? A two-toed sloth?'

'No, no, no!' said Frankie, laughing as she got out of the car

ESCAPE TO THE COUNTRY GARDEN

and feeling glad that she had already managed to lift her aunt's spirits. 'Much simpler than that for once, although I would love to rescue some ex-battery hens at some point. Ah, here's Louisa – do you remember her from when she brought Holmes and Watson?'

'Hello, Frankie, Sylvia,' said Louisa, hugging them both. 'Good to see you. How are those peacocks getting on?'

'They're doing brilliantly,' said Frankie. 'We're going to let them out soon.'

'I'm glad they found such a good home. And now it's a dog you're looking for?'

'That's right. I know we talked about it when I took the peacocks, but now it's the right time. Don't worry,' said Frankie, turning to Sylvia. 'I know it seems sudden, but I asked Dad a while ago and he's happy, and I've got loads of advice on how to introduce a new dog to Moriarty and Ava.'

'And we know that Feywood is a suitable home,' said Louisa. 'So we're good to go. And we do have a dog I think might be ideal. He came in a couple of weeks ago, and I thought he'd go quickly because he's beautiful.'

'Why hasn't he?' asked Frankie.

'He's sad,' said Louisa, looking unhappy herself. 'I think it puts people off. He's a golden retriever and normally families snap them up as they're so gentle, but he keeps getting overlooked. It's such a shame, because he's the sweetest boy. Come on, I'll show you.'

They walked through the office building and out to the pens where the different animals were kept. Louisa led them to a pen at the far end, in which lay a large, golden-coloured dog, its beautiful head on its paws. It barely looked up when they approached. Louisa disappeared for a moment, then came back with a chair for Sylvia.

'Would you like a cup of tea or anything?' she asked, looking worried.

'No, no, thank you, I'm much better now I'm sitting down. Thank you for noticing. I can see why you run this sanctuary... maybe I should leave Feywood and come and live here,' she said with a smile. 'I'd be less trouble for everyone.'

Frankie put an arm round her aunt and gave her shoulders a squeeze.

'You're no trouble at all, Aunt Sylvia, and we certainly don't want you rehomed.'

'So, this is Aslan,' said Louisa. 'Named after the lion from *The Lion, The Witch and The Wardrobe*, of course, because he's huge and golden and good. He's about four years old and was living with a young man who had a serious congenital condition and sadly passed away. Aslan was well looked after and had a quiet life, and we think he's grieving for his previous owner. He'll need a lot of love and patience, but he'll be a perfect pet. He's got a history of being good with children and other animals and he has no medical issues. We can't tempt him with much, but he has shown a liking for carrots and blueberries. I know he looks sad,' she added, looking at Frankie and Sylvia, who were both wiping tears away, 'but I think he needs to be back in a loving home.'

'Oh, he *will* be!' burst out Frankie. 'We'll look after him, Louisa, I promise.'

'Yes,' said Sylvia, without taking her eyes off the dog. 'He'll have a perfect home at Feywood.'

'Good,' said Louisa, smiling. 'Shall we get him out and you can meet him?'

She went into the cage and crouched down, speaking gently to the dog, then she clipped a lead on and encouraged him to get up. He walked slowly, his head low, eyes dull.

'Hello,' said Frankie, holding out her hand to the dog, who sniffed it disconsolately. 'I do hope you'll be happy with us.'

Sylvia also held out her hand and, to their surprise, Aslan nudged it slightly, then sat down next to her and laid his head on her lap. She stroked his head and soft ears, talking to him quietly.

'Look at that,' said Louisa. 'He knows he's going home.'

When they arrived back at Feywood, Rousseau was waiting for them with Moriarty and Ava on their leads.

'I'm going to have a lie-down in my beautiful new room,' said Sylvia. 'Bring Aslan along later, won't you?'

'Of course,' said Frankie, giving her aunt a gentle hug. 'Do you need any help getting there?'

'Not yet, my darling,' said Sylvia, and gave the big dog a pat before leaving.

'Thanks for having them ready, Dad,' said Frankie, watching as the three dogs sniffed each other carefully. 'The sanctuary said that a short walk on leads was a good way to introduce them to each other.'

They set off towards the village, Frankie keeping up a stream of chatter in the hope of distracting her father from asking her any questions about Nathan. *I'm doing so well. If I can keep up a brave face, then surely it will stop hurting so much?*

But when they got home and she took Aslan to show him his basket, where he immediately curled up and looked up at her trustingly, she couldn't hold it in any longer. Burying her face in his furry, sympathetic shoulder, she sobbed, feeling as if her broken heart might never mend.

TWENTY-EIGHT

Nathan dragged himself through the next couple of weeks. He found consolation in his work, pouring his time and soul into it, and he knew it was the best he had ever done. But the moment he laid down his pencil, or shut his laptop for the day, his mind was instantly filled with thoughts of Frankie and how readily he had let her go. The family was tremendously kind to him, steering clear of the subject, although he was sure he caught Donata looking at him sometimes with an expression that said *stupido uomo*: stupid man.

Lucia, he knew, was delighted to see the back of Frankie and had been warmly friendly and attentive towards him. They had often spent an evening chatting over wine or going for walks together when the heat of the sun had cooled in the early evening and he had enjoyed her company, until Henry, looking embarrassed, tapped on his door one day while he was working.

'Sorry to disturb you. Is work going well?'

'Very. What can I do for you?'

His brother perched on the side of the bed, looking uncomfortable.

'Look, I didn't want to bring this up, but Allegra told me I had to, and she's right.'

Nathan frowned.

'What is it?'

'Uh, well, it's just that since Frankie's been gone, we've noticed you spending a lot of time with Lucia.'

'And?'

'The family thinks... well, they think that you make a smashing couple and are holding their breath, but I don't think that's how you're feeling at all, is it?'

Nathan shook his head.

'No, you're right. Lucia's good company, but I hadn't thought about her as anything other than a friend.' He flushed deep red. 'Does, er, does she think differently?'

'I think so,' said Henry. 'I mean, obviously she hasn't confided in me, but that's the general, er, consensus.'

Nathan ran his hand through his hair and sighed.

'All right. Thanks for letting me know. I'll sort it.'

Henry stood up and clapped his brother on the back, then left. Nathan sat for a moment, feeling nothing but exhaustion. Another failure to understand a woman, and maybe someone else's feelings hurt. *Stupido uomo.* He pushed back his chair and, standing up, grabbed a hat and a bottle, which he filled with water. It may be the hottest part of the day, but he needed to get out. He couldn't avoid thinking about this any longer.

He jogged quietly down the stairs and slipped out of the front door, walking briskly down the long drive. He only relaxed his shoulders once he was out of sight of the house and unlikely to hear his name called. He slowed his pace, but only slightly, taking long strides as he drove himself to think about Frankie. Had his brother, his wife and her grandmother been right? Had he jumped to conclusions and let Frankie go unnecessarily? A little flame of hope jolted within him, making him catch his breath and he slowed his pace slightly while he recovered and let an opposing voice have its say: *no, you were right and anyway, do you want that chaos back in your life?* As he was about to counter this with a further possibility, he heard voices shouting his name. He stopped walking and looked around, finally seeing two faces peering at him over a hedge on the other side of the road: Fable and Orion. He looked around himself, surprised. Had he walked that far already that he had reached their house? They shouted again and he lifted his hand to wave.

'You must come in!' yelled Fable. 'I'm coming to open the door for you now!'

Nathan hesitated for a moment, then crossed the road. He didn't want to go back to Villa Torre yet, knowing that an awkward conversation with Lucia awaited him and anyway, the temptation to spend time with people who knew Frankie well, who might be able to let in some light, was strong.

The door was flung open, and he had a moment to register Fable's welcoming, smiling face, before he was once again swept into a tight embrace.

'So good to see you,' she said, finally releasing him. It had been easier to hug her back this time; she was so openly friendly that it would have been difficult not to respond.

'And you,' he said, meaning it. 'I didn't realise I had walked so far.'

'Coming past our house was an *accident*?' she said, her eyes widening.

He nodded.

'Yes. I was walking aimlessly.'

'Aimlessly!' Orion's deep voice made him jump, but he was ready for the hug this time. 'You mean you *thought* you were aimless, but your subconscious plainly brought you to us.' Fable was nodding vigorously, and it crossed Nathan's mind that they might be right. 'Come in! We were about to have a *Spritz* – you must join us.'

Nathan followed them out to the terrace, which brought

back strong memories of the party. It was quiet now, of course, and he could appreciate the beautiful view over the Tuscan countryside. He sat down and gladly took the glowing orange drink, garnished with fruit, from Fable.

'Where's Frankie?' she asked. 'Back at the villa? Oh, I was so happy to see her the other night, it had been far too long. Why don't you give her a ring and ask her to join us?'

Nathan swallowed and tried to speak through a tight throat.

'Frankie's gone back to England.'

'Oh gosh, it's not her aunt, is it? She mentioned she was waiting for surgery.'

Nathan shook his head.

'No – well, I don't know.' He had wondered about Sylvia's health many times since Frankie had gone home, having become very fond of her. 'Frankie left because...' He trailed off, then gathered his courage. 'She left because of me. We were... that is, we had... Well, we were becoming more than just friends.'

'Of *course* you were,' said Fable, grabbing his hand that wasn't holding the drink. 'We could see it, couldn't we?'

She turned her gaze on Orion, who nodded.

'Yeah, for sure. What gave, man? You two seemed so aligned.'

'Really?' spluttered Nathan. 'I don't think so at all. We're too different.'

'Nah,' said Orion. 'You complemented each other – well, at the party you did. Can't speak for the rest of the time. Weren't you getting on?'

'No, no, we were, very well. It was the party that showed up the differences that I – well, we – well, look, me anyway and probably Frankie, too, had been worrying about.'

'What was your worry?' asked Fable, finally releasing his hand.

Nathan shrugged.

'You know her well; you know how full of life she is. I'm the opposite. I like quiet. I would have bored her, in the end.'

Fable fixed him with a penetrating stare.

'Did you ask her that?'

'No.'

She let out an impatient noise.

'Pah! There's more to it than that. No one breaks up with someone because they think they're going to bore them.'

'Well, she did break up with me, so I think that proves it.'

'I wonder. What I want to know, what I *really* want to know, is what you were scared of, for yourself.'

'I'm sorry?'

'Okay, so you think you would have bored her. We'll leave that there for now. What was it in Frankie that you were shying away from?'

Nathan looked from Fable to Orion. Both were looking back with such kindness that the words came spilling out of him.

'She reminded me of my parents. They were artists, not particularly successful ones, and their lives were chaos. My brother and I brought ourselves up through the madness of it all: the midnight flits because rent hadn't been paid; living in communes; not being sent to school; alcohol and drugs. I slipped in and out of all that myself, emulating then rejecting them.' He took a sip of his drink. 'It was always going to go one way or the other and I chose to be as sensible and stable as I could. When I first met Frankie, I knew her life had been similar, but she didn't *feel* chaotic, or wild. Just vibrant and clever. Unconventional, yes, but in a way that was freeing, rather than alarming. She began to bring it back out in me, my creativity and vision, which I had locked away with everything else that resembled my parents.'

He stopped abruptly and had some of his drink.

'So, what changed?' asked Fable quietly.

'At your party,' said Nathan. 'She was having such a good

time, and I couldn't join in, couldn't unbutton myself enough.' He stared out across the hills, then gave a dry laugh. 'I've fitted myself out too well as dull and conventional. There's no going back, and I couldn't bear to stultify Frankie.'

'Two things,' said Fable, speaking gently, but with steel in her voice. 'One: do you think for a moment Frankie would *allow* herself to be stultified? And, two: I thought you said *she* left *you*? From what you're saying, it was very much your decision.'

Nathan frowned.

'No, I don't think she would. Let herself be stultified, that is. That's why she ended things and why I didn't argue.'

They all sat in silence for a moment, then Fable poured everyone more *Spritz* and said, 'I'm going to share a conversation Frankie and I had; I don't think she'll mind. The thing is, she thought that *you* couldn't possibly stay interested in *her*.'

'But why?' asked Nathan.

'Because she thinks you're so wonderful and she's not good enough for you,' said Fable bluntly.

'*What?*'

'That's what she said. I can't understand why you weren't honest with each other.'

Nathan shook his head.

'We were,' he said slowly. 'At the time, we both utterly believed in what we were saying. But I've done a lot of thinking in the past couple of weeks, thinking about how I have let my fears and insecurities from my past dictate everything, and how that is no way to live. I've made changes, refused 'safe' work and now I'm branching out on my own, doing work I've always wanted to do. It was losing Frankie, recognising my own self-sabotage, that pushed me forward. I can't and I *won't* go on living half a life.'

'So, what now?'

'Now,' said Nathan, a smile broadening across his face. 'Now, I think it's about time I got on a plane.'

TWENTY-NINE

Frankie pressed the buzzer, and the door clicked open for her to go into the ward where her Aunt Sylvia was recuperating after her operation. A nurse directed her to a numbered space, its curtains drawn around it. Quietly, not wanting to disturb her aunt if she was asleep, she poked her head in.

'Frankie, come in, come in.' Propped up on three pillows, Sylvia looked pale and fragile, but she was smiling as she waved Frankie in. 'You'll have to pull that chair over,' she said. 'Take those things off it but don't forget to put it all back when you leave, otherwise' – she lowered her voice to a conspiratorial whisper – 'the woman next door sends her husband in for it so that they have two.'

Grinning, Frankie did as she was told, and sat down.

'How are you feeling?'

'Like I've been charged by a bull, but they said the operation went well and I'll be home in a few days.'

Tears sprang to Frankie's eyes as she lifted her aunt's hand and kissed it.

'I'm so glad. We've all been so worried.'

'I can't pretend I wasn't a little concerned myself, but I'll be fit as a fiddle in a few months, and we'll have forgotten this ever happened. I'd much rather talk about you.'

Frankie looked wary.

'What about me? I've got things moving for the orangery; it should be looking great by the wedding.'

'I wasn't talking about work, darling, as well you know. I want to know what you're going to do about Nathan.'

Frankie looked surprised.

'Do? I wasn't going to *do* anything. Well, other than pack up his things.'

She raised a small smile.

'Has he asked you to?'

'No, but he must need them.'

'So you were going to send them back without contacting him?'

Frankie shrugged.

'I haven't heard from him in three weeks – I don't know what else to do.'

She looked dejected, and her aunt frowned.

'What do you *want* to do?'

Frankie looked at her, her face drawn.

'I miss him so much. I think... I think I was wrong. I was so sure that I hadn't changed, that I couldn't be trusted, that he was far too good and kind and grown up for me, but since I've been back, I've missed him so much. I still love the garden and the orangery and working on them, but I miss talking to him and drinking tea while we try to work out what to do next and laughing at the peacocks together.' She picked at a loose thread on the blanket. 'When I left Dylan, I didn't miss any of it, any of that stuff I'd been doing for years – the late nights, the parties, the drinking, the craziness. I felt relieved that I didn't have to do any of it anymore. And that never changed. The party at Fable's house was fun, but I don't need to do it every night.'

'And couples can have different interests, you know.'

'I know. But Aunt Sylvia, what is Nathan thinking?'

Sylvia laughed, then started coughing. Frankie quickly poured her a glass of water from the plastic carafe on the side table and helped her sip it until the fit had subsided.

'Sorry, darling,' she said hoarsely. 'Serves me right for laughing at you, but what a question! How should I know what Nathan thinks?'

'Do you think he hates me?'

'Well, of that I *am* sure – of course he doesn't. He was mad about you only a few short weeks ago and I very much doubt that's changed.'

'Even after that party?'

'Absolutely. And before you ask, we've been over this before and I still think that he hasn't been in touch because he wants to respect your wishes.'

'So, what do I *do*?'

'What you need to *do*, my girl, is talk to him. Honestly, with all the communication methods at your fingertips these days. The younger generations seem to find it incredibly difficult to put any of them to good use. Send him a Snapchat, ping him on TikTok, Facebook him, DM him, use WhatsApp or Messenger or email or just pick up the bloody phone and call!'

Now, it was Frankie's turn to laugh.

'Aunt Sylvia! How do you know all those different sorts of social media?'

'Well,' she replied modestly. 'I am an old hand at Instagram, as you know, because I run the cookery school account, and I follow Juliet on various things.'

'You're amazing. Maybe I should go back to the Belminster animal sanctuary and see if they've got any carrier pigeons.'

'Send one of those ridiculous peacocks if you must, just get in touch!' She pulled a face of complete frustration, then looked serious. 'Darling Frankie, I'm not guaranteeing that everything will work out perfectly, but you must see that you have to try.'

Frankie nodded.

'I know. And I will. Now, let me show you a photo of Aslan I took yesterday. He'd cheered up so much since we got him from the sanctuary, but he's been a picture of misery since you've been in hospital. I thought I might be able to swing a visit with him if I passed him off as a therapy dog, but when I rang to check, the nurses were having none of it.'

'What a shame, I miss him already. Oh, is that him with the peacocks?'

'Yes. They're out of their cage now and roaming around wherever they like, screeching the place down. He's terrified of them, but they like him, and they keep following him around.'

'Poor Aslan. Well, soon he'll be able to help me recuperate. I can take him for lots of slow walks.'

'He'll like that.' Frankie switched off her phone screen and took her aunt's hand again. 'And so will I. I'm so glad the operation went well.'

Sylvia smiled.

'So am I. Now we just have to get you and Nathan speaking. After that we can work on your father's wedding and kicking Martha and Will into doing something other than gazing longingly at each other when they think no one's looking.'

Frankie grinned.

'Sounds like a plan.'

THIRTY

Frankie stood in the orangery later that day, her heart and mind fizzing with sudden possibility. She felt so light after the sadness of the past weeks that she thought she might lift off her feet and be able to tackle the weeds that flowed across the domed glass roof without having to bother with a ladder.

'I'm going to do it, Aslan,' she said out loud to the large dog, who was sitting by her side. 'I'm going to work off some of this energy on the weeds and for once in my life I'm going to think about what to say. Then I'm going to – well, what do you think I should do? Text him? Call?'

Aslan looked up at her, his face open and trusting. She knelt down and flung her arms around him.

'Oh, darling Aslan, I know you'd help if you could. Maybe you could just be with me when I do whatever I do. That would help. I'd ask Holmes and Watson, but they'd probably start squabbling down the phone and we wouldn't be able to hear each other. And hearing each other' – she stroked the silky golden ears lovingly – 'is well overdue.' She kissed the top of the dog's head and stood. 'Right, time to get down to business, or rather, up.'

She had asked Will earlier that day to bring a ladder from one of his outbuildings so she could reach the ceiling of the orangery.

'What length of ladder do you need?'

'*I* don't know,' she had replied in surprise, waving her hand airily. 'One that will reach the top and that I can manage on my own.'

Will raised an eyebrow, although she knew he was unsurprised by her request. He had lived at Feywood long enough to be used to the vagaries of the Carlisles.

'Well then, I'll pluck one out of my vast store of Ladders For All Occasions, shall I?'

Frankie grinned.

'If you could. Thanks, Will!'

And the lightweight aluminium stepladder had appeared later that morning, when she had been visiting Sylvia. Seizing her secateurs, she climbed up it now and started hacking away at the invasive creepers.

'The thing is, Aslan,' she said as she reached up and chopped through a particularly thick stem, ducking to avoid it as it fell to the ground. 'I still don't know for sure if I'm right. Well, I know that I'm right in that I'm pretty crazy about him, and that I'm not such a ridiculously bad bet as a girlfriend. But what makes me feel wobbly is not knowing what he's thinking. What if I've put him off for life?'

'You haven't.'

Frankie gave a little scream and nearly dropped her secateurs.

'Aslan?'

'It's me.'

Her heart thumping – *could that truly be Nathan's voice?* – Frankie grasped the top step and turned. There, in the open doorway, was a large lemon tree in a pot. As she watched, the foliage was pushed to one side, and Nathan's face appeared, smiling.

'Oh!'

Frankie scrambled down from the ladder and rushed over to him.

'Nathan! What on earth is this? Can you even get in through the door?'

'It's incredibly heavy – hang on.'

He gave the tree a firm push and it slid forward on the tiled floor, allowing him enough room to step in beside it. For a moment, they stared at each other, then spoke at the same time:

'What are you—'

'Frankie, I—'

Then they laughed and for a moment, until she remembered, it felt to Frankie as if nothing had changed. *But everything has changed*, she reminded herself. *He might only be here to collect his things.*

'Go on,' said Nathan. 'You first. But tell me who this handsome fellow is.'

He bent down and scratched behind Aslan's ear and the dog immediately collapsed to the floor and rolled over, tongue lolling out, gazing giddily at him.

'That,' said Frankie, rolling her eyes, 'is Aslan, and he has clearly developed an instant crush on you.' *Not that I can blame him.* She had forgotten how handsome Nathan was and seeing him standing there in the familiar soft plaid shirt and jeans, the sun warming his auburn hair, grinning down at the dog, she felt at once shy and as besotted as Aslan. 'Let's go and sit down and he can drool all over your knee.'

They went over to the cast-iron seating and sat, Frankie automatically settling into her cushion nest, which was still there. Aslan padded after them and put his head on Nathan's knee, nudging his hand to be stroked, a dribble of pleasure trickling out when Nathan complied.

'I told you so,' said Frankie.

'When did you get him?' asked Nathan. 'He's beautiful.'

'About a month ago. He was terribly depressed when he joined us, but he quickly realised he'd landed in doggy heaven and cheered up. Now he's missing Sylvia, but you seem to be adequate compensation.'

'Is she all right?' He looked up, worried.

'Yes, fine. She had her op yesterday and it all went well.'

'That's excellent news. Please send her my love.'

'I'm sure she'd be glad to see you – if, you know, if you're sticking around a bit. I mean, I know you've probably only come to get your things, but...' She trailed off, feeling foolish. 'Anyway, what's with the lemon tree?'

They both looked over at it.

'It's for you,' said Nathan. 'Or, rather, it's for the orangery. Even though it's lemons. It's from Tuscany.'

'You can't have brought that over with you!'

'Well, not exactly. I ordered it and collected it on my way here. As we'd talked about having citrus trees in here, I thought... It was probably stupid.'

'Not stupid at all, inspired. Thank you.'

Nathan nodded, and Frankie saw the familiar blush start to creep up his neck. She longed to rush over and sit by him, take his hand, hug him, but was still unsure of why he had come and desperate not to make another wrong move.

'Good.' He nodded again, then took a deep breath.

'Look, Frankie, I didn't only come here to bring you a lemon tree, or to get my stuff.'

'You didn't?'

'No. I came because... I came because I couldn't not. Frankie, you've made me happier than anyone or anything else, ever. I know you said we shouldn't be together, and I know we'd barely got started, but I came to ask you, to see if, well, could we try again? I'm not as exciting or creative as you or your friends, I know that, and I'll probably never strip off and leap into a swimming pool in the middle of a party, but if you don't mind that...'

'Don't mind!' interrupted Frankie, a broad smile spreading across her face. 'Of *course* I don't mind. I thought *you* minded!'

'Minded what?' Nathan looked bemused.

'Minded that I'm so silly and unpredictable and maybe a bit chaotic sometimes, and that I have bonkers friends and buy peacocks and say what I think, or sometimes things I don't think but they pop out, anyway.'

'But those are the things I love about you! Well, they are now, now I've spent so much time with you and then so much time without you. Don't *you* mind that I'm boring and overly cautious and have spent most of my career planting box hedges for the council?'

'No!' said Frankie vehemently. 'And you're not those things, anyway. I mean,' she added, pulling a face. 'I admit that I *did* think that, a bit, but then I realised that actually you're stable and kind and grown up and probably couldn't be doing with a flibbertigibbet like me.'

'A what?' said Nathan, laughing and pushing Aslan's head gently off his knee as he went to the bench and sat down next to Frankie.

'A flibbertigibbet,' she replied, giggling. 'Don't you want someone all elegant and sensible – like Lucia?'

He frowned at her.

'Not you as well?'

'I assume the family had noticed, then? It was blindingly obvious, but I suppose you were oblivious?'

'Yes, until Henry pointed it out. Lucia's a very nice woman, but she's – well, Frankie, she's not you.'

Now, it was Frankie who turned red. Nathan put his hand to her cheek.

'I didn't know you blushed,' he said.

'Only when I'm very, very pleased,' said Frankie, looking into his green eyes and finding them full of emotion to match hers.

And he leant in to kiss her, on and on, neither of them noticing the golden retriever flop down contentedly at their feet.

EPILOGUE

'What a perfect morning for a wedding,' sighed Martha, opening the front door for Frankie to go out and the marquee hire people to come in. 'Dad and Sindhu will be thrilled.'

'It is,' agreed her sister. 'When September gets it right, it's better than any other time of the year.'

'That's very romantic,' said Martha. 'Love suits you, Frank.'

Frankie tried to roll her eyes, but couldn't stop herself grinning happily as she went to tell the marquee people where to go, then walked round to the back of the house to feed the peacocks. It was true. She felt happier than she had ever been. It wasn't a wild excitement or a daring thrill or a happiness born of relief when you had been expecting something to go wrong and it didn't. It was a feeling that was somehow calm yet enlivening, a happiness of finally feeling secure but also having so many unknown pleasures to look forward to.

'Morning, fellas,' she said, unlocking the cage and stepping inside. 'I've got your breakfast. I'm afraid you can't go out this morning, not until they've finished setting up the marquee, but I've brought you some berries as a treat to make up for it.'

'Don't feed them the entire wedding breakfast, will you?'

Frankie turned to see Nathan. She chuckled.

'If these two find out there's watermelon, we'll be in trouble, but Dad and Sindhu will probably be down here themselves to share it. The animals in this house are ridiculously spoilt.'

'They're loved,' said Nathan. 'And that's different.'

'True,' said Frankie, stepping out of the cage, locking it and then wrapping her arms around Nathan. 'It brings out the best in all of us.'

For a moment, the wedding was forgotten as they kissed, oblivious to the cantankerous squawks of the peacocks, annoyed to have their morning routine changed, and to the three dogs thundering down the lawn towards them. It was only when Aslan pushed his soft, golden head in between them that they sprang apart, laughing.

'Are you *terribly* deprived of attention?' said Frankie, stroking him. 'It must be – ooh – a whole two minutes since you left Aunt Sylvia's side.'

'Do all three of them sleep in there with her now?' asked Nathan.

'No. Ava is in with Juliet and Léo, and Moriarty with Martha, but they all join her and Aslan every morning because they've worked out that's where the breakfast Bonios are.'

'You don't mind too much that Aslan has adopted Sylvia?'

'No, it's been amazing for her recovery – and for his too. And anyway, I got him because I felt so sad about not being with you. He did his bit to keep me going until you turned up with that ridiculous lemon tree, so he's moved on to where he's needed, like some kind of canine Mary Poppins.'

'Although I can't see him ever leaving Sylvia.'

'True. I think they've found their forever people.'

Neither spoke for a moment as the phrase hung in the air between them, then a bellowing shout made them jump.

'They're putting up the marquee,' said Nathan. 'The florist will be here soon; we'd better go and check the orangery over.'

Hand in hand, they walked over the damp grass to the now fully refurbished building. Its stonework, which had been thoroughly washed, glowed in the morning sunshine, which also glinted off the spotless glass, its cracked panes replaced and the grime scrubbed off. Inside, they stood for a moment to admire their work. Elegant palms curved up on either side, almost to the ceiling, highlighting the dome. The clematis had been trimmed and trained to show it off, and it was still producing copious scented flowers. The pool, now fully revealed, cleaned and mended, had little orange and silver fish darting around in it and it was surrounded by banks of lush ferns. The statue of two simple leaf shapes that Nathan had made under Rousseau's tutelage stood on the small plinth in the corner. There were now two glossy lemon trees, heavy with fruit, which had been placed either side of a table that stood in front of the back doors nearest to the house. Two chairs covered in green silk were in front of this and other chairs had been placed in short rows for the guests.

'Oh!' said Frankie. 'I didn't know it had been set up! Doesn't it look beautiful? I'm so glad they decided to have the ceremony here.'

'So am I,' said Nathan. 'It does make a perfect venue. Was Martha saying something about hiring it out?'

'Yes,' replied Frankie. 'It's no more than an idea at the moment, but now that we've seen it can work, and we've got the licence, it could be a great stream of revenue for us, especially if people use Léo and Sylvia for the catering. We've got the guest rooms up and running in the house already from the cookery school and obviously having a marquee is no problem.'

'It's a fantastic idea. If it takes off, you might be able to renovate one of the rooms indoors eventually, if people prefer that.'

'Exactly. It's funny, we've lived here for years with the place falling down around us, perfectly happy, but now we're getting used to the idea of sharing it, everyone's fired up. And we're actually getting good at this stuff. Juliet put a wash on the other day without checking with anyone which programme to use, and everything actually came out clean.'

Nathan laughed.

'Today the washing machine, tomorrow the world?'

'Something like that. Right, I'd better go and get changed. It would be too like me to be late for a wedding in my own house.'

An hour later, Frankie stepped out of her room to find Juliet and Martha waiting for her on the landing.

'Well, girls, this is it,' she said. 'At least we've all scrubbed up well.'

She twirled to show off her orange silk tunic, which fell to just above her knees and had flowing slit cape sleeves.

'It's sensational, Frank,' said Juliet. 'And nice to see you in something other than black.'

'You can talk!' said Frankie. 'Queen of the LBD!'

'Well, not today,' said Juliet, smoothing down her violet linen shift dress. 'Yours is gorgeous, too, Martha. Where did you get it?'

'I made it,' she replied, looking down at the elegant voile maxi dress in swirling shades of pink and white. 'You inspired me to try something new as well, Frankie, so I've been learning dressmaking.'

'You kept that a secret!' said her youngest sister.

'Because I didn't want to find myself with commissions for you two and no time to make my own,' replied Martha, grinning.

'Ooh, you're toughening up!' teased Frankie, and gentle Martha shrugged.

'Maybe a little. I figure if you two can change your lives, then maybe I can too. Now come on, we'd better get downstairs or the bride and groom will beat us to it.'

. . .

The ceremony and meal were joyful and soon the marquee started filling up with guests for the evening reception. Frankie sat with Nathan, holding an elderflower and lemon cordial in one hand and his hand with the other.

'They look so happy, don't they?' she said, watching her father and Sindhu swaying together on the dance floor, talking and laughing as they danced. 'I'm glad he met someone after Mum died.'

'Someone else is looking pretty happy too,' said Nathan, nodding in the direction of Martha and Will, who were standing close to one another at the edge of the floor talking. As they watched, he took Martha's hand and they joined the dancing.

'She looks blissful,' said Frankie. 'It's about time those two got together.' Nathan nodded, but a slight frown creased his forehead. 'What is it? Don't you agree?'

'I do, yes, but – well, it's probably nothing.'

'What?'

'Well, the other day he mentioned something about family in Scotland and maybe going up to be with them.'

'*Will* did?'

'Yes. I've probably got the wrong end of the stick.'

'I've never heard anything about it. He'd better not break her heart,' said Frankie fiercely.

'It doesn't look like it from here,' said Nathan. 'Try not to worry about it tonight, anyway.'

'I'll try. The day has been too perfect to spoil with worry.'

'Do you like this song?' asked Nathan suddenly.

'Yes, I love it. Reminds me of my wasted youth, but in a good way, for once.'

Nathan stood up, put down his glass and held out his hand.

'Then I think we'd better dance to it, don't you?'

Frankie put her glass beside his and took his hand. As she rose, he pulled her close to him.

'Are you going to dance with me, Nathan Brooks?' she whispered. 'I didn't think it was your sort of thing.'

'Maybe not, Frankie Carlisle, but you very much are my sort of thing, and I think it would make you happy.'

'You make me happy,' said Frankie, her voice catching. 'Happier than I had ever imagined.'

And, still wrapped in each other's arms, they joined the other dancers on the floor.

A LETTER FROM THE AUTHOR

Dear reader,

I want to thank you from the bottom of my heart for choosing to read *Escape to the Country Garden*. I do hope you enjoyed Frankie's journey; I loved sending her on it and seeing her find her happy ending. If you haven't already, do check out *Escape to the Country Kitchen* for her sister Juliet's story, and an introduction to Frankie.

If you want to join other readers in hearing all about my new releases and bonus content, you can sign up for emails from Storm:

www.stormpublishing.co/hannah-langdon

Or for my monthly newsletter here:

www.hannahlangdon.co.uk

If you enjoyed this book and could spare a few moments to leave a review, that would be hugely appreciated. Even a short review can make all the difference in encouraging a reader to discover my books for the first time. Thank you so much!

I started writing about the three sisters living at wonderful Feywood several years ago. The image of each one was strong in my mind's eye – severe but soft-centred Juliet; gentle, dreamy Martha; and feisty, funny Frankie, who couldn't help getting into trouble but craved stability and love just the same. The challenge was creating a hero who would be right for her, and I hope you fall in love with Nathan, who I think is totally dreamy!

Thanks again for being part of this amazing journey with me and I hope you'll stay in touch – I have so many more stories and ideas to share with you.

Hannah Langdon

facebook.com/hannahlangdonwrites
x.com/hmvlangdon
instagram.com/hannahlangdonwrites

ACKNOWLEDGEMENTS

Writing a book often feels like a solitary process but, by the time it reaches readers, it has been shaped by many wonderful people. I am hugely grateful to each of them. I must start, as always, with the fantastic team at Storm. Everyone there is always so professional and supportive, and I couldn't ask to be part of a better team. Particular thanks go to my editor Kathryn Taussig, who somehow made time to read and edit the manuscript before going on maternity leave: thank you so much, I can't tell you how much I appreciated it. Massive thanks also to Kate Smith, who took me on in Kathryn's absence and has been brilliant to work with – the way she embraced my work has meant so much to me. Thanks also to Rose Cooper for another beautiful and enticing cover, and to the whole Storm team, particularly Alexandra Holmes, Amanda Raybould, Catherine Lenderi and Naomi Knox.

Thank you to my friend Asuka Nonomiya Inoue for ensuring my Japanese was correct.

Employ My Ability is a fantastic organisation that offers vocational training for students with special educational needs and learning disabilities. Based at the Walled Garden at Moreton, Dorset, they inspired Nathan's involvement with the fictional ILM.

Sarah, thank you again for your swift and invaluable early read of *Escape to the Country Garden*. Your insights are always brilliant, and your meticulous eye catches every little error.

Mum, I am forever grateful for your unwavering support of my writing and my life.

Rose, although I haven't written anything you'll read just yet, it's all for you, really. Thank you for always being so excited to receive the first copy (and the brownies)!

And finally, John. I have to thank you properly for your professional advice on the correct storage of old documents, but, more importantly, for being you and being with me. There is more than a bit of you in Nathan – he has your sincerity, integrity and gentleness. Like Frankie, I know that 'still waters run deep'. She and I are lucky women.

Printed in Dunstable, United Kingdom